Sealing Fates

Sealing Fates

K.A. Shady

Kyra Shady

For all the dreamers, never stop chasing stars.

Contents

Dedication   v

One
In Which the Thief Is Taken   1

Two
In Which Things Are Missing   6

Three
In Which Demons are Hunted   15

Four
In Which the Oracle Gives Advice   23

Five
In Which The Search Begins   37

Six
In Which a Lead is Found   51

Seven
In Which the Thief Leaves a Trail   65

Eight
In Which Aegis Follows   74

Nine
In Which the Road is Long   82

Ten
In Which a Beacon is Lit 95

Eleven
In Which the Thief Is Saved 107

Twelve
In Which Decisions are Made 115

Thirteen
In Which Feelings are Confessed 122

Fourteen
In Which the Tribe is Found 136

Fifteen
In Which the Thief is Tended To 145

Sixteen
In Which the Trials are Set Forth 160

Seventeen
In Which the Second Seal Is Secured 168

Eighteen
In Which the Veil Is Crossed 177

Nineteen
In Which The Gargoyle is Lost 185

Twenty
In Which the Thief Runs Off, Again 193

Twenty-One
In Which The Palace is Infiltrated 204

Twenty-Two
In Which Truths Are Learned 211

Contents - ix

Twenty-Three
In Which Discord Falls 219

Twenty-Four
In Which It All Comes to an End 231

About The Author 237

One

In Which the Thief Is Taken

Lilith

There's a lurch, then a bounce, my body flying up and rotating. I land in an awkward position on my shoulder. I try to scream, but no sound comes out. Another bounce and my face hits a wooden surface, I feel blood fill my nose as I gasp for air. Warmth wraps around my wrist and races up my arm, the pain fades but with it, so does my awareness.

***

I'm pulled to my feet by my arm, my injured shoulder shoots pain down to my wrist and I cry out as I try to get away from whoever has grabbed me. They hold fast and drag me along, muttering under their breath. When I try to open my eyes, the world blurs, so I slam them shut again. I'm jerked around, fumbling and falling down a set of stairs before I hear a cage door swing open.

I'm shoved forward and tumble to the ground, I'm unable to catch myself as my limbs refuse to cooperate. My face lands and hits the floor, dirt and damp seeping into my cheek. I hiss out a pained breath, but the strange warmth returns and the world settles.

"You said she'd come with you willingly," a strange voice snaps, "We're not equipped to handle her magic."

"She chose them," another voice replies, I almost recognize it but there's something that doesn't feel right. "I drugged her to get her complacent, then gave her more on the way here. She won't be functional for a while yet, and that'll give us time to get the chains."

"What if she fights back? Or worse, they come looking for her?" The other man snaps, his voice becoming shrill.

"They won't, they'll think she took the charm... which she technically did." I finally place the voice as Gavin's, my stomach dropping as the full depth of his betrayal sinks in.

"Where is it? You said you'd get it."

There's a moment of silence. Someone grabs my arm, wrenches my shoulder back, and the man curses, "What the fuck? You gave it to her?"

"No! She grabbed and it won't come off of her. Maybe the Speaker can get it off."

"You better hope so!" the man snaps, then drops me on the ground again and I hear them stalk off. My heart pounds as my body registers the myriad of pains all across it. Trying to reposition, pain causes darkness to engulf me.

***

I'm unsure how much time has passed when I wake up. My limbs are numb with cold, my shoulder is throbbing with pain, and my mouth is dry. I shift and sit up, my shoulder screaming in pain when I put even the slightest weight on it. I scoot back and lean against the stone wall of the room I'm in and take in my surroundings.

The room is dark and I can tell from the chill invading my clothes that it's underground. There's a cell door in front of me, a small cot on my left, and nothing else. I lean back and look above me, hoping for a window, but there isn't one.

I lean back with a groan and try to roll my shoulder, only for it to protest with another shot of pain. I hiss at it, "Gotta get it together."

A quick flex of my shoulder lets me know it's not dislocated, just jammed into the socket. Gripping my elbow with my hand and my magic, I pop the joint. I groan in pain, panting as the pain subsides and I can think again.

I close my eyes and reach out with my magic. My awareness snakes through the shadows, each one leading me through the building I'm locked in. It's a home, average sized, with a few rooms that appear to have never been lived in. The only unusual thing is the fucking basement dungeon.

I pull my magic back; it feels sluggish and I don't want to wear myself out if I need it to protect myself. The pain in my shoulder has already eased, so I get to my feet to get a better look at my cage. I walk to the gate and inspect the lock; it looks pretty simple. But before I can investigate further, I hear footsteps above me and a door slam.

I scramble away from the door and fall on my ass in my haste, instead of trying to get up, I lie on the ground. A few moments later, the door opens, multiple people sets of footsteps clomping down the stairs. Three people stop in front of the gate, "She moved," one says, their voice familiar from when I was first brought in, "but it doesn't look like she's awake."

"Get in there and put the chains on her," another snaps, "We can't afford for her to wake up and try to leave."

I wait as the cell door creaks open; I hear someone moving toward me, but just as they get close, I try to jump into the shadows. As if they knew what I would do, I hear a loud crack and the room fills with light. The shadows disappear and I'm kicked from the darkness. "Fuck!" I cry out as I'm slammed against the wall by a thick arm.

"Nice try," the man hisses, his arm pressed across my throat and cutting off my air.

I glare at him, "Can't blame a girl,"

He grunts, then looks over his shoulder, "Gavin, get those fucking cuffs and collar on her."

My eyes narrow as Gavin comes around with the items in his hands. "Don't fucking touch me!" I shout, trying to shove the man holding me away.

He slaps me hard, and I groan as my vision dances. "Shut up."

I'm too dazed to resist further as I feel chains clamp around my wrists, followed by a collar being buckled around my neck.

The restraints make it harder to reach my magic. I glare at them as I can focus again, "What the fuck do you want?" I demand.

"We'll be asking the questions," the third person finally speaks.

My captor drags me to the middle of the room, where the third person is standing with the end of a chain in their hands. This person has an odd air to them, as if they're not quite present. I scowl as they link my cuffs to the chain. As soon as I'm secured, the chain rattles as it's pulled through a loop on the wall.

I cry out as they pull the chain taught, yanking my arms above my head. I'm standing on my toes when they stop pulling on the chain, my entire body stretched to its limit. The third person, who is clearly in charge, smiles serenely at me.

"I need a few things from you, darling. I need that," they gesture at the charm on my wrist, "And I need to find the second seal. The first seal has attached itself to you, which means you can find the second. So, you can either help us find the second seal and we'll be kind to you. Or you can resist, and we'll make your life a living hell while we find it."

Glaring at them, I'm unable able to pin down their features, like their body is being blurred in front of me. "I'm not giving you any-thing. I work for Aegis and will not hand over a dangerous artifact."

They back hand me, making my head snap to one side and busting my already bruised lip. "Fine, you won't help... Tyler, beat her into compliance." With that, they stride from the room.

Gavin hesitates in the doorway as the other man, Tyler, walks up to me, cracking his knuckles. I grin wickedly at the two of them, "I'll make you regret every blow, so tread carefully."

Tyler grunts at that and rolls his eyes, then punches me square in the nose and all goes black.

Two

In Which Things Are Missing

Philip

The library door slams open, startling from me from the depths of my hangover. "What the fuck?" I snarl, shifting to glare at Marie, who's in the doorway looking panicked.

"Uh, the um," she stutters.

"Spit it out!" Damien roars, making my head throb in pain, I haven't been this hungover in a long time.

"Lilith is missing!" She shouts, "So is Gavin, and... and the artifact."

I swear those words make my entire world stop. Everything becomes suspended in that tattered, fractured sentence, and the first thing I can think, the only thing I can believe, is that it's not true.

Damien is on his feet faster than I can process everything that's going on. There's shouting and it makes my head pang even further. I hear more movement, but I get to my feet; I have to see for myself. She has to be in bed, the training yard, the garden, somewhere.

I slam into her room; the blankets disturbed, some of her clothes thrown about as if they'd been gone through in a hurry. She's nowhere to be found. I don't listen to the shouting behind me as I make my way to the training room, there's no evidence that she's been in here.

I turn to sprint away, but find a crowd outside Sam's office. I look inside and Sam is kneeling next to his safe, which is open but unharmed, and he's staring into it. Next to me, Riley snaps, "I knew she was a lying thief! We never should've let her in here."

I snarl and reach out to grab her, but Damien grabs my arm and shakes my head, "Don't,"

"She's throwing around accusations! We don't know who- "

"There aren't many who could unlock the safe and it is undamaged," Damien says, his voice low.

"This is bullshit! Lilith would never steal from us! You've got to know that, got to believe it! For fuck's sake Damien! She was heartbroken at the thought we'd kick her out after last night."

"Yeah, and maybe she saved herself the possibility," He says, not meeting my gaze.

He knows he's spouting bullshit; I turn to ask Samael's opinion, but my boss is gone. I gesture behind Damien, "Where did he go?"

Damien turns and frowns, "I don't know, he's..." he inhales and scowls, "his scent is gone. Fucker is hiding from me."

Marie looks around, as if Sam is just going to reappear, "What? Where would he have gone?"

Damien shakes his head, "Searching for him won't turn anything up. Roland, get the grounds keepers to search all the gardens and the stable. Look for any trace of Lilith or Gavin. Marie, do the same inside, if we can find traces, we can find trails."

Everyone stands there staring at him for a long second, before he barks, "NOW!"

They scatter, but I stand in front of him with my arms crossed, "You don't actually believe any of this, do you?"

"I can only believe what I know," he gestures at the safe, "It's all gone Phil. If you had stayed to listen to Marie, you'd also know that Lilith asked to go outside alone this morning, and she never came back in. That was almost three hours ago. The evidence is all there, not to mention that Sam fucking bolted, don't you think if he saw something to put any doubt in this he'd tell us?"

I open and close my mouth a few times, not sure how to respond to the logic. I look at the safe again and close my eyes, "I can't believe it."

"It won't change the truth," Damien says, then pats me on the shoulder and walks away.

Damien

I walk outside and take a deep breath, I can't catch Lilith's scent in the early morning air. The wind is blowing and making it hard to pick anything out of the chaos that comes in from the city. I want to tear off into the city searching for everything, anything, that could help us find her. Though as I think about it, I'm not sure what I'd do when I found her.

On one hand, if she stole the artifact and ran off with the damned mutt, then we're screwed in more ways than one. But if he took her, if he hurt her. I close my eyes again and clench my fists, trying to keep myself steady as I search the grounds.

I only get halfway down the drive when a courier runs up, panting with wide eyes, "Is this Aegis?" he asks, his hands on his knees.

I nod, "Yeah, what is it?"

"Message from the police station on fourth, by the docks. They said they found another body," his eyes are wide and frightened.

I scowl, "What? Are you sure?"

He nods, "Yes sir, they didn't give me too many specifics. Just said to come here and let Aegis know that they found another body."

"Fuck. Phil!" I shout, my voice carrying across the drive. I pull a coin out and hand it to the boy, "Thank you."

The lad runs off as Phil appears glaring at me, "What?"

"Message from the docks, they found another body."

His expression falters, "Fuck," he looks behind us then shakes his head, "Okay, we should head down there."

One of the stable hands is walking by and I grab his arm, startling him, "Tell Helga and Roland that we've got urgent Aegis business at the docks. We'll be back when we can."

The boy nods then rushes off into the house, slipping a couple times on the fresh snow. We jog down the street before the boy makes it into the house.

We get to the docks as fast as we can, not wasting time trying to hail a carriage. Walking into the precinct makes a chill run down my spine, the entire place is somber and muted. None of the normal bustle I expect from what's usually a busy office. I walk up to the desk, "We're with Aegis,"

The man looks at me with wide eyes, "It's... I've never..." tears gather in his eyes and I frown.

"Where was the body found?" Phil asks, "We'll head over there."

Another man walks up, his eyes pinched, "We couldn't leave them on the street how they found 'em. It was a..." he shakes his head, "It's bad, sir."

Phil and I exchange a look, then nod, "Show us the body and afterwards we will inspect the scene for anything that's left."

The man nods, taking us through the office and into the morgue.

"Why did you let everyone see?" I ask.

The man shakes his head, "We had little choice..."

I frown again and keep silent as he opens the door to the morgue, but stays planted outside of the room. The first thing that hits me is the smells, blood, death, and demons.

I cough and cover my mouth, "Fuck," I hiss, Phil also covering his face.

"How many?" Phil asks, looking over at the officer.

He swallows hard and looks away, "We're pretty sure it's three, but it's hard to tell."

My stomach drops as Phil and I make our way inside without the officer. The mortician is sitting next to three tables covered with cloth, staring at the bodies with a blank expression. His eyes staring but not seeing, when we approach he startles and looks up at us. "Ah, you must be with Aegis."

Phil nods, "Yeah, what can you tell us?"

"I've seen nothing like this, even that other man that was brought in a couple weeks ago wasn't this bad. They're in... pieces..." he chokes on the last word and looks away from the tables.

Phil and I exchange another look and he walks up to the man, resting a hand on his shoulder, "You go wait outside, we can move them into the cases too if you need us to."

The old man nods and stands, "I'd appreciate that, they're in the last three slots." He waves at the far end of the room, then rushes out without another word.

We stare at each other for a while before he moves to the first table. As he pulls the sheet back, we both go still.

Philip

Damien and I stare at the table. What's there scarcely looks human anymore. It's shredded pieces of flesh clinging to blood-dark bone. Most of the body has been eaten. The only thing that shows it isn't an animal is the hand at the end of one piece, it's such a horrific sight that it turns my stomach. I cover my mouth with my arm and try not to vomit. I've seen some fucked up shit, but it's been a long time since I've seen something like this.

Damien coughs and covers his mouth too, "Fuck," he growls, "Fuck! Do they all look like this?" he demands, looking at the other sheets and going pale. Based on the way the sheets lay across the tables, I'd say they all are.

"We won't get much from these this way," I say quietly, "We'll have to rely on scent." I look at him, waiting for an answer.

He grimaces and nods, "I can definitely smell demons. I'll need a few minutes to sort out what kind," he slowly uncovers his face and coughs again, "Go see if you can get any info about where they found them."

I nod and leave the room; the smells making me nauseous. I step into the hall. Both the officer and the mortician are waiting for me, staring at each other with hopeless expressions. I clear my throat and they jump, then look at me, "What?" the officer asks, his voice a croak.

"Just wanted to get some details on where they were found," I explain.

The officer nods, "Yeah, they were uh," he shakes his head, "They were in an alley near tenth and the docks, someone came across the remains and initially thought they were some poor chicken or something that'd gotten caught by wild dogs. Then... then they saw the hand." He shudders.

"And then came and got the officers, I take it?" I offer.

He nods, "Aye, we got to the scene and... honestly I think everyone who went threw up. It's horrific," he looks over at me with earnest confusion, "Three people, what could possibly do that to three people and would just... leave them there?"

I shake my head, "We're not sure, my brother is looking at the remains, but we need every detail we can find. Is there someone who can take me to the scene? And bring my brother after?"

The officer nods, "Yeah, I'll take you over. We got all we could of their bodies... but the whole alley was a mess, like there was a fight." He leads me out of the building when Damien shoves the door open, scowling as he storms closer to us.

"What?" I ask, frowning at his expression.

He runs a hand through his hair and exhales with a huff, "The main smell I got was that of some sort of swarm, small, scaled, lots of teeth and claws. But I also smelt their blood and found a few pieces of horn and scale, something bigger seems to have come through and eaten the swarm."

"But left the bodies?" The officer asks, frowning, "Why?"

Damien gives me a long look that seems like he's got something else to tell, but is keeping quiet, eventually he says, "Probably wasn't hungry after the swarm, or doesn't care for human flesh. We still need to look at the scene," he waves toward the front of the building, "lead on."

The officer looks conflicted, but nods and heads for the door. I hang back with Damien and we follow a few paces behind, so I can whisper, "What is it?"

"I think I smelled..." he shakes his head, "it seems unlikely, but I think I smelled Parsley."

I scowl, "What are you on about? The swarm tried to season them?"

He shakes his head, "Not the herb, you idiot, the chimera."

I stop walking at that, "What? You think *they* made it across? Why the fuck would they do that? They don't even have a food source on this side of the veil."

"Apparently they do if swarms are making it across. I just don't know why they came through in the first place or where the fuck they would've gone off to."

"Are you two coming?" the officer calls from the end of the street, looking perplexed.

"We'll talk more at the scene," Damien hisses, then marches off, leaving me standing there baffled.

Damien

We get to an alleyway and the officer stands at the entrance staring at it with a pale face, "Here," he waves down, "I... I've got to go." He walks off without giving us much explanation.

Once he's out of sight Phil turns to me, "What do you mean you smelt Parsley?"

"I mean just that, I'm pretty sure I detected Lilith's fucking Chimera's scent."

"What the fuck? They've never tried to come across before."

"They were never able to get through on their own. If the veil is thinning, they may be trying to find her." I run a hand across my neck, "Look, we can discuss it later, right now we need to see what we can gather from this crime scene." I turn to look at the alley.

Phil frowns at it too, "This is a mess," he says in a whisper.

I nod in agreement as I take it all in. There's blood on every surface, the ground, the walls of the surrounding buildings, the various containers, and boxes. The trash, boxes and even some pieces of brick are scattered across the ground. I swallow and inhale, smelling blood and death, just like at the police station.

I run a hand through my hair, "We need to scout around, look for any demon pieces and maybe anything to suggest Parsley was here. If they are on this side, they might be able to help us find Lilith."

He nods and starts his way down the alley. I frown but turn to look at the walls; the blood has dried somewhat. However, I can still see that some of it dripping down the brick, that realization makes me swallow, it's so much blood.

"Damien," Phil calls from down the alley, startling me slightly.

I look up at him and he's holding something up with an arm over his face, "I found one of our swarm."

I come closer and grunt, covering my face as well, "Fucking hell," I mutter, the scent of rotten meat and sulfur turning my stomach.

"What type?" I ask when I get a little closer and can't tell what I'm looking at.

"I can't bloody tell, but..." he trails off and looks at the walls.

I look at the walls as well and spot what he's seen. All along the surface of the bricks is a thick coating of the red blood, but mixed into the gore is a wide swath of putrid green. I swallow and step up to the wall, inhaling deeply to see if I can identify what foul being may have left it behind.

I inhale again and look away, "Fuck, I think that's a pack of fucking leeches."

"Of course," Phil groans, dragging a hand over his face, "Of course it's one of the few FUCKING things we'll have a hard time with."

"We need a witch," I mutter to myself.

Phil looks up at me and smiles, "I know a witch who could help, if she'll admit to it."

"Leah?" I offer, and his grin widens.

Three

In Which Demons are Hunted

Leah Mortimer

I pace the parlor, wringing my hands and trying not to mutter incantations. Dante is sitting on the couch a few feet away, watching me pace and keeping a calm expression on his face. I stand in front of him and plant my hands on my hips, "Something is wrong," I announce.

He opens his eyes comically wide, "Oh? I never would have guessed."

I scowl at him, "Don't be an ass. I'm serious, there is something wrong and I cannot figure out what!"

"You're not a seer, love." He stands and cups my cheek, "I know your intuition is good but it's not magical. If something is wrong it very well may be in your head."

I lean into his touch and sigh, "All right, all right. I'll try to calm down."

A knock at the front door has us both jumping and turning. It's not often anyone is able to sneak up on our house. Usually one of the wards goes off. I rush to the door, that feeling of wrongness increasing as I approach.

I open the door and find Philip and Damien standing there. Damien looking his grumpy self, and Phil looking almost as dour as his brother. "What's wrong?" I ask.

"No hello, how are you?" Damien asks, turning his head to one side.

"No, something is wrong, " I state flatly. "I can feel it in my gut. You two wouldn't just show up on my doorstep unless something was wrong. So, out with it."

Damien snorts and gives his brother a look, the happier twin sighs and rubs his neck, "We need a witch. Not a mage like Marie, but a proper witch who can work with blood."

I recoil and take a step back, "Why come to me for that?"

They exchange that loaded look again and it's Damien who snaps, "Maybe because you are a witch mated to two vampires and kin to a werewolf. Maybe, it's cause we trust you to actually help and not bolt as soon as something goes wrong. *Maybe,* Graves has low-key being trying to bait you and your family into joining Aegis for years."

I open and close my mouth a few times, Dante starts laughing behind me and puts a hand on my waist. "They've got you there, love. Let them and see what they need."

I sigh and wave for them to enter the building. As we make our way back to the sitting room Dante and I had just left Andre appears with a frown on his face, "What's going on?"

"We need your wife's help," Damien says. "We're running into a problem downtown. there's a swarm of hell-beasts near the docks and we, unfortunately, are unable to track them."

"Can't you smell like a hound-dog?" Andre asks, frowning at Damien.

"Yes but it has its limitations. I can't really pick out the scent of a swarm in a blood covered alley. Thankfully, it looks like something else managed to kill a few of them, hence the need for a witch who can work with blood."

"So, are you going to help or did we waste our time?" Phil snaps, his tone mimicking his brother's.

I cross my arms and eye them both, "Fine, but I'd like you to take a message to Lilith for me as well."

Phil tenses and Damien asks, "What is it?"

"Ask her if she'd like to join me for tea in a couple days. I understand if she's unwell because of the nastiness at the ball."

"I'll let her know as soon as I see her," Damien promises with a nod, "Now let's go, we're losing daylight."

Philip

We escort Leah and Andre down to the crime scene at the docks. As we near it the vampire hisses and covers his nose, "How the fuck did you two manage to even go in there?" he says through his suit sleeve.

"Practice," I grunt, "We've been around for a long time and seen plenty of shit."

Leah winces and covers her nose too, "Okay, where is this corpse you talked about?"

I march to the end of the scene and crouch next to what remains of the hell-beast. An adult one isn't much larger than a chicken, however they move in swarms and have teeth sharp enough to pierce dragon hide. Leah follows me through and crouches next to it too, "This is probably the smallest monster I've ever seen," she says quietly.

I nod, "Yeah, but we need to track these down before they get too far. They're dangerous in large numbers, and they breed far too fast."

"Like rats," Leah says with a nod, "All right, stand back."

The witch pulls a stick of chalk out and draws a circle around the remains, muttering as she goes, "Goddess I hope we catch these. The sheer mayhem I'm getting just from their blood is outrageous."

She stands in front of her circle and puts her hands on her hips. With a nod she holds her hand out to her partner and he walks up, using one of his fangs to pierce the tip of her finger. "Does that not interfere with the magic?" Damien asks with a frown.

Leah shakes her head, but Andre replies, "Not enough to cause problems, no venom just the wound."

"I've also had plenty of practice making sure the slight variance doesn't do anything." Leah says, turning her hand over and letting a single drop of blood fall onto the chalk circle.

As the blood lands, the circle lights up, magic suffuses the entire space and makes the hair on my neck stand on end. Leah chants softly, her words blending together into a spell I don't recognize. I drag my hand down my neck a few times, making the hairs settle.

When the chanting settles, a thread of light leads from Leah's fingertips into the alley. "Damn," Damien says, watching the thread disappearing into the maze of spaces.

Leah nods at the thread, "We can follow this. I don't think we can be much help with any fighting, I'm certainly not capable." She looks at Andre.

The vampire shakes his head, "I'm not going to put myself at risk, sorry."

I nod, "Fair enough, lead on."

Parsley

We dig our claws into our meal, the meaty chest tears easily and blood splashes our faces. Its screams echo in the stinky tunnel, warning the others that we are coming. Our snake head swallows the remains as our owl begins to look deeper into the darkness.

Stalking deeper into the tunnel we soon find a large space. Multiple tunnels leading away from it in different directions. We cannot smell Mother down here, but we're unable to ignore the gnawing hunger either. So we continue to search for the leech nest.

Inhaling deeply our lion is able to pin-point where the leeches' scent is strongest and we follow it. It's not long before we can hear them, the small, chicken-like creatures building burrows out of the debris of the stink-tunnel. We burst into another larger room and the leeches screech again, all of them trying to swarm us at once.

Gleefully we lash out, claws, teeth, and tail working in sync to tear through the little beasts. It doesn't take long for us tear through not only the leeches but their nests too, leaving no creature alive as we begin to eat through the dead.

We're curled up in the middle of the carnage when a hole opens in the roof of the stink-tunnel. Light pierces the darkness and we snarl at it, wishing it would go away. A moment later two beings drop into the tunnel. They look like humans, at least in shape, but we know them. Their familiar scents weave past the stench of the tunnel and we stand up, stalking toward them.

"Holy shit," the blond one says, staring at us, "Is that who I think it is?"

The dark one grunts, "I think it is, but they do not look friendly at the moment."

We roar at them, "Mother! WHERE!?"

They cover their ears and the blond stumbles, "Yep, not in a good mood at all. Parsley, you've got to-"

Owl cuts him off with another screech, this one making them drop to their knees in pain. "We can't understand!" the dark one shouts over our cries.

Lion roars and we leap over them, using the hole they created to crawl from he stink-tunnel and into the fresh air. Lifting our nose to the air we race off into the forest of buildings searching for mother.

Damien

After we're able to get our bearings, Phil and I search through the nest of leeches and find that Parsley has cleared it out. Everything is dead and most eaten.

When we climb out of the sewer, Leah and Andre are standing where we left them looking terrified. "What the hells was that?" Andre demands, pointing in the direction I assume Parsley went. Leah is hiding behind him, her face pale and terrified.

"Chimera," Phil answers, looking in that direction too.

"That is not what I thought we were tracking." Leah says softly.

"It's not," I reply wiping some of the blood and muck off on my hands. "They cleared out the leeches for us, we should be good now."

"So, that's it? They're just gone?"

"The beasts, yes. As for the Chimera..." I trail off and stare down the alley, "I'm not sure what it means that something that large has made it across the veil, likely by chance. They're intelligent to a degree but Parsley was clearly distressed and wouldn't have crossed over without good reason."

"What kind of good reason? Also, did you call it Parsley?" Andre asks.

"I think they're looking for someone," Phil says, "And yes, we know that particular Chimera."

The two of them exchange a concerned look but I shake my head, "No time now, you two head home we need to report this back to Graves. Thank you for all your help." I start walking away from them without waiting for a reply from either of them, or Philip.

***

We walk back into the manor, and everything is eerily quiet. There's no smoke coming from any of the chimneys, there's nobody in the yard, and the paths are covered in snow. Phil and I look at each other with concern, usually, the house would be teeming with activity.

I walk into the kitchen and stop short when I see Roland, Helga, Cook, and Marie at the table looking like someone's died.

"What's going on?" Phil asks, looking at everyone.

"Lord Graves came back," Cook says quietly, "Won't say where he went."

"Okay, where is he now?" I ask, walking toward the big man.

"Office," he says, not looking up from the table.

"Why do you all look like someone died?" Phil snaps.

"Ask Graves," Roland says dourly.

Phil looks at me and I shrug, not sure what is going on either. Making our way up to the office, we find Graves sitting at his desk, the papers organized, the safe closed, and he looks as serious as his namesake.

"What's going on? Half the house staff is sitting in the kitchen looking like someone died." I ask, jerking my thumb behind us.

"I'm more concerned about what our plan is to find Lilith." Phil interjects, shoving me aside to walk up to Sam.

"There isn't one." Graves says, not looking up from the papers he's sorting.

Phil freezes where he stands, his mouth opening and closing.

Graves flips a paper over and looks up at me, "How did your hunt go? Judging from the muck and blood on you, I hope it went well."

I shake myself and the clutch of icy fear that's wrapped around my heart, "Yeah, it went well. Leah helped us track down the beasts that attacked, they were a type of swarming creature, so we dispatched the entire nest."

He nods and makes a note on his page, "Excellent, we'll continue to monitor the area, but hopefully they remain at bay."

"What do you mean?" Phil suddenly breaks out of his stupor with a shout.

Graves raises an eyebrow at him, "I mean, I hope the swarm will not return. I didn't think it was that confusing of a-"

"Not about that! About Lilith? What's our plan to find her?" Phil demands, marching up to our boss and slamming his hands on the desk.

Graves sighs and pinches the bridge of his nose, "There is not a plan to find her, at least not one that involves anyone in the house. I've established a bounty with the constabulary and-"

"You WHAT!?" Phil roars, his human glamour fading away.

Graves sighs again and looks my brother in the eyes, "I established a bounty with the constables. They will make up posters and work to find Lilith, Gavin, and the Seal."

"You can't honestly think that Lilith did this!"

I take a step back and look at Graves, trying to read his expressions and failing. Graves shakes his head, "It's not about belief but evidence. There isn't anyone else we know of who could've gotten into that safe without breaking it. You two certainly didn't take it, which leaves only one option."

"Then let us find her," I blurt, getting both of their attention.

Graves shakes his head again, "No, I don't trust you two to find her and not try to protect her. I need you both to handle the demons that are invading."

"So that's it, everything that's happened in the last months you're just going to throw away? Because of, of..." Phil trails off, clearly at a loss for words.

Graves closes his eyes and I swear he shudders, the first sign of emotion other than annoyance. When he opens his eyes, he looks at both of us and speaks slowly, as if we're too dense to understand otherwise. "I cannot deny the evidence. Despite what I may wish to believe, I cannot ignore the facts that lie before us. I expect you, and everyone else in this house, to do as you've been told and tend to your normal duties.

Four

In Which the Oracle Gives Advice

Marie

My hands tremble as I do everything in my power to prevent myself from throwing the vase I'm cleaning at the wall. It has been almost a week since Lilith disappeared, and it feels like the entire house has turned on its head. Damien is eerily calm, Philip has a hair-thin temper, and Lord Graves has turned into more of a recluse than ever.

Not only that, but Graves has forbidden everyone from looking for Lilith. He acts as if she's guilty, as if she would betray us, betray him. When the rest of the fucking house is certain that she loves him at least as much as he loves her.

I'm roughly dusting a bookshelf, causing it to shake, when one of the scullery maids, Abby, appears, panting. "Marie! You have to come quick, there's, there's..." she waves her hands helplessly for a moment, "it's bad."

I drop the cloth in my hand and follow her. We get to the kitchen to find Cook, Roland, and Helga standing around the table, staring at a box. I come up next to them, shoving Cook aside to get to the container and freeze as well. Nestled inside is a massive stack of posters with Lilith's face on them, wanted posters.

"What the fuck," I mutter, staring at the page. "How... why?" I look up at Helga, who's standing across from me.

"I don't know, don't make sense." she says with a shrug, "Lad is smitten with her, not a damn reason for this."

"Do you think he's being manipulated somehow?" Roland asks, "Maybe there is a spell that we missed?"

"That one of the twins wouldn't have sniffed out?" I demand, "Damien makes a fuss when I use new cleaning spells!" I throw my hands in the air and walk away from the table.

"Then," Cook says quietly, "She did it."

I spin on the big man and glare, "That's the biggest load of bullshit that's ever been said inside these walls. She loves him! And we all know damn good and well that he's in love with her. Hell, so are both the twins! I wouldn't be surprised if she felt the same toward them."

"Lilith belongs here and they know it! Someone had to take her, someone had to do something to her and they're acting like a bunch of fools because of the past! If they won't look for her, maybe we should." I put my hands on my hips and lift my head.

Helga and Roland exchange a look, then Roland says, "Well, so far, the posters are just here. They aren't on the streets, perhaps he's still considering the options?"

I scowl at them, "I'm not going to just sit here and speculate then. He's got to provide some fucking answers." I snatch the first poster off the top of the stack and march my way over to Graves' office.

Lilith

Being in a windowless basement has fucked with my perception of time. I remember what happened when I was first brought in, but it's hard to say how long it's been. Between the pain, the disorientation, and the drugs, I'm pretty sure they've given me at least twice. Everything feels distant and intangible. I'm lost in my thoughts as they swirl around almost aimlessly. I wonder if the guys are looking for me, if it's been long enough, or if they're still unaware, I'm gone.

I press my eyes closed and try to push away the fear that threatens. Tears pool at the corner of my eyes and I shake my head to disperse the feeling that everything is going to collapse. I take a deep breath and open my eyes again, surveying the space before me and finding it just as bleak as before.

I hear them before they even open the basement door. Raised voices and heavy footsteps that seem to stop just outside. I turn my head slightly, hoping to decipher what they're saying. I close my eyes and focus, but not everything is clear. Whenever one of them shouts, I hear a few words, though their voices are distorted by the door.

"... don't have time..." a shrill voice cries.

"... come around!" comes the reply in a lower voice.

"Too much..."

"... fine..."

"... too long and... insane!"

".. don't know-" the deeper voice is cut off.

"I've seen it before!" the higher voice shrieks, making me wince. That seems to subdue the other person, and the conversation becomes too quiet for me to hear properly. A few more moments pass, then I hear the door at the top of the stairs open. I let my head fall forward, acting like I'm asleep or unconscious.

The cell door swings open and I keep still as the single set of footsteps approaches, "I know the look of an unconscious person lass, yer not fooling me."

I try to keep still, but there's a grunt and the cell door closes. Thinking that they're gone, I lift my head to look. I freeze as I make eye contact with the man who knocked me out, Tyler; I think.

He smirks when our eyes meet, "I thought you'd be less predictable. Given that Aegis was falling all over themselves for you."

I raise my chin at that, "Fuck off,"

"We both know I can't do that," he says, his smirk faltering as he looks me over, "Yer in a bad way, you know that?"

I frown, "What do you care?"

"Ye aren't what I was expecting when I was hired. As luck would have it, I ain't got a choice in it anymore. I'd rather not have to hurt ya anymore, so why don't ya drop this stubborn act and cooperate?" He gives me a look that seems soft.

I snort, "You expect me to believe that? I'm not an idiot."

He frowns then sighs, "Don't say I didn't try, lass."

I scowl at him, but then he hauls off and punches me in the ribs. I hear and feel the bones crack and I choke on air. Coughing and sputtering as I try to catch my breath, my now injured ribs protesting as I inhale hungry gulps of air.

To my surprise, the man pauses until I've caught my breath before dealing another blow, this time to the other side of my ribcage. I cough and hack as I catch my breath for a second time, my throat and ribs burning with every inhale.

"Ready to cooperate?" he asks roughly.

I lift my chin and scoff again, "It'll take more than that."

He sighs again then punches my jaw; my head cracks to the side and I feel blood pool in my mouth. The sensation is, unfortunately, familiar, and I spit the blood out as my vision clears.

I bare my teeth at him now, knowing that they're bloody and horrific, "Please, sir, may I have another?" I taunt.

He grunts, then shakes his head and punches me again, this time in the gut. I cough up more blood, spraying it across his face as more blows land. He doesn't pause long between each blow anymore and doesn't bother asking if I'll cooperate. I watch his face as he lays into me and can practically see the war going on in his head. I wonder which one of us will break first, will he succumb to his guilt or will I stop being stubborn?

The last thought has me grinning, which causes him to hesitate, my stubbornness is what's kept me alive this long, I sure ain't going to stop now.

Damien

I walk down the stairs and flex my hands, needing to generate some activity. It's been a little over a week and Samael has insisted that we don't search for Lilith. I understand why he might not trust us if we were to find her, but to rely on humans to find her. It's absurd and I'm half tempted to suggest he get some of the magical agents to being looking. I get to the bottom of the stairs and Marie is standing in front of Sam with her hands on her hips.

"What in the world are you thinking?!" she shouts, "You can't be serious about, about," she waves at the kitchen.

"I am serious. There are only a few people who are capable of getting into that safe, and quite frankly the fact that she's not come back is enough to make the decision."

Her hands clench, "That's a lie! You know it! She would never steal from you! Not permanently anyway. Don't you dare put those out!"

I try to ask what she's on about when the kitchen door slams open and Phil is standing there. He looks a mess from his hair to his boots, I knew he'd been out in the city, but I didn't realize he hadn't been taking care of himself. "What the fuck is this?" he screams, a piece of paper clutched in his hand.

Graves looks at it, his face impassive save for the most minor twitch in his jaw, "It's a wanted poster."

Phil hisses, baring his fangs and shifting to his paler form, wings and all, "Why does it exist? What sort of bull shit is this?"

"Yelling isn't going to get you answers any quicker," Sam says with a dry tone, "I'll tell you the same thing I told Marie, there's not many people who can get into that safe. And, the fact that it's been a week and she's still gone? Miss Callam is more than capable of escaping any kind of bonds, If she weren't involved she'd be back. Initially I had decided to let the constables handle it themselves, however I realize that she's too elusive for them and will be calling in other Aegis Agents." He doesn't give them any more time to argue with them before he turns and marches up the stairs.

When he passes me I can smell fear and frustration, I turn to watch him and when he gets to the top he glances back down at the three of us. I spot a wariness in his eyes as if he's trying to communicate something without having or being able to put to it into words.

I frown at him but he disappears before I can really read what he's trying to convey. I turn to look at the two at the bottom of the stairs, "Can you believe this?" Phil asks holding the poster out to me.

I shrug, "He already told us his stance, it'd take new evidence for him to change his mind."

Phil snarls, "You're just going to let it be? You're not even going to try?"

I shrug again and finish my descent, "Like I said, he's the boss."

He hisses at me, baring his fangs, "Fucker!" then he storms off.

Marie looks at me with sorrowful eyes, "Are you really okay with this? Is he?" she gestures at the stairs.

I frown at her, glance at the stairs, then look after Phil, "I don't know; I guess we'll find out." I follow after Philip before he goes and makes a mess of something.

Following him through the city, listening to him bitch about

Samael makes me smirk, it reminds me of the *very* first time we met Lilith. I had a similar reaction to her…

Deimos

I watch the front doors of the palace closely, waiting for our 'subtlety expert' to arrive. I'm still irritated that Samael thinks we need help from some hellion in order to be subtle.

Next to me, Phobos bounces on his toes, "You're going to scare them off before they get here if you keep glaring like that," he taunts with a huge grin.

"I don't see why Boss thinks we need help, we've been managing just fine." I snap, "It's not like subtle is going to make this any easier."

"It's not just being subtle," he says, "apparently they know the ins and outs of the locals better than we do. Hopefully, he gets down here before they arrive though, I'm not sure how they'll respond to us."

"I don't give a shit how they respond to us, I'm only down here cause Samael said to be."

Phobos shrugs and rocks back on his heels, "Hope you don't end up regretting that."

As if he heard them coming, the doors open and someone clad in sea-green enters. My mouth drops open as I realize it's a woman, the outfit she's wearing unlike anything I've seen. A sleeveless bodice hugs her torso, then cuts open as it reaches her hips. The fabric moves to reveal breeches that look like they fit as snugly as the bodice, but she moves in them with ease. Bare feet pad silently on the marble floors and a veil of black hair cascades down her back as she approaches us.

She comes to stand in front of us with an appraising look in her eyes. I scowl, there's no way this is our supposed subtlety expert. She stands out like a fucking flower in winter, her bright clothing a stark contrast to the grays of the hall. A moment later a dark form appears at her side, this must be our expert, he's wearing an all black suit with black hair pulled back into a neat tail at the nape of his neck. He moves as silently as the woman, but his movements are much smaller, more contained.

None of us speak for a long moment, the woman leans toward the man and whispers something so quiet I can't hear it. Which is perplexing, since my senses are much stronger than most. The man huffs out a laugh then steps forward, "Is King Samael available? We are expected."

"He got held up in a meeting," Phobos says as he takes a step forward, "We can help you get settled in your rooms," he glances at the woman, then back to the dark man. "Uh, do you have other servants with you? We were only informed that one room needed to be prepared."

The woman snorts and gives my brother a droll look, "Whomever you received your information from clearly left things out. I suggest you inform Samael we've arrived and do so quickly."

"No need," Boss's voice booms across the space as he appears from the side hall that leads to his office.

The woman turns, and a smirk spreads across her face as he walks up, "There you are Sammy, I was beginning to think you'd forgotten about me."

I expect him to snap at her for daring to use a nickname, but he grins and holds his arms out, "One would be a fool to forget you, Lilith. And Pray forgive my tardiness, a meeting with some governors from the nearby towns went long."

To my surprise, she steps into his embrace and Samael looks over her head at the shadowy man, "Errill, yes?"

"Yes sir," the man replies, "I'm honored that you recall my name."

The woman steps out of Samael's arms and flounces over to the man, draping her arms over his shoulder and grinning, "Mores the fool who dares forget it, Errill. It is, after all, unwise to forget the name of he who tempers chaos."

"You flatter me My Lady, we both know that you're the one who tempers me." The man says with a smile at the corners of his mouth.

The woman, Lilith, kisses his cheek, then turns to look at Phobos and I with amusement in her eyes, "Who're your boys, Sammy? I don't recall them from my last visit."

I bristle and growl "Watch your mouth, I'm no child and you have no right to act so fucking casual!" I start towards her, and her expression darkens.

Before I can take more than a couple of steps forward, ropes of shadow leap up from the ground and grip my legs, then wrap around my arms and up my neck until I'm immobilized.

My eyes flick to the man, Errill, and I growl again, "Release me! I won't let this disrespect stand!"

"Deimos," Samael says, his voice taking on that tone that makes me want to hit him, like I am an errant child, "Errill is not responsible for your restraints. And, given that she is colloquially known as the Queen of Shadows and Chaos, I suggest you reign your temper in before Lilith decides you have been too disrespectful."

My attention snaps to the woman who's walked up in front of me, her eyes glowing green as she cranes her neck to look at me. I open my mouth and one of those ropes clamps over my mouth, preventing me from speaking. "Hold your tongue for a moment and think before you try again. I recognize your name now, Deimos, you're one of those Immortals who Samael took in some years ago. I knew one of you had a temper, but I didn't expect such blatant sexism."

"Uh," Phobos says, "if I may interject?"

Lilith looks over at my brother and raises an eyebrow at him, "You may."

"I don't believe it is your sex that has informed my brother's behavior, so much as your attire. We were told to expect an expert in subtlety and stealth, and your clothing does not exactly align with what we're used to with those skills."

She snorts, but the shadows holding me in place loosen, "I suppose that's reasonable. Though, in the future, if you wish to retain my help, you will be respectful to me."

The gag over my mouth falls away and I scowl at her, "Whilst you're disrespectful to my king?"

Her gaze cuts to me and I go still, her eyes bore into my soul and I can't help feeling like I've been stripped bare. As if she can see through all my bravado right down to the lost, scared child I truly am.

I swallow hard and drop my gaze.

She shakes her head before looking away, "You'll do well to remember that your king is my friend, and has been for longer than he's been king. I'll forgive your insolence this time, given that you were ignorant. I won't be so lenient in the future."

In the next breath, all the restraints dissipate and I fall to the ground. Lilith turns away from me and says, "Are my usual rooms prepared, Samael?"

"They always are," Samael replies.

I hear them both walk away as I stare at the floor.

Once the footsteps fade, someone walks up in front of me and I see Samael's boots, "You're one lucky bastard," he says dryly.

"How so?" I ask, not looking up and still trying to gather myself after feeling like my soul was laid bare with just a look.

"Lilith is not referred to as a queen for nothing. She's an Eternal, with a penchant for recklessness and mischief. If she had decided your behavior wasn't tolerable, she'd have killed you, or turned you green for a while, depending on her mood. And that's just speaking of Lilith herself, Errill is a Primal and only Lilith can stay his rage. Had she not stepped in, we'd be cleaning pieces of you off the floor."

"Am I to be punished, then? For trying to defend my family?" I ask, still not looking up.

"I think you've learned your lesson," Samael says, amusement lining his tone, "Get yourself together before morning, you do still have to work with her."

His remark hits me hard, making me realize the depth of my fuck up. He says nothing else, just walks away, leaving me to my stupidity.

Philip

I storm into Sarah's shop, the scents of herbs and oils hits my nose and makes me wince. I walk up to counter and slam my hands on the surface, "Sarah!" I shout at the top of my lungs.

I hear the door behind me close and the steady footsteps of my brother behind me. I tried to scream at him too, but apparently this whole thing doesn't fucking phase him.

"Yelling at the oracle isn't going to help," Damien says dryly as he leans against the wall to my right.

I glare over at him, "Why are you even here?"

"Because," Sarah says, appearing seemingly from nowhere, "Damien is frustrated with the turn of events, despite his apparent calm."

I bare my teeth at her, "Where is she?"

"I don't know," Sarah says with a sigh.

"How do I find her?" I push, slamming my hands on the counter again.

"I don't know," she shakes her head.

I growl and drag my claws against the counter, tearing gouges into the wooden surface, "Do you know anything? What's the point of having an oracle around if they can't help?!"

I turn away from her before she can reply and throw my hands up, "Things are falling apart! Lilith is missing, Samael has closed off so bad we can't even get a reaction from him, the rest of the household is on edge. And now he's made up fucking wanted posters!"

"I'm aware," she says dryly.

I spin and slap the counter again, the wood cracking under the pressure, "Tell us how to fix it!"

The look she gives me is full of pity and she shakes her head again, "You can't. The only ones who can fix this are Lilith and Samael, they're the only ones with the power to overcome Discord. You need to trust them."

"Trust them?" I snap, "Lilith is missing and, despite how much I hate it, there's solid evidence to suggest that she took the first seal and ran off with it! Meanwhile, Samael has become despondent and has no choice but to assume that she took it and now... now..." I groan and rub my forehead.

"Now he has to start a manhunt for someone he's fallen for," Damien says quietly, "He's being betrayed by a woman he loves, again."

"You must trust them," Sarah repeats.

I turn back and slap the counter, "How? How can we trust them? We've been chasing them through lifetimes for a thousand years. A thousand years of repeatedly losing them, watching them break under the pressure of their powers, or die to power-hungry people. And you expect us to just... just let things happen? Why is this time so different?"

She stares at me for a long time, her eyes sad. At length, she turns around and picks up a mirror in an elaborate frame. She turns back and sets the mirror on the counter, "This is a person, the frame is the body and the glass is the soul."

Damien and I exchange a look, but we both know better than to interrupt her just as she's started explaining things.

"When Discord fought them a thousand years ago, they separated the souls from the bodies. Without the soul, the bodies died," she separates the frame and the glass, setting the frame aside, "and then Discord took their souls and- "

"And cast them out into the rebirth cycle," I interrupt, "We know."

"No," Sarah snaps, then drops the mirror, causing the glass to shatter on the counter, a spider-web of cracks spreading through it and separating each piece, "Then they shattered the souls and sent them into the rebirth cycle."

I frown, "What does that mean?"

"It means that each lifetime was simply larger and larger collections of the shards coming together and manifesting the correct soul signature." She pushes the pieces together.

I stare at it as she slides the pieces back together, "So the difference this time?"

She finishes reassembling the mirror, save one piece, and looks up at me, "This time, all but one shard is present in each of them. Every lifetime prior did not have enough of their souls to handle the weight of what they were. This time, they are nearly whole, and all that remains is for them to embrace the final shard of who they are."

"And where are the final shards?" Damien leans over the mirror and inspects it.

"The last pieces are held in the seals."

"So, if Lilith has the seal, she's whole?" I ask hopefully.

"No," Sarah shakes her head and places the last piece of the mirror in its slot, but nothing else changes within the mirror, "The shard is there, but she would not be whole. She must accept that piece as well to repair the fractures," She taps the glass, and it fuses back together.

"And how do we help her do that?" I prompt.

"We can't," Damien says, "She's gotta figure it out on her own, we can tell her, but it won't be enough."

I turn to glare at him.

Sarah sighs, "He's right. All you two can do at this point is stay with them, support them, and trust them."

I want to reach across the counter and shake her, "So that's it? We're supposed to just... wait?"

"Yes," she nods.

"Lilith is in danger! We can't just sit here and do nothing!" I shout, trying to get it through to her.

"Lilith will call for help when it's time," Sarah replies, "For now, you can only wait."

I lose it at that and launch myself over the counter, before I can get my hands on the Oracle, Damien grabs me and drags me back, "Phil! Stop."

I fight to pull away and snap my teeth in his face.

He starts to shift too and then shouts, "Phobos! Enough!"

The use of my true name makes me stop short, I'm panting as Sarah stares at the two of us with that sadness in her eyes again. "When?" I demand, "When will she call?"

"When it is time," Sarah says, shrugging slightly.

I almost leap at her again, but she turns and plucks something off a shelf behind her, "I need you to take this to Samael, he commissioned it a few weeks ago."

She holds a cloth bag out to me, looking entirely at peace with the fact I tried to attack her.

I sigh and take the bag, "What is it?"

A small smile is all she gives me before waving us away and disappearing into her workroom.

Five

In Which The Search Begins

Lilith

The cold that creeps in from all directions has numbed out the semi-rhythmic strikes against my battered body. The pain is distant and so is my mind, I've zoned out as far as I can to protect from what's being done to me. It's not the first time I've had to cut myself off, but last time I didn't feel my life slipping away. I swear I can feel a sweet, blissful darkness lurking nearby, waiting for me to give in and sink into it.

But I keep myself away from it, I hold on because I'm certain that somewhere out there I'm being looked for. If I can just hold on, I'll be found and saved from this torment.

The tempo of my torture shifts and it draws me back to the present. Pain bursts across my mind and body, as does a keen awareness of all that surrounds me. The room is ice cold and I can hear a steady drip behind me. My arms are above my head, my hands clasped in shackles that are dampening my magic, and heavy drugs are running through my system, preventing me from fighting back. I cry out when another blow lands, earning me a rough grunt from my assailant.

Before I can recover, he renews the force of his blows, making me cry out again as tears stream down my face. I hear the door open but my captor doesn't, three more blows land in my midsection, knocking what little air I have left out of me. He doesn't stop his assault until a familiar voice snaps, "Enough."

The massive man steps away as the cell door creaks open, "What? You said no more chances today."

My ears are ringing from a blow I'd received to my head, so everything sounds distorted, "Things changed," the new-comer's voice says, "Is she conscious?"

"No idea, but she started screaming again a few minutes ago," it's all the warning I get before I'm soaked from head to toe in water.

I splutter and cough as the water tries to fill my mouth and nose. I rapidly blink and peer out at the two men standing in front of me. They blur once before I can focus on their faces.

On the left is the man who's been torturing me for the last week, his dark eyes crinkled with concern and blood, my blood visible on his knuckles. Gavin stands on the right, his expression somewhat sympathetic, but I now know better than to take his expressions for sincere. "Ready to comply?" Gavin asks, his tone coaxing.

I shake my head, the chains that are holding my arms to the ceiling rattling as I look up and smile, "Not. A. Fucking. Chance." I spit a large glob of blood and snot that lands on the cell floor with a wet plop.

"Oh?" Gavin asks, his voice almost amused, "Not a chance, eh?" he gestures behind him and I still as another person comes forward. I recognize Riley with a sneer on her face. I open my mouth to make a smart remark, but Gavin snatches a piece of paper from her and holds it up in front of my face.

I blink at the page for a few moments, trying to read it, but the letters swim before my eyes. After a second I realize I'm looking at an image of me, it's fairly accurate, but the most concerning thing is the large, bold, letters at the top. I mutter the words aloud as I read them,

"WANTED: Lilith Callam.
By order of Aegis, for theft from the organization..."

There is more on the poster, but tears fill my eyes before I can finish reading it. I choke on a sob and Gavin clears his throat.

"Shall I finish reading it for you?" he asks, but doesn't wait for a reply. "For theft from the organization. She's to be brought in alive for a reward of 5,000 marks. And any information that leads to the apprehension of Miss Callam will be rewarded."

I shake my head, "T-tha-, that can't be. They wouldn't..." I trail off as Riley's expression becomes down-right gleeful.

"They're not looking for you," she snaps, "Lord Graves has declared that the Twins aren't allowed to search for you! And none of the other staff will, you're not as important as you thought Lillian."

I frown at her, tears still dripping down my face, "What?"

"You were just a means to an end," she says, ignoring my question, "nobody cared about you. Lord Graves just wants the artifact back."

I shake my head again, "No,"

Gavin makes a soft sound of concern, "I told you they were no good, Lil, you should have listened to me. I know you were being stubborn because you thought they'd come rescue you, but now that you know the truth... Are you ready to cooperate, Lillian?"

I drop my head as tears and blood drip down my face, "Y-yeah. I'll cooperate, just... don't let them... don't let them lock me up."

Gavin gestures to the wall and the tension on my wrists releases, letting me collapse to the floor in a heap. I sob again and try to curl in on myself, the cold damp of the dirt floor strangely soothing to my frayed nerves.

The shifter crouches in front of me, gently moving a few strands of hair from my face, "I won't let them take you. You know I never wanted to hurt you, right, Lillian?"

I shy away from his touch as more tears fall, but don't reply to his question. He grunts and shakes his head, "I'll give you time to calm down, then we can discuss what we need from you."

Riley makes a noise of protest as he ushers her out, "I thought you said she was going to be punished! This, this isn't what I wanted!"

"I don't fucking care," Gavin snaps, then the door shuts and I can't hear anymore.

I curl myself tighter as the sobs become even heavier. Then squeeze my wrist where the seal has secured itself and whisper, "Send help, please."

At first, nothing happens, then warmth spreads from the seal and something that feels like a memory surfaces. It's a rune, imbued with magic, and I'm not sure what it does, but I hope it'll call for help. I roll so I can see the floor and use my broken and bloody nails to scratch the rune into the dirt.

Graves

I press my hands against the top of my desk and count backward from ten. It's been a long time since I've had to extensively rely on meditation to keep my magic in check. The desire to lash out at anything and everything has gotten stronger with each day, I worry I'll lose all control soon. I shake my head in an attempt to dispel the dangerous thoughts that creep in, only for my office door to slam open.

Looking up, I find myself face to face with Earl Evans and his family. I blink at them, "Can I help you?" I ask, suspecting what brings them here, but not wanting to give it away if not.

Leah marches forward, a piece of paper clutched in her hand and slams it on my desk, "I sent word with the Twins over a week ago asking if Lilith could come by for tea. I assumed she'd need some time after the ball, but I never heard back! I decided I'd come visit her myself only to find that these," she slaps the paper, "Are being made up and put out on the streets. What in the world, Graves?"

"I thought the posters were fairly self explanatory, I put all the necessary details on them." Refusing to look down at the poster. I'm too afraid to face at the image that stares up at me.

"Do you seriously believe that Lilith Callam would steal from you?" She demands.

I wish Sarah had gotten me that damn spell already as I reply, "I don't owe you an explanation, but I suppose it won't hurt. I'm not sure how much stock you put in Clarissa's accusations during the Solstice, but a few of them were correct. Aegis hired Lilith to steal something from the vault at the Solstice Ball. During the festivities, Lilith slipped out and stole said artifact." I let them process that.

Charles is the first to speak, "Okay, and?"

I raise a brow at him and continue, "And she delivered it as expected. However, the next day the artifact was stolen from the safe that I put it in."

"That doesn't mean she did it!" Leah shouts.

I glare at her, "The bracelet, Lilith, and her friend Gavin all went missing at once. As Lilith is the only one who has the skill to break into the safe, I can only assume that she was at least complicit."

"You don't think that this Gavin fellow could've done something?" Andre chimes, "It is obvious Miss Callam holds immense loyalty to Aegis, and to you."

"Gavin is her friend, she is more loyal to him than to us." I say, the words tasting vile and dragging a pang of jealousy from me.

Leah throws her hands in the air, "This is absurd!"

I hear heavy footsteps a moment before Phil appears at the door, Damien at his heels. "What the fuck?" Phil demands, throwing about five pieces of paper in the fire, "It's one thing for you to have them made, but actually putting them out?"

I sigh now, unable to contain my annoyance as I get ready to repeat my logic. "Wait," Damien says, putting an arm out to hold Phil back. The gargoyle pulls a pouch from his coat and tosses it to me on the desk, "From Sarah."

My eyes widen and I snatch the pouch off the table, pulling it open, I dump the contents into my palm. It's a small poppet, a doll about the size of my hand that has Lilith's hair woven into the top and a strip of fabric tied around its middle. The fabric bears embroidery of various symbols and emanates a soft but powerful magic.

I let out a sigh of relief and sit down, all my composure disappearing as my hands shake, "She gave this to you today?" my voice is equally trembly as I stare at my best friends.

"Yeah, we went to ask her some things, and she said to bring it to you." Damien says, his eyes on it, "What is it?"

"It's a poppet!" Leah shouts, "Are you trying to control her? How dare you?" She lurches toward me, but Dante holds her back.

"I don't think that's it," the man says quietly, his eyes not on the doll but on me.

"I wouldn't dare control Lilith. I've seen what happens to those who cross her," I open one of my desk drawers and sift through it until I find the small lock box hidden inside.

I put the box on the desk and unlock it; I pluck the near identical poppet from the box and set the two on the desk side by side. The other poppet looks like me, my hair, and a different color of fabric, but is essentially the same. I could weep with relief at having the doll here, I'd ordered it before everything went to shit, but I demanded Sarah finish it sooner rather than later.

"Close the door," I say quietly as all of them stare at the two dolls.

"Is that..." Phil says slowly, coming up to the desk and hovering his hand over them.

"What does the poster say?" I gesture to the one still on my desk, "I'd like all of you to read it out word for word, please."

Leah scowls, then snatches up the poster and reads it out "Wanted: Lilith Callam for the crime of theft from the Aegis Organization. By order of Lord Samuel Graves, she is to be brought in alive for a reward of 5,000 marks. And any information that leads to the apprehension of Miss Callam will be rewarded."

I turn my head to the side, all four of them read it the same. Lilith and Samuel. The twins are frowning, though I'm not sure if it's in confusion or concern.

I sigh and rub my forehead, "I'm not surprised by that, but before I explain what the purpose of these are, I need your word that it does not leave this room."

Damien grunts, "Are you sure this is wise?" he asks, his eyes skating across the others who are giving us concerned looks.

I look down at the poppets and pick up Lilith's, looking into its face, "I'm not. But I have to do something, I can't..." I close my eyes and count to ten, my magic getting away from me as emotion overwhelms me. "I can't lose her, we have to find Lilith, whatever the cost to me."

Damien nods, "Understood,"

"What?" Leah asks, looking between the two of us, "What's going on?"

I turn to them and rest my forearms on the desk, "These poppets are the anchors for two powerful enchantments. They are complicated and can only be created by an Oracle. They make it so the only people who can use Lilith or my true name are those who can be undoubtably trusted by us."

"So, what to those people hear instead?" Evans asks with a glance at the twins.

"For Lilith it would be Lillian, for myself it's Samuel."

"Wait," Andre says, "Your name isn't Samuel? Does that mean you can't trust us?"

"Not necessarily," Damien says, "It simply means that there are some circumstances which might cause you being untrustworthy. However, that you hear Lilith's name correctly means that you can be trusted with her safety."

"Which is more important at this point," I supply, "For now we need to figure out a plan on how to find her. I'm just hoping that Lilith notices the spell is in place."

"Would she even realize what it means?" Phil asks with a frown.

I grimace, "I hope so, she's aware of the spell for me."

"So, what do we do then? Just wait?" Leah asks, "I'm not going to just wait around while she's in danger!"

Phil clears his throat, "Sarah said that when the time comes, Lilith will- " he cuts off as an image shimmers into view in the middle of the room.

It starts as a shadow but gradually gains features until it becomes a very clear image of Lilith. She's standing there with her arms wrapped around her waist. She's covered in bruises, cuts, and looks like she's shivering and crying too. My heart clenches as I take her in.

I try to take stock of how badly she's injured and what state she's in, but the image fades before I can get a good look. The flames roar up in the fireplace and wind kicks every loose object around the room as the ice covers the glass panes and cracks them. "Help," she says, her voice echoing around us faintly, "Please, someone... help. Don't leave me alone."

My magic flares further as a pang of her emotions hits me, loneliness, sorrow, a sense of betrayal, and a despair so deep it brings tears to my eyes. "We're coming," I say hurriedly, trying to push the words back to her, trying to reach back out. My tears fall as my anguish mixes with hers and becomes overwhelming. I don't know how I know, but she believes we're not coming.

Instead of reacting to my words, she sobs and wraps her arms around herself, curling forward and whispering, "Help," one more time in a hopeless voice.

The image disappears and my magic explodes, the disarray I kicked up before becoming a maelstrom. The windows shatter, the flames leap from the fireplace and catch on some papers flying around.

"Fuck!" I hear someone shout distantly.

I feel my magic spread further until someone grabs my shoulders and Philip's voice breaks through the chaos, "Samael! Enough!"

"Did you see her?" I demand, but even so wrangle my magic back enough that the fires go out and the wind settles. The chill from the broken windows is quickly chasing away what little warmth was present.

"Yes, I think we all did." He nods, but he moves to grip my face and force me to look at him, "I've seen that type of call before, she called out to who she can trust to help her. But if you lose it right now, we won't get the chance to get her back. You need to hold it together because you're the one with the plans."

"The plan is to find her!" I shout at him, unable to keep my frustration contained as tears continue to fall.

"No shit," Damien's voice cuts in from the doorway, the Evan's family is outside the door and Damien has transformed, standing between me and them. "That's the basic plan, but we need an actual plan if we're going to get her back."

"Right," I nod and sit down again, "Right..."

Philip

I don't think I've ever seen Samael react this violently to anything in this lifetime. He sits down and drops his head into his hands, "She... she thinks we aren't coming. Someone showed her a poster," he whispers, his voice trembling.

"Was that not the plan?" Leah says with a frown.

"It was, but planning it and feeling her despair because of it aren't quite the same," he says, his voice broken and scratchy.

"Well, what's next?" Evans says.

"I need someone to take over Aegis's operations here," Sam says flatly, "The Twins and I are going to go find her."

"How?" Dante mutters, "That projection didn't exactly give many clues."

"I can track it," I say, "There's a bit of a signature trail, even though it was a projection."

Samael nods, "Good, who do you think can lead while I'm gone? There are still demons in the city, we may have to call in some of the stronger agents from outside."

"I'll do it," Evans and Leah say at the same time, then look at each other with raised brows.

Damien chuckles and looks at Graves, "Look at that, Boss. The Evans and Mortimer Families *finally* deciding to step in to help Aegis."

The four of them glare over at him. "Perhaps we just needed the right motivation," Leah argues.

Sam makes a derisive noise and shakes his head, "Regardless, we need to get moving." He stands up as if he's going to leave the room.

I grunt and put a hand on his shoulder, "No, you need to get things written up so the four of them have the authority to be in charge and send messages to everyone who needs to hear about the shift. Maybe tell Helga, Marie, and Roland where we're going? I'm willing to bet Marie is still ready to fight you after this morning."

There's suddenly a knock on the door, Graves raises his head, "Open it," he says.

Damien pulls the door open and, as if they heard their names, Helga, Marie, and Roland stand there. The three of them march in and Marie steps closest, her hands on her hips and her head held high.

"We are here to submit our resignations," she says, her voice wavering as she finally takes in the room.

Graves' eyes widen, "All three of you?"

"Da," Helga says, her arms crossed, "Won't stand by while you attack Lilith, no matter how much we care for you, Samael."

Sam huffs out a laugh and drags a hand down his face, "Well then, I have good news for you. The twins and I are leaving as soon as possible to go find Lilith. I just need to write up the proper paperwork to transfer my authority as the head of Aegis over to the Evans and Mortimer family here."

The rigid postures of the heads of the household all deteriorate and Marie even sobs, "You are? What about the posters?"

"What do you think Lilith would do if she were kidnapped?" Sam asks, giving the woman his signature raised eyebrow.

Roland frowns, "She'd be stubborn and difficult..." his eyes widen, "Which would just get her in more trouble."

Marie's eyes widen too, "And she'd continue to hold out until you found her... but if you went looking," she goes deathly pale, "They would've hurt her more. Tried to use her."

Sam nods, "Sarah said that Lilith would rather..." he shakes his head, "It doesn't matter, the posters were to make Lilith believe we aren't coming. It's the only way to make her cooperative enough to not be in more danger. Did you see..."

The three of them nod, "Yes," Marie says, "we did. What do you need us to do?"

"Keep things quiet from the other staff, enough of them dislike Lilith that they may cause problems if they find out. Give any help you can to the Evans' while we're gone," he glances to the windows, "Over see getting those replaced."

He pulls out papers and starts writing, "Phil, Damien, go try to track her."

"All right," we both turn and leave, not waiting for further instruction.

Lilith

I hear movement on the stairs and get to my feet; I sway, the rune I etched into the dirt took a lot of magic to make. Between the physical torture and the drain coming from the cuffs, I'm rather impressed that I got it working at all.

A few minutes later, I hear them coming down the stairs. When they get in front of my cell, I don't lift my head to look at them, just raise it enough to see them through my lashes. This time the one in charge is with Gavin and Tyler, and they have a strange, absent expression on.

"I hear you're willing to cooperate now," they say, their voice sounding like someone drugged out of their mind, "Is that so, Lillian?"

"It seems I've nowhere else to go." I squeeze my arms around myself and close my eyes as tears gather, "No point being stubborn and loyal if they have abandoned me and marked me as a traitor."

"Smart woman," the odd one says, "I am the Speaker, I represent our illustrious patron. Now that you're going to cooperate, we will leave immediately."

"To go where?" I ask opening my eyes to look at the Speaker.

"To the second seal, of course. You have the first one there, and if you focus, you'll be able to find the second. So, let's begin."

I frown and look down at the charm wrapped around my wrist, "What should I focus on?"

"Just think of the seal, focus on finding its partner. It will lead you,"

I frown, still not quite understanding what they're saying, but wanting to get this over with none the less. Closing my eyes, I grip my wrist and press the charm as close to my skin as I can. I bring my hands to my chest and whisper, "Take me to the second seal, please."

Nothing happens for a moment, but then magic surges from the seal and hits me hard. My vision shifts, like I'm being dragged from the damp basement and through the city streets. It's hard to identify everything that passes by, but things slow for a moment and I see that I'm at the east gate. As if it's waiting for me to understand what I am seeing, the vision shifts again and I'm being pulled further into the countryside.

I don't know how far the vision takes me, but it stops when I'm outside what looks like a town. The small collection of buildings is dull and empty. I suspect I need to find what I'm looking for to proceed. I spot a sign, it reads "North River" as I read the words everything goes black.

I shake my head and look around me, I'm on the floor of the cell, everything aching as I lie there and try to reorient myself. Gavin is holding me up looking concerned, "What the fuck just happened?" He asks, his attention snapping over to the Speaker instead of me.

The Speaker smiles, "You saw where we're to go."

I nod despite it not being a question, "Out the East Gate, toward a town called North River."

The speaker grins and claps their hands, "Excellent! We leave at once," they turn and look at Tyler, "Bring her; do *not* remove the bindings."

Gavin looks like he's going to argue, but I shove away from him as Tyler reaches for me. He holds out his hand, which I take and let the muscular man help me to my feet. He looks over my shoulder and shrugs at Gavin, who I can almost feel fuming behind me.

"Come along Lillian!" The Speaker calls from the top of the stairs.

Tyler pushes me forward, making me stumble on unsteady legs. I turn to glare at him, but then I see he's cut Gavin off from getting to me as he pushes me up the stairs.

I'm filled with a surge of gratefulness for the large man's inter-ference as he pushes and prods me up the stairs, being equal parts antagonistic and helpful. We step out into the street and I wince as I'm blinded by the sunlight, "How long was I down there?" I ask, the question not directed at anyone.

"A week," The Speaker says brightly, "You held out a whole week, I'm quite impressed Lillian. Most people do not endure darkness as you did."

"Darkness doesn't scare me," I reply simply, "We've always been friends."

The Speaker laughs as if that's some sort of inside joke, then gestures at the carriage before us, "In we go, it's off to North River!"

And with that, I'm shoved inside and promptly chained to the floor, the others climbing in after us.

Six

In Which a Lead is Found

Damien

I inhale deeply as we pass a rather rancid smelling alley way. The scent makes me cough and Phil says, "You gotta time those better," his tone is attempting to be light but fails.

I glare over at him, "I'm just trying to keep the trail; it's actually getting stronger, so we must be getting close." I turn another corner and frown at the rows of well-kept houses.

We both stand there staring for a long minute, I swallow hard and say, "This is ominous,"

"Yeah," Phil agrees, "If... if she's here, or was here..." his voice cracks and I put a hand on his shoulder and squeeze.

"Come on, let's keep moving. The sooner we find a lead, the better," I push him forward slightly and he grunts, but we both start walking down the road at a fast clip.

I keep inhaling periodically then come to a stop outside a large house, I immediately recognize the crest on the mailbox and feel my hackles raise, "Hurst," I growl.

Phil nods, "I see it, this is a rental property though," He points at another symbol under the crest, "Who knows if they were even aware someone was here."

I growl again, baring my teeth at my brother, "Come on, we're going in."

He doesn't argue as we walk up to the door; the home is unlocked and the door swings open on silent hinges. The first thing I notice is how mundane it looks. There aren't any heavy chains, no dark corners and broken furniture, nothing. Then I'm struck with the scent of a scrubbing spell, which is making Lilith's scent fade from the space.

"Fuck!" I shout, rushing into the building, trying to beat the spell to any trail that may remain.

Phil comes in after me, fanning out in a different direction, looking for clues as well. I hear a door open as her scent becomes even more faded. A few seconds later I hear Phil make a noise, "Dem," he says, his voice choked.

I rush into the kitchen to find him staring down a staircase, his eyes wide. I walk to his side and catch the scents of blood, fear, and Lilith wafting up toward us. A heartbeat later, we're both rushing down the stairs and into a modified cellar.

Someone carved out the space from the basement, doubling what I'd normally expect from a building this size. They sectioned off one half with metal bars to form a cell. A chain drapes from the ceiling. Despite the cleaning spell, I can still see flecks of blood on the chains and ground, and someone's feet have scraped the dirt, leaving a clear mark.

I swallow hard, my entire being rejecting what I'm seeing, despite having seen what she looked like when she called to us. I want to say it isn't possible; when I look over, I see that Phil's entire expression has fallen, his body beginning to curl in on itself. Rushing to his side and grab his shoulder, "Phil, brother, Phobos!" I shout his name at last and he looks right at me, but doesn't see me.

Phobos

Dem and I run up to the compound as a roar tears from somewhere inside. I slide to a stop, many warning bells ringing. Deimos stops next to me as we both stare up at it, "What do you think that was?" He asks quietly, his eyes scanning the building.

"No idea, but it can't be good." I reply, drawing one of my swords, "We need to stay alert."

We step as one toward the front of the building, only for Samael to run out. The Eternal stops to catch his breath when he sees us, "Thank fates," he says with a sigh, "There you two are."

"What's going on?" I ask, holding an arm out to steady him.

"We found Lilith," he says with a wry grin, "And the compound has between ten and twenty minutes before Errill loses his shit."

"Okay, so let's get out of here." Deimos says, grabbing my other arm and tugging on me.

"No," Samael says with a tight smile, "You two need to get to Lilith before Errill loses it."

"What? Why?" Dem demands, glaring at our king and friend.

Samael puts a hand on his shoulder and looks into my brother's eyes, "Because, if Lilith is still in danger, when Errill loses his temper, the entire realm will fall to his wrath. Aside from myself, you two are the only ones I can trust who also have the power needed to break her out of whatever containment she's in. She's on the south side of the building, I'm pretty sure it's the top floor."

"Why us?" Dem asks again, trying to shake Samael's hand from his shoulder.

Samael smiles, darkness covering his features as his wings take on a dangerous hue, "No time, go!" He shoves us both toward the south.

Dem snarls but takes to the sky, his axe in one hand. I sprint under him, plowing through the few enemies that dare approach, though many are preoccupied with the roars coming from the main part of the house.

We near the south side of the building and Deimos lands on one balcony, "Fuck," he calls down, "She's in here."

I slide through the stone and up to him; I hear the glass break as he shoves his way into the space. We both go still. A cramped area, hardly a room, containing only a cage and chair placed outside of it.

Curled up on her side, her clothing dirty and torn, is Lilith. "Lilith?" Deimos asks, his voice going soft as he slowly approaches the cage.

She startles and scrambles away, pressing her back to the bars furthest from us, "W-what d-do you want?" she stammers, tear tracks are all over her face, her eyes puffy and red as she stares at us.

"We're here to get you out," I say softly, "how do we let you out?"

She turns her head to one side and stares at me, almost with disbelief, "That's a new one, letting me out. Stupid really, giving me hope."

"What the fuck are you on about?" Dem snaps, ever the impatient one, "We're trying to get you the fuck out of this shit hole, Hellion, stop being difficult."

Her eyes widen at that and her attention snaps to my brother and his big mouth.

"Dem!" I snap, "Yelling at her isn't going to-"

"Deimos?" Lilith cuts me off, the distant, frightened look fading from her features as she zeros in on his face, "It's actually you?" she looks over at me, "Both of you."

"Who else would it be?" Dem snaps still, his voice becoming a growl.

Lilith doesn't answer, but she points at something behind the chair, "There's the key, it'll unlock the cage."

"They just left it in here?" I ask, even as Deimos grabs the key and hands it to me.

As I turn the key in the lock, I feel the magical seal break too, realizing that they must've been using the cage as a way of containing her magic. I yank the cage door open. Lilith throws herself into my arms, a sob breaking free as she presses her face to my shoulder, "Thank you," she whimpers, "Thank you."

I grunt and hold her tight, "Of course, we'll always come find you."

She nods against my shoulder, then says, "We need to get out of here, I can feel Errill close by. As it stands, I'm not sure I've got the strength to protect you both from him."

"What in the hells is he that we need to be protected so badly?" Deimos asks, even as he sticks his head out the window to survey the area.

Lilith doesn't reply, but tries to stand and ends up with her knees buckling.

"Fuck," I hiss as I catch her and pull her into my lap, "How can I help?"

"Blood," she breathes, her tongue flicking out to lick the few drops of demon blood on my shoulder, "I need to recharge some, blood is fastest."

"You're fucking vampiric?" Dem snaps, "Can't Phobos just carry you?"

"After some blood," I argue, "She needs to be able to stand on her own, literally and magically."

Deimos growls, "Fine! Hurry."

Lilith presses her face to my shoulder, "You sure?" she whispers.

"Anything for you," I vow, meaning the statement with my entire soul.

A small smile is the only warning I get before she sinks tiny fangs into my shoulder, her venom makes the world go fuzzy for a moment, then it all clears as she pulls away and stands up. "Okay," she says with another small smile.

"Finally," Dem says, wrapping an arm around her waist and taking off before she can protest. I jump out after them and land right as another roar tears through the compound. I turn around in time to see a giant shape burst through the middle of the building, causing it all to collapse.

"Holy shit," I mutter as Dem lands next to me.

Lilith is clinging to his shirt and her other hand darts out to grab me when they're close enough, "He's not that threatening," Deimos says as we watch what sort of looks like a cross between a wolf and a dragon tear into the structure.

Lilith chuckles and pulls us all closer together, "He's still exercising restraint," she looks around and takes a deep breath, a dome of shadow rises to cover the three of us and as the dome closes she lets out a single, drawn out note. It's something akin to a screech and a whistle, it carries over the decrepit landscape and makes my ears ring.

The moment it reaches the behemoth in the distance, the beast's head swings in our direction. There's a long moment of silence, then the beast returns the note, the sound seems to sunder the ground and definitely causes the building to finish collapsing. My mouth drops open as Lilith smiles indulgently toward the dark beast.

"Shit," Dem whispers, and I see his arm flexing to pull Lilith closer, "Remind me never to piss him off,"

Lilith giggles at that, "If he gets pissed at you, it's already too late. We're safe in the circle, he won't get close to it, so we'll just hang out here until he and Samael are done."

She pulls herself from his grasp and sits down, hugging her knees as she watches the devastation wrought by her companion.

Graves

I'm standing in the empty kitchen, Roland sent most of the staff home, and stuffing non-perishable foodstuffs into a saddlebag. I shove a few more things in when Marie comes in from outside, "Here, Sarah had me make these a few days ago, she didn't explain what they were for, but I suspect you'll need them." She produces two potion bottles, both of which are sealed closed with wax that she's pressed her sigil into.

"What do they do?" I ask, taking them and setting them into the saddlebag.

"One neutralizes poisons, and the other helps accelerate healing," she explains, "Sarah said that I'd know when to use them, I assume the same goes for you."

I nod, "Thank you, I hope... I hope that these don't end up being needed, but I'm glad to have them."

"I agree, I hope you can find her before it gets that bad," she smiles sadly and covers my hand with hers, "You need to stop holding back, Samael. I fear that everything you are is going to be put to the test before this is all over."

I stare at her for a long while, not wanting to acknowledge the truth in her statement. I know I've been too careful, too concerned with image and what could potentially go wrong. I thoroughly think through things. And I can't stop thinking any more than I could control Lilith, both are pointless pursuits.

I'm still lost in my thoughts when the Damien slams the door to the kitchen open with enough force that the whole house shakes.

I look over and glare at the gargoyle, "Don't destroy the house any more than I already have."

He grunts, then walks past me toward the armory, a magic switch making the hidden door open and revealing weapons and armor. I look at Phil for answers as to why his brother has devolved into a grunting beast.

Phil runs a hand over his face, looking like he's seen some shit in the last hour or so, "We found the place she was being kept. It's a townhouse, but nobody was there and someone set a scrubbing spell so we couldn't get any scents or magic traces."

"So I need to take a look," I say, "Can you find the owners of the property?"

"About that..." he rubs the back of his neck and looks away, uneasy surging around him like he's more afraid of my reaction than what's gone wrong.

"Spit it out," I snap.

Damien reappears at the door. He's armed to the teeth with blades, a pistol at his hip, and leather gloves stretch over his knuckles with small pieces of metal embedded in them, "It belongs to the Hursts. Fucking Clarissa housed whoever the fuck took Lilith! There's a fucking dungeon in the basement, for fucks's sake! And they, they... FUCK!" He throws a punch into the wooden door frame and it cracks, his anger rushing out from him in a burst.

At his words, a feeling washes over me, which I can't quite describe. To call it anger seems like an insult to it. Even rage falls short of the intense burn in my veins. My heart pounds even as my stomach drops, if Clarissa and Gavin are working together Lilith is in far more danger than we'd originally thought.

I close my eyes and try desperately to pull my magic back, despite my efforts the room heats and things blasted off shelves. When I finally open my eyes, I level my gaze at Damien, "Get the horses. We'll go by the house to see if I can find anything, then directly to the Hurst Estate."

"What are we going to do?" Phil asks, even as he cracks his knuckles and looks ready to fight.

"I'll decide on the way," I snap as I make my way to the armory to grab my gear.

***

We get to the house where they held Lilith and I stare up at it. It's a nondescript building, a comfortable size with soft colors and a bit of a garden. I scowl at it as I make my way up to the door and I don't bother knocking as I push it open. I can already sense that there's nobody inside.

Damien sneezes as soon as we walk through the door, "ugh," he says, "The scrubbing spell has had more time to work, it just smells like some random bitch's magic now."

I nod, "It is good we could identify who owns the place, then. I'm still going to do another sweep of the building. Where's the entrance to the basement?"

Damien grunts, leading the way through the house and into a cellar. A cell is revealed at the bottom of the stairs. I go still as the air feels cold and damp, almost unnaturally so. I walk into the cell; the door swinging open silently. Phil stands on the stairs, staring down at us like he's almost afraid to come all the way into the space. "Phil?" I whisper.

He shakes his head and backs away, "Can't," he says hoarsely, "Being down there earlier already fucked with me. There's a chain on the ceiling, check that."

I do as directed and freeze. The chain runs through a loop and a section of it sags toward me, the rest of it coils back until it gets to an attachment point on the wall. I walk over to the contraption and see that it's designed to wrap the chain around, hoisting whatever's bound off the ground.

My stomach churns as I reach up and wrap my hand around the chain. Searing pain fills my entire body, it's like I've taken a beating or ten. Everything hurts like I've been kicked, punched, cut, and all manner of other pain. I yank my hand away and double over, Damien moves toward me and Phil makes a concerned noise from the stairs. I hold up a hand and gasp, "Look for any runes, she had to have sent the message somehow and the fact that there's a trail at all..."

Damien sets to work scouring the walls. When I'm able to move again, I cross the room and stop about midway to the door. Turning in a circle, letting my thoughts and my magic move about the space, looking for the source of tension in my gut.

Damien grunts, "Found it," He points at a spot on the ground, there, scratched into the floor, is a shape that looks like swirling lines.

I crouch down and run a hand across the rune, reaching for it and hoping to catch some trace of magic. Instead, I'm hit with emotion so strong and so raw it makes me fall back. When I look up, the Twins are both crouched next to me, even as I can feel tears sliding down my face.

"She was here," I say, my voice hoarse as the tears burn down my cheeks. The pain and despair of betrayal chokes me, "All I got was emotion... there's not enough here to give us a direction."

"Then we go to the Hursts' Estate," Phil says quietly, a deadliness in his tone that I've rarely seen in him, "They had a hand in this, even if all we get is who they rented the space to."

"Yes, we need to get going." I get to my feet and look at the chain again, a chill runs down my spine as I turn away, "Let's make these people regret hurting Lilith."

Philip

We ride up to the Hurst estate and I swear I can see Damien getting more irritated as we've gotten closer. Sam, on the other hand, looks eerily calm, like he's got perfect control of the situation, but I suspect the mask is fragile at best. I find myself re-living the same memories over again. The last time we were all looking for Lilith together, I shake myself before I get lost in remembering, and turn my attention to the others. Hoping that they have an idea of what to do next.

I hop from my horse and look up at the estate, "What's the plan?"

"Go in there and beat the shit out of them till they give us answers." Damien snaps, stalking toward the door and flexing his fists like he's already imagining the ways to make it hurt.

"No," Samael says, his voice taking on a hint of magic that makes Damien stop in his tracks, "We're going to go in the same way we always enter a noble estate. We will not begin with violence, despite how much we'd all like to."

"Why the fuck not?" Damien roars into Samael's face.

Boss meets his gaze with a tight smile, "Because we need answers. If we go in there looking for a fight, that's what we'll get. So, we're going to be civil, at least as long as it takes to get the answers we need. I understand your anger, Damien, but I will *not* put Lilith in more danger with rash decisions and short tempers."

Damien looks ready to haul off and punch Graves, but manages to get control of himself. My brother rolls his shoulders, then walks to his usual post at Graves's side. "Lead on then, *Boss.*"

With a precision that only comes with years of practice and familiarity, the three of us walk up to the estate and Graves knocks, using the end of his cane to make the sound stronger. It takes a few minutes before the door swings open, a butler stands in the doorway looking confused, "May I help you?" he asks, his eyes flicking over the three of us as if trying to place why a noble is at the house at this hour.

"Tell Clarissa that Samael Graves is here," Graves says, using both of their first names and drawing looks from both Damien and I.

The butler's eyes widen, and he sweeps back to let us in. We're ushered inside and off to a small room before the Butler disappears.

"What the fuck was that?" Damien growls as soon as the Butler is gone.

Graves raises that insufferable eyebrow at my brother and says, "It'll put her guard down and get her in here quickly."

Damien's eyes narrow, making him look even more annoyed, then grunts and steps back into his usual guardian stance. If this didn't have to do with Lilith, Damien would've started a fight with Samael by now. But, as always, he keeps his mouth shut for her sake. We both do. We're all uncomfortably silent for the few minutes it takes the Butler to return.

However, it's not the butler that reappears in the doorway, it's Clarissa. She flounces into the room and practically throws herself into Boss's arms, "Samuel! How good to see you!"

I tense at the relaxed energy she brings in, but then she gets to Sam's side and lays her hands against his chest. I'm about to snap at her and lose my cool, even before Damien does.

Samael beats me to it and catches her wrists before she touches him, giving her a tight smile, "It's nice to see you too, Clarissa. However, I do ask that you keep your hands to yourself. I may have changed in ways but retain my dislike of casual contact."

Clarissa pouts, then sighs and pulls her hands away, "Very well, I just thought since you'd come to visit..." she trails off and bats her eyelashes at him.

Damien growls and takes a couple of steps forward, which earns him a haughty look from Clarissa. As if the shifter just now noticed a small smile curls her lips, "Oh my, is my nose correct?" She inhales deeply and looks at the three of us, "The little tramp is gone, her scent isn't on any of you. I'm surprised the dog didn't go with her." She waves condescendingly at Damien.

"The only person who's a dog here is you," Damien snaps, taking a step toward her with his teeth bared and a gray pallor overtaking his neck.

Graves clears his throat, drawing Clarissa's attention back to him before she can taunt Damien again. "That's not what we came to discuss. We were actually following a lead in regard to a theft. We have reason to believe that whomever took the artifact used your home on Ninth as a hideout."

She makes a face, "What makes you think that?"

"We found traces of the culprit's scent," Damien says, his voice more growl than words.

Clarissa laughs and turns away, "If they were using my home, it was not with my permission. When you find the culprit, let me know and I'll level my own charges at her."

She turns back to Graves and steps up to him, "Is that all you wanted to speak of?"

Graves nods, "Yes, that's all we were concerned about. We'd like to, if able, get access to the rental records of the property."

She sighs dramatically, "I can have them sent over, but it will be a day or so before I can get them." She waves her hand dismissively, "Martin is out of town for the time being, it may take more than a few days for our people to reply. They're not as considerate to me."

I'm half a breath from grabbing her wrist myself, but my decision comes too late. As soon as her hands land on Graves' chest, he grabs one wrist, wrenches it behind her back and slams her face first against the wall. With her captured wrist pulled up behind her to an uncomfortable angle.

"What?" she screeches, "Let me go!" she tries to struggle away from, only to find out the hard way that Samael is stronger than he looks.

"Not happening," Graves replies, his voice calm despite the scowl on his face, "Don't lie to me, Clarissa. Do you really expect me to believe that you don't have those documents in your office right now?"

Clarissa whimpers, "What are you on about? I don't-" she cuts off as Graves twists her arm further.

"Ah, so that's it. You already know who was there and what was going on," he says in a deadly whisper, "What do you know?"

"What do you care?" She demands, trying to shove him away but finding it far harder than she expected and looks terrified, "I-I saw the posters that were put up! I know that you're looking for that little tramp. You should've been more careful, letting someone like *that* trollop into your home."

Graves twists her arms again, and she cries out in pain, "Keep spouting insults and I'll make you wish Damien had gotten to you. Now, tell me who you rented the house to and why they want Lilith."

"What does it matter?" Clarissa wails, her voice shrill and making my ears hurt, "She's just a street- "

With a hiss, Graves presses the shifter's shoulder against the wall and leans in close to her, "I thought I was clear enough at the Solstice, anyone who goes after Lilith with cruel intent again will pay for it. I suggest you give me the answer before I make good on my promise."

Clarissa's crying stops and the color drains from her face so quickly you'd think she was being drained by a vampire. She opens and closes her mouth a few times, then says, "They were the leader of a religious group, called themselves the Speaker of Disorder. All I know is that they were looking for the same thing you were and, and that the shifter friend of hers was going to help."

Graves grunts and lets Clarissa go, causing her to fall to the ground in a heap as he turns away and brushes his hands on his pants like he's touched something vile, "When did they end their lease and leave?"

"They left this morning, said something about Lillian finally giving them a heading and that they were going east." Clarissa weeps as she stays leaning against the wall.

"Good," Graves says. He stops in the doorway on his way out, "Oh, and Clarissa,"

She looks up at him; her face tear stained and puffy. He smiles cruelly, "Good luck explaining to Martin why all your assets, income, and properties are being seized."

Her mouth opens and she screeches, "I answered you!"

Before she can, Samael raises his eyebrow at her, "I made my stance clear. You're lucky I didn't decide to kill you." With that, he leaves Damien and I on his tail and looking at each other in shock.

Seven

In Which the Thief Leaves a Trail

Lilith

I scowl at the dark curtain pulled across the window of the carriage, not daring to looking at the other people inside. I don't want to see them, to acknowledge them even. They've left me alone thus far, apparently giving them an exact city to look for is enough, for now.

As if thinking about their presence made them aware of me again, the Speaker leans forward, "Tell me, Lillian, is the seal in North River?"

Glancing over at them, I try to ignore the ache that blooms when I see Gavin beside the strange person. "I don't think so, that's just where the vision stopped. I'm hoping that as we get closer, I'll see something else."

"Hmmm," the Speaker says slowly, "You'd best be telling the truth, if not you're going to suffer pain like you've never known."

I snort and roll my eyes.

They scowl at that, "Do you doubt me?"

"Physical pain is not an adequate threat," I reply as I turn away to stare at the window again, "You can ask your torturer there, he's bloodied me up plenty and I didn't cave."

The Speaker's eyes cut to Tyler, who looks like he's going to throw up, "Perhaps, but he had orders to keep you alive. If you're lying, then your use will have expired, so I may do what I wish."

"If you try to kill me, I'll take every one of you with me," my eyes flick to Gavin, "Even with my hands and feet bound I'm more than capable of taking on a shifter, a human, and whatever the hell you are." I turn my eyes back to the Speaker.

"You bitch!" They lash out and slap my face, bursting a scab and making my head snap to one side. Before I can recover, their hand strikes from the other side, this time causing blood and saliva to hit Tyler, who's stationed beside me.

Blood fills my mouth and I turn back to the Speaker, a feral grin overtaking my face as my magic seethes with impotent anger, "Done with your tantrum?" I ask sweetly, noting the lighting shifting ever so slightly as my eyes glow with magic.

The Speaker's eyes widen in response and Gavin leans back in his chair, "You can't access your magic," Gavin accuses.

"So you say. Wanna test it?" I ask, feeling a touch maniacal as I reach deeper into my magic, which causes the light in my eyes to brighten. I know I can't use the magic, but trying to pull on it makes it fill me enough to show like I can.

The Speaker mutters something under their breath and presses their hand to a locket on their neck. A moment later, a shock rips through my body. It starts at my feet and races up all the way to my hair. I scream and try to writhe away from the pain, I can't escape and instead lose my grip on my magic and my consciousness.

***

I wake to Tyler leaning over me with a damp cloth, I'm laid out in a bed and he dabs the cloth on my face. When he sees that my eyes have opened, he grunts, "I'm not sure if you're incredibly brave or incredibly stupid."

I laugh harshly, but it quickly turns to a cough, my throat too dry to do much more. Eventually I clear my throat, "I've been called both and worse." I flex and most of my muscles protest, but I get myself sitting up, "How long was I out?"

Tyler leans back to give me some space, but watches me closely, "We got to North River, the Speaker dosed you with sedatives to keep you asleep while we traveled."

I sigh and rub a hand down my face, "That's why my mouth feels like sandpaper and my head hurts like a bitch."

Tyler snorts and sits back in his chair, as he hands me a glass of water, "Luckily for you, they didn't shock you more than once. If they had, I doubt you'd be so mouthy."

I laugh aloud at that, "You ain't seen nothing yet, I'm barely at a little mouthy. Though, if there are more of those shocks to come, then I'll probably tone it down unless absolutely necessary, too much strain on the body." I sip at the water and sigh as it soothes my throat.

"How are you so relaxed about this?" He demands, leaning forward to look right into my eyes, "You're being transported as a fucking prisoner across the country while leading a religious zealot and someone who betrayed you to a powerful magic artifact. Yet you're acting like this is just another day for you."

I shrug and look up at him, "At this point all they can threaten is my life. If I'm honest, death would be a reprieve from the bullshit my life has been. Besides, like the Speaker said, once I've outlived my usefulness, they'll kill me. The way I see it, if I'm going to die, it'll be on my own fucking terms, most likely while being a brat."

He shakes his head and scoffs, "I don't understand it, a woman like you, young and smart, acting like life is barely worth living. It doesn't make any sense."

I shrug, "Sorry to break your perspective on the world," I chug the rest of the water, then look around the room.

There's two cots, a bucket, and that's it; not even a window to give me the illusion of freedom. I turn my head to one side and sigh, "Why are you the one in here with me?"

"The Speaker doesn't trust Gavin not to bend to your whims and babysitting is beneath them. So yer stuck with me, Lillian, at least until they can gather up some other guards to monitor you."

I groan and put my head in my hands, "All right, all right. Can I convince you to give me a bit of privacy while I take a piss?"

He glances at the bucket in the corner and sighs, "Yeah, that's fine, just don't try to leave."

"Where, exactly, am I going to go?" I ask, gesturing around the room with only one exit.

He grunts and shakes his head, "Fine, fine," he stalks to the door, unlocks it with a key in his pocket, then goes through and I hear it lock again on the other side.

I stand up and explore the room a bit more, no bags, no food, no weapons. Figures they'd keep as much as possible away from me, though the second cot is unexpected. I shake my head, no need to wonder if they'll leave someone in here with me, they won't. It's most likely that I'll be locked in and someone left to keep watch, seeing as if they left the person with the key inside I'd just take the damn thing.

I rouse myself from my thoughts before I allow myself to get too caught up in escape plans. I finish my business and survey the room once more. Fidgeting my fingers, the desire to leave a sign getting stronger the longer I stand here. I hear the lock turning and shake myself, there's not a good reason for me to leave a sign. I'm on my own, as always. The door swings open and I brace myself for the verbal war.

Tyler is the one that comes back, followed a moment later by the Speaker.

The latter smiles in that distant, loopy way of theirs and says, "We've made it to North River, Lillian, where is our next heading."

"I haven't seen anything else from the Seal," I admit, rubbing the artifact on my wrist.

Their eyes narrow on me, that distant expression disappearing in an instant, "Then look again. If you cannot give us another clue, then you've worn out your usefulness."

I grunt and close my eyes, fighting the urge to fight them, I can't take them as I am. I take a deep breath and pull both my hands to my chest. Wrapping one hand around the seal and focus intently on the subtle magic that emanates from it. I'm not sure how long we sit there, but it's like time stands still. I take another deep breath and the warmth races up my arm and swells to fill me.

At first, it feels like I'm hovering above myself. Like the seal is some cosmic entity watching my life. I focus intently on the seal, and nothing seems to happen. It worked before, but doesn't seem to be anymore. I grunt and squeeze the charm harder, to no avail. I grapple desperately for something to guide me, but it feels like it's out of my reach.

Suddenly, jolting magic races up from my ankles, ripping through me as if it's trying to tear me apart. I scream and drop to my knees, the warmth of the seal warring with the static sensation of the chains shocking me. Trying to move away from the pain only for it to become stronger. I scream again and finally something snaps, my body goes limp and I feel myself drift from consciousness.

When awareness returns, it doesn't seem like I'm being guided. Instead, it feels like I'm recalling a dream, or maybe a memory.

***

I stand on the edge of a forest, my arms tucked against my sides as I stare out at the trees. A sense of desire, of longing, but also fear, is so strong it's like a tangible thing pulling at my chest as I watch the branches sway in the breeze. A large form walks up and drapes a cloak over me, "Come on, Miss Lilith, we shouldn't linger here."

I turn and Philip is looking down at me, his bright blue eyes filled with worry. "Why did Damien bring us here? If it's unsafe?" I stare up at my friend, searching for answers in his eyes.

"He... he wasn't thinking straight. We shouldn't be here, there are dangerous people in this forest." Phil explains, still trying to lead me away from it.

"Philip," I put a hand on his arm, "Tell me the truth."

He stops and looks down at me, his hand comes up to cup my cheek, his entire expression softening, "Promise not to be mad at him."

I frown, "Why would I be mad?"

Phil sighs and presses a kiss to my forehead, "You're always so nice to him. This forest used to be a way back home for us, it hasn't been for a long while. But..."

I grab his hand, pinning it to my cheek, "Spit it out."

"He brought you here because you remind him of her and he's hoping that being so close to home will help you remember."

I swallow and look at the forest again, that confusing feeling pulling at me again, "I..."

"You don't," Phil finishes for me and starts pulling me away, "You don't remember because this isn't home, not really. All he's done is put you in more danger because he's desperate."

That strange sensation becomes a full-out pull, something dragging me toward the forest. "Wait," I tug out of his grasp and make a dash for the trees, my heart pounds in my ears and my breathing comes in gasps as I dart through a few rows of trees.

I can't deny the pull, can't deny the need driving me into the forest. I have to get to where it's pulling, there's something there for me, something important. And even though my dearest friend is chasing after me, calling my name, I cannot stop.

Suddenly a branch snaps, I tumble forward, falling down, down, down into a ditch. I gasp for breath at the bottom, staring up at the stars that peek from between the branches. I hold my hand up to the sky, peering back at the stars through my fingers.

I know the fall has damaged something essential. I'm not sure how I know since the shock has rendered me numb, but I can feel my life slipping away. As I lay there staring up at the stars, there's another snap and someone is standing over me, someone I don't know.

They look concerned and crouch next to me, dark eyes scan me and swirling tattoos paint their face. His markings are dark, looking like mud on the man's face. The lines swirl in a way that's familiar. Three lines on his forehead, two on each cheek and one down the nose. The mark of the Eternal Tribe.

They open their mouth to say something, but I don't hear it as darkness seeps into my vision. The last thing I see is Phil bursting out of the trees, eyes ruby red, teeth bared and aimed for the stranger's throat.

***

I wake with a jolt, gasping for breath and rolling onto my side as pain lances through every inch of me. The pain is a phantom one a remnant of the memory clinging to my mind. "About time," the Speaker says from somewhere nearby, "Do you know where we need to go?"

I cough and roll onto my side, only distantly aware of Tyler and Gavin also standing nearby. "I... I think..." I groan as different pains war within me, making everything muddled.

"Don't think, answer me, Lillian!" The Speaker yells, their voice becoming harsh and making me wince.

When I don't reply right away, there's another jolt of shocking magic that makes me finally cry, "The forest, the Black Forest to the north, it's there I saw the Eternal Tribe. I think they have it. I'm not sure exactly where, but I'll try again when we're closer."

They make a disgusted noise and stand up, "Very well, it's a heading I suppose." I don't see them coming until their foot is on my throat and they're glaring down at me, "If I find out that you're playing us, I will make you suffer for it."

I manage a manic grin, "You say that like I'm not already suffering."

Their scowl becomes darker and the press of their foot stronger.

I cough once and then say, "Can't help you if I'm dead."

They let off the pressure and scowl down at me.

My grin widens further and I lift the wrist with the charm on it, "This thing drives people batty, right? But not me," I tilt my chin, "I'm still sane, or at least as sane as I was before the seal. How many others can say the same after almost two weeks with it?"

Their expression shutters for a moment, but then they step away and that dopey look returns, "You're right, can't lose our best asset. Regardless of my feelings toward your attitude." Before anyone can reply, they leave the room.

Gavin and Tyler continue to watch me as I let my head hit the ground and laugh. A moment later Gavin leaves, then Tyler, who's standing over me, looks down and shakes his head, "You're an enigma, Lillian, I don't know if that was brave or stupid."

I smirk up at him, "Don't you know that there's only a fine line between the two?"

He frowns again then leaves the room, the lock clicking into place seconds later. I chuckle to myself as I continue to lie on the floor, maybe this thing is driving me a little batty. I shouldn't be reckless with my life, taunting the person who holds it in their hands, but I just can't find it in myself to care. My eyes close for a second when something clicks.

My eyes snap open and my heart races, *Tyler called me Lillian.* I think back through the last few days, trying to recall when they've addressed me. They've all been calling me Lillian, even Gavin. Is it the same spell as Samael's? Probably, cause Gavin absolutely knows my name.

If that's true, Sarah is still on my side and trying to help, at the very least. At best, so is Aegis. My chest tightens, remembering the words on the wanted poster. Wanted by Aegis, by the people I thought I could trust. But maybe, if I'm supremely lucky, I still can.

I shouldn't be so hopeful, I shouldn't let myself believe that I'll be rescued when people have only ever let me down. But a deeper part of me insists that they're coming, that they would never leave me like this.

I sit up and look around. Needing to leave a trail without using too much magic. I prod my lower lip until the scab breaks and I get a good blood flow.I crawl halfway under the bed, still poking at my lip to keep the wound dripping. Closing my eyes, I focus on the charm and instantly feel its warmth spread along my arm.

I carefully draw a symbol along the floorboards, my blood almost instantly soaking into the wood. As I finish with a whispered plea, the blood dries and darkens to an eerie, scorched black.

I run my thumb along the mark and smile, a drip of blood falls near the symbol. Oddly, the contrast between the fresh blood and the symbol sends of a sense of satisfaction through me, but when I hear the lock engage again I scramble out from under the bed and throw myself atop it.

Eight

In Which Aegis Follows

Damien

It's late on our first day of travel when I smell it, the subtle hints of sage reaching me first. I slow my horse and look around. Phil senses the change in my attention first, also starting to slow down and calling ahead for Samael.

Graves comes back toward us, "What is it? We're kinda in a hurry."

"I smell her magic," I say, looking around as if she's just going to pop out of the trees or something, "She's been here and tapped into her magic."

There's a moment of silence, then Graves nods, "All right, fan out and we'll see if we can find any clues to where they may have gone. Let's just hope they haven't veered off the road."

We scatter into the trees, each looking for any indication that Lilith has been here. Something feels off, move my way through the trees, searching for further traces of Lilith's magic, but I can't pick anything else up. I'm only a few yards away from the road when the scent of her magic disappears. I lift my nose and inhale deeply, still nothing. It's like she didn't get the chance to actually use her magic, just begin gathering its strength.

I wander back to the road. Sam and Phil are already there, both of them looking concerned. "I can't see any indication that they were here," Graves says, "It seems to be just on the road. Though I am detecting some powerful emotion and another source of magic, just nothing that's strong enough for me to make any sense of."

"Yeah," I agree, "I guess we should keep going. I had hoped she'd gotten away from them."

"I don't think she'll risk it," Phil says as we move.

"Why not?" I ask glaring over at him, "Why wouldn't she jump at the chance to get free?"

"Cause she thinks we're hunting her too," Graves says quietly, "She'd probably rather be with them where she knows what's going on, rather than getting herself into trouble when she's not sure what'd happen if we found her."

I scowl at that, then look away, "You're right, she'd be dumb to expect anything other than conflict with us." I close my eyes, remembering the devastated look on her face when she'd told me how often people had abandoned her.

When I open my eyes, Phil is looking at me with a sympathetic stare, his expression pinched. I glare at my brother and he offers me a tight smile, "We'll set things right once we find her."

"Right," I mutter and look away, "Cause she'll just forgive us for even suggesting that we'd abandon her."

He makes a pained noise in the back of his throat, then tries to smile at me, "She's forgiven us for worse before."

"Not in this lifetime," I snap. His face pales and he drops the subject. I wonder if that piece of information is strong enough for him to question what might happen.

Lilith

I walk along the wagon that we'd traded for the carriage; it creaks along as the horses pull it like it's a weight too grand for them. A handful of men from North River have joined us, and many of them watch me with something between pity and interest. It's been a few days, and my smart mouth got me kicked off of the wagon rather than being allowed to ride in it. As it stands, the Speaker is riding in it with their nose in the air as they regard us all with what I can only describe as contempt.

Gavin drives the wagon, keeping the pace steady, but just a touch too fast for me to walk comfortably. So instead I have to trot to keep up. Thankfully, all the running Damien made me do allows me to keep up with them easily, only needing to break every couple of miles. Which seems the same distance that the horses need before they refuse to move.

I lag behind again and one of the men we'd picked up grunts and, of all things, slaps my ass and says, "Keep moving, bitch."

I stop in my tracks and spin on him, unable to contain the flash of absolute rage that rushes through me. My magic refuses my call, so I swing one leg out and knock his feet from underneath him. Another motion and I'm poised over him, the chain connecting my wrists pressed against his throat, "Touch me again and I'll tear your fucking hand off."

He scoffs, despite choking against the chain.

Leaning closer and I see the slight reflection of green in his eyes as I speak, "Don't believe me? I've fought vampires and gargoyles, even killed a demon a couple weeks ago. I *will* find a way."

His eyes bug out as I press harder against his throat, then Tyler is there and drags me away from my captive and up to my feet, "Enough," the big man snaps, glaring down at me.

I glare back up at him, and when the man on the ground moves, I slam a foot down on his hand, making him scream. "I didn't say I was done with you," I snarl.

Before I can do any more, Tyler backhands me, sending me sprawling away from the man and busting the cut on my lip. "I said enough!" he shouts, "If you don't knock it off, the Speaker will shock you again."

I look up from where I'm braced on the ground. The Speaker is standing up in the wagon, regarding me with annoyance. I bare my teeth at them, "I'll tolerate abuse from you, Gavin, and Tyler, the rest of these rubes are fair-game. If you cannot keep them from touching me, I will."

Tyler looks over at the Speaker, who's annoyance drops into that dopey smile, "I can respect that, though I will not permit you to kill them."

I grunt and get to my feet, "Fine," I spit out a mouthful of blood, directly at my assailant, who's still on the ground.

The Speaker chuckles and turns away, "Let's keep moving, we haven't time to waste!"

Tyler helps the man to his feet then ushers me away from him, "Yer one reckless lass," he hisses in my ear.

I grin at that, but still don't take my eyes off the man in front of me, "You haven't seen the least of it, *lad*."

Philip

The village of North River has seen better days. Most of the buildings are in disrepair and the citizens eye us with suspicion before scattering as if they can tell with a glance that we're dangerous. We aren't a threat to them, for now. Near the center of town is a pub and inn, the sign above proudly labeling it the 'Flying Falcon' even though it looks just as run down as the rest of the town.

We tie up our horses and walk up to the inn, Damien and I fall into formation behind Graves as he walks in with his head high. The room goes silent when we enter, all eyes turning to us. The tavern is about half full, the smells of stale ale, unwashed bodies, and fresh bread fill the air. One man stands, "We don't we get strangers very often."

Graves looks over at him and raises his eyebrow, "Good thing I don't care. We're looking for someone and we can pay anyone who has information."

A few of the men exchange glances, then the man behind the bar says, "Ain't nobody passed through this way in a while."

Damien growls and Graves sighs, "Not even an entire question out of my mouth and I'm being lied to."

Samael raises his head and looks at the surrounding group, then draws his gun and pulls the hammer back. "If you don't know anything or aren't willing to share it, leave."

Everyone scrambles to their feet and races for the door, parting around us. The bartender tries to back away, but Graves levels the gun at him, "Not you."

The man freezes and swallows hard, "I, uh, I don't know nothing." He stammers.

"Which implies you know something," Graves says as he walks up to the bar and sits down. He lowers the hammer of the gun and sets it on the bar, resting his elbows there as well to regard the man. "You have two choices. Either you tell us what you know and we leave with our newfound knowledge. Or, you lie to me and make us drag the information out by force. I would rather not inflict any harm on you, but if you refuse to cooperate, I'll do whatever it takes to get what I need to know."

Swallowing again, the bartender walks back up to the counter, "Okay, what do you want to know?"

"Recently, a group of people would've passed through here. I don't know everyone involved, but there would've been a shifter and a woman with black hair and green eyes."

The bartender shifts his weight, "Aye, they passed through. Said the lass was a dangerous prisoner, and they needed help to transport her."

"What the fuck!" I shout, cutting him off and slamming my hand on the counter, "You just let them drag her off without asking what her crimes were?"

He recoils, "I didn't say that! The leader of the band said she was a prisoner. But after they asked around for anyone willing to help them, another went around telling everyone she was innocent."

I frown at that, Damien and I exchanging a look over Graves' head.

Samael nods, "I see. And how many people opted to help them?"

"Only about five. The lass didn't look too dangerous and was nice to everyone who they let speak to her. With how nice she was and the one man saying she was innocent, most weren't keen on potentially harming her."

"But also not brave enough to rescue her," Damien growls.

The bartender shrugs, "We ain't fighting folk, besides none of us were sure she was innocent. Better to stay out of it than get involved."

Samael sighs and pinches the bridge of his nose. "Very well. What did they purchase, and which way did they go?"

"They got thicker clothing, coats and such, then a wagon and rations for about two weeks. They were heading north, but didn't say anything else." The bartender rushes to say, his eyes still flicking to the gun periodically. Even though I'm certain that Damien is the bigger threat at this point.

"When did they leave?" Graves asks, raising an eyebrow at him.

"Two days ago."

Graves winces, "Shit, we've fallen behind, we should get going."

"Where did they keep her?" I ask, getting a look from Graves. I shrug, "We may be able to find a clue."

"They probably scrubbed the place like last time." Damien snaps.

"Worth a look," Graves says as he stands up. "Show us which room."

Graves

The bartender leads us through a few rooms and into a main floor room that looks converted from storage. "What the hell?" Damien growls, looking around the sparse room.

"The leader demanded that the girl be put in a room with no windows. Somethin' bout her being too slippery," He says hurriedly.

I step inside, and the strange scrubbing spell has been cast in here as well. "Fucking hell," I growl, "they scrubbed this one too, it doesn't even leave behind emotional impressions."

Phil walks in now, shoving Damien out of the way, "I smell blood," before Damien or I can react to that revelation, he grabs the cot and throws it aside with a crash.

I startle when I see a swirling symbol on the floorboards, "Shit, is that the same as the other one? Why didn't we see anything?" I go to his side, staring down at the symbol alongside him.

"No," Phil says, running a hand across the marking, "It's not the same, it's more like a trail marker rather than a call, just meant to be like a magical rune."

"Let me look with my magic," I say, crowding closer to him.

He grunts and moves aside. I drop to the floor and wrack my brain for any recognition of the symbol. The swirling lines are imperfect, but something about the way they spiral feels familiar.

I try not to focus on the familiarity of it as I press my hand to the surface of the wood. At first there's no change, nothing to suggest that I've even tapped into whatever message is imbedded with it, but then I'm hit with a wave of energy.

Lilith's magic swirls out from the rune, lacing around me and almost weaving its way up my arm. Then it hits me with pain, frustration, fear, but and only a scant trace of hope. Unfortunately, it doesn't give me a direction and the signature fades before I'm able to track it further.

I pull my hand away then slam it on the wooden surface, "Nothing, it doesn't seem like she's hoping someone's coming. There's something else there too, I just got hit with the emotions first. Maybe one of you can get a better read."

Phil shrugs, "Worth a shot," and presses his hand to the mark as well.

A moment later, he pulls his hand away and looks over my head at Damien, "I just... I saw a memory. They're going toward the Eternal Tribe."

Damien hisses and scowls, "That's not good."

"The Eternal Tribe, aren't they a myth?" I ask with a frown.

Philip sighs, "I fucking wish. They used to follow the Lost Gods, but it's been so long since they were active that who knows what they believe now?"

"All right then, that gives both a direction and a target. If we can't find Lilith directly, we can find this tribe and hopefully enlist their aid in finding her."

"Hopefully," Damien says dourly.

I frown at him, then shake my head, "Come on, we need to keep going. We're two days behind."

Nine

In Which the Road is Long

Philip

I stare at the small clearing and rub the back of my neck. The remnants of the campsite are sparse. Based on the lack of footprints in the snow and the ice on the cinders remaining in the fire pit, it's been days since anyone has been here.

Damien is storming through the surrounding woods, making enough noise to wake the fucking dead as he curses about not being fast enough. Samael is sitting on a stump not far away, staring despondently into the fire pit as if it'll have the answers we need. The worst of it is the stump has blood smeared across the side, forming the rune that drew us here.

I tilt my head to the sky, trying to rein in my reactions. My companions need me to stay optimistic, even though this is the third time we've come across a site like this. Both are too realistic for their own good; they see the failures and refuse to consider that we're still making progress. I take another breath, then hear a branch snap.

I spin, ready to yell at Damien, but he's standing a few yards away with his mouth hanging open and staring at something behind me. I frown and turn, but his eyes widen in panic as something leaps over my head and lands in the fire pit. My mouth drops open at the creature now standing in the center of the camp staring Samael down.

Parsley stands in the middle of the circle, even though we saw them in the city, this is the first time I'm getting to see them clearly. The center head is a lion with a red mane with streaks of gold. On the right is a black screech owl, its head swivels eerily on its neck, taking in all three of us. And on the left is a horned snake, it has its head pulled back against the main part of the body, but its eyes are glaring at us and it's in a strike pose.

"Sam, don't move." Damien says, holding his hand out toward our very mortal charge as he moves to block the chimera's line of sight.

I swallow as the owl head spins to look at me. A second later, I feel a push of feelings, of thoughts, of questions. Just like in the sewers, I gasp and put a hand to my head, their thoughts overwhelming and confusing. When I don't react, the owl screeches and the cry makes me wince. The lion's head focuses intently on Damien, and I see him wince and step back too, making the lion roar and stamp its paw in the dirt.

All three of the heads turn their attention to Sam, who is sitting still as a stone. I try to take a step toward it but before I can move Sam winces and puts a hand to his head, "Whoa, whoa, slow down," He says, holding a hand up to the chimera.

I frown as the beast seems to settle slightly, then focuses on Graves again. Samael winces again and closes his eyes, "You're looking for someone?" He asks, then winces, "Fuck, I can't keep up with that. Slow down!" He shouts the last, and the Chimera goes eerily still.

Neither Graves nor the Chimera move for a long moment before Sam says, "Your mother? I don't know your mother."

The next thing that happens is a mental shout, "MAMA!" three voices scream, but before we can try to get more clarity, the beast leaps away and disappears into the forest.

Graves

We all stare after the creature and I look at the twins, "What was that?"

Damien and Phil exchange a look, then Phil says, "Uh, it's a creature called a chimera."

I give him a bland look, "I actually knew that. Now answer my actual question: how in the world did it communicate with us and why?"

Damien clears his throat, "It's clearly distraught and lost. It'd be hard to say what exactly it was after-"

I raise a brow at him, "You two can stop pissing around the truth any time now. It was looking for someone and thought that we could help it. Why?"

I keep my gaze steady on them both for a long while. Phil is the one who ends up caving, he sighs and runs a hand through his hair, "It knows us. They were the queen's pet... so she's the mama they're looking for."

I get to my feet, "So we could follow it to the Queen?" I prompt, even though I know damn good and well that Lilith is the Queen, something makes me hold back from telling them. They've been so tight-lipped about everything from that past that it almost feels like I need to keep my awareness to myself, at least until the right time.

Damien's eyes widen and he looks in the direction the creature went, "Shit, we might have been able too. But they don't listen to anyone but the Queen, so it's not like we could've gotten them to cooperate."

I groan and run a hand down my face, that was the answer I was afraid of. They're too distraught to be of much help, anyway. It would've been nice to know that the creature is connected to Lilith before it ran away. I'm tempted to yell at them both, they should have been up front with us about the truth the whole time. I take a deep breath, they probably have their reasons, but I doubt I'd appreciate any of them at the moment.

So, instead of dragging out a problem that I know we're unable to address, I look up at them, "We'll camp here for the night." They both nod and we split up, each going to our designated camping tasks.

***

I stare into the fire as the cold sets in further. Phil sits across from me and is also staring at the flames. Damien wandered off, cursing and complaining, but supposedly looking for more firewood. I know the angrier twin is losing what little control he has over his temper. He's preparing for the worst when we finally find Lilith. But that doesn't prevent me from being annoyed at his attitude.

Philip, on the other hand, is exceedingly calm and has barely shown any doubt. I study the vampire from where I'm seated, I'm wondering why he's so certain everything will be all right. But more than his reasons, I need to hear it. I need someone to reassure me that Lilith is going to be okay. That when we find her, we're she will let us make amends, that she'll understand the decisions we, that I, have made.

"How do you do it?" I ask.

Phil looks at me and frowns, "Do what?"

"Keep so calm and optimistic? This whole thing is a mess. We're chasing after someone who thinks we hate them, who has captured by people who do hate them, and you're seem so confident that everything will be all right. How?"

He watches me for a few moments, then says, "Lilith is smart, resourceful, clever, and strong. I don't doubt that she will keep herself safe until we can find her. I've never doubted her abilities, though there have been times where I've been painfully aware of how mortal and fragile she can be."

"I'm calm because I'm certain that Lilith has figured out that Sarah's spell is in place. She knows that there are still people looking out for her, even if she's not sure who. And I hope, I hope she will understand the choices that were made. I hope she can forgive us for not coming for her sooner," he smiles tightly at me and hope isn't the only emotion shining through the expression.

I open my magic to his emotions and I'm hit with everything at once. His hope, fear, confidence, trust and, most importantly, love. He harbors a deep, intense love for Lilith, the emotion feels so old and so entwined with who he is that I know without a doubt it originated back when Lilith was his queen.

I'm almost ashamed of prying into his feelings, the complexity of feeling seeming almost too intimate to disturb. Then he shakes his head slightly, and shoves that emotion down, pushing it back and under all the others until it's almost undetectable.

I frown at that and before I can stop myself, say, "Why do you do that?"

Philip looks at me with confusion, not replying. I wonder if I should just drop it, but I can't. I can't just continue not knowing why this immortal hides how much he loves Lilith.

So, I ask again, "Why do you hide how you feel about Lilith? Just now you were talking about her and your emotions were full of love and care, but then you shoved it back. Why?"

He stares at me, his mouth dropping open before he says, "You never noticed before."

"I usually make a point not to pry into my friends' emotions; but I needed to see how much of what you were saying was truth and how much of it was to placate me," I admit, "And now I'm wondering why in the world you're hiding all that you feel."

Phil frowns and looks away, "I... I hide it because..." he hesitates, then sighs, "I hide it because I've seen the way she looks at you and I know you share those feelings. I will not get in the way of that."

I frown, "So you'll just keep hiding a love that fierce just because you think I- what? Think I'm more deserving? What sort of sense is that? You've never doubted her, not for a moment, and you think I deserve her affection more?"

He shakes his head, "You don't understand,"

"Yeah, I don't, because it makes little sense," I snap, suddenly furious that he's been keeping this a secret. How long has he felt this way and kept it to himself? The entire time? Even before we died the first time?

He looks up at me and says, "She cares about you, I've seen it in her eyes. I've never seen that affection directed at me. I'm not about to complicate everything when Lilith deserves whatever makes her happy. And I refuse to put either of you in that position."

"What position?" I snap again, the flames jumping in my ire, "A position where the woman I love and my best friend are all happy and open about their feelings? You may not have seen her look at you with the same affection you've seen her turn to me, but it's there. She cares about you as deeply as she does me. She just shows it differently."

He stares at me, his eyes wide, "What?" then he shakes his head, "That's not the point. Look, Samael, I don't know why you're upset about this. I'm telling you, I have no intention of pursuing my feelings for Lilith. Besides, we can't be sure she'll forgive us for what's happened, so this seems completely unwarranted."

I scowl at him, then sigh and look away, "Fine, but I think you should tell her."

He grunts, "Maybe, if I ever get the chance."

Lilith

I walk down the hallway with purpose. I have to find Fate, he's got answers, I've got questions. I push the library door open and my mentor looks up from his books with an amused expression, "Yes, Lilith?"

I scowl at him, "Don't act like you don't know why I'm here. I know what I am, and you're going to tell me how to, to be it."

"That's not how this works," he says with a sigh.

I cross my arms and sigh dramatically, "Fine, I'll tell you what I am then. I am freedom! No rules, no restrictions, nothing!" I toss my arms out.

He snorts and returns to his book, "Sounds to me like you're trying to get away without consequences."

"So?" I snap.

He looks up at me, his eyes scanning my face for something. I can only assume he finds it when he stands up, "All right, let me show you something."

I grin and skip after Fate, my excitement bubbling up and making me giddy. He leads me down a few hallways and into a dark room. A clap of his hands illuminates the room, and I gasp. On the far side of the room, in a darkened alcove, is an enormous creature. They're in a cage, which is wrapped with chains, and locked with padlocks.

I leap through the shadows until I'm standing next to the cage. Reaching for one lock and it shocks me, sending me stumbling back. I spin on Fate, my heart pounding in my chest with equal parts outrage and terror, "What is this? Let them out!"

"No," Fate says with a shake of his head. "I will not let them out, given that they willingly put themselves in. This is one of my brothers, Aggression. He entered that cage and bid that I bind him within. It has been thousand or so years ago now."

"Why?" I ask, staring at the cage with concern.

"No rules, no restrictions, nothing. Nothing to keep his power or his temper in check," the Primal says, his voice full of sadness. "Aggression, when loose upon this world, cannot truly control his nature. Wherever he walks, violence and conflict follow. Whenever he speaks, it is an attack. He made the decision that it was better for him to remain in this dormant state than to be 'free' to roam the worlds wreaking wanton destruction in his wake."

I walk up to the cage again, my hand outstretched but not daring to touch the chains again, "So freedom isn't what I am, is it?"

"I cannot answer that question for you, it is something you must find within yourself," Fate says softly, putting his hands on my shoulders and turning me to face him. "Your experience in the world, your skill with your powers, all those things are still fresh. You are scarcely more than a child, do not think to have found your truth so soon. It took me almost a hundred thousand years to find my true purpose, no need to rush it."

I look down at my feet, "I just want to be useful, I want to know what I am so I don't have to be so confused."

Fate pulls me into a hug and kisses the top of my head, "I will keep you safe until you've figured it out. I swear. Besides, it is not often that an Eternal such as yourself can narrow themselves to a single word. Come along."

I hug him too, then pull away and he goes to leave the room, "Wait! Can- can Aggression hear us?" I ask, looking at the caged Primal.

Fate looks at the cage as well, then nods, "He can, though he won't be able to respond to you in any meaningful way."

I shake my head and walk up to the cage, avoiding the chains and the metal. I put my hand on the Primal's side. Fate doesn't move as I close my eyes and reach out with my magic, "I'm sorry, Aggression, that you're trapped like this. I'm sorry that your very nature is also what keeps you from enjoying the world. One day, you can be free and live happily. I'll be back to keep you company."

Nothing happens, just like Fate said, but I turn away from the cage and my mentor is smiling at me, pride in his eyes, "Your compassion is admirable, I hope you never lose it."

I grin up at Fate, unable to keep my excitement in check, "Do you know if Aggie likes books?"

He laughs, "Yes, he's quite fond of stories, anything to take him away from..." he trails off and glances behind us.

I nod and hook my arm with his, "Let's go then, to the library!"

***

I wake with a start, the memory still fresh in my mind. My heart isn't pounding and my stomach is free of the nausea that usually accompanies the memories. I look up at the stars and take deep breaths until I feel calmer. Closing my eyes, I reach out with my magic, letting it flow across the ground and through the shadows of the night. My magic stretches through the darkness until I catch a wisp of magic, it's somewhat familiar but I can't place it. It calls to me and I'm on my feet in a flash.

I use a touch of magic to silence the chains around my ankles and hands, weaving through the tents as I make my way to the edge of camp. I step through the faint barrier and look around, a soft humming sound coming from nearby makes me turn. The voice strikes a note of familiarity to me, so I whisper, "Hello?"

The humming cuts off and I hear hurried movement before a creature stands before me. I stare at them for a long second and they stare back at me. Their face is covered in small, iridescent scales, and their nose looks flat to their face. Their entire body seems to be covered in the scales as they make their way down their neck and under the loose robe they're wearing.

After a few moments, they smile. The expression is too wide for a typical smile, and a soft, feminine voice says, "Oh! It is you! I didn't recognize you at first! What with your soul being all fractured like that." She waves her hand at my entire body.

I frown and try to open my mouth. But they grab my jaw and pull me close, looking inside my mouth, "Ohhh, you're in a mortal form, I see, I see. I take it you don't remember everything either? No?"

I shake my head, but they've still got my mouth pried open so I can't speak.

"Unfortunate. I suppose the incident which took you from us caused the fractures?" once again, they continue to speak without allowing me to respond, "Which also explains the mortal form, probably put pieces back together over lifetimes. Though you have all your pieces now, I wonder why the fractures haven't healed."

I grunt and then, using my magic, shove them away and rub my jaw, "As enlightening as you're being, who the fuck are you?"

They blink at me a few times, then their expression falls and they look sad as their eyes fill with tears, "Oh Lilith, my queen, my... friend. I've missed you so."

I relax at the use of my proper name, "Can you answer me? Who are you?"

Their smile returns, though it's subdued from its former brilliance, "Sylvia Snyder," they bow low with a flourish, "Chief Researcher and Head Librarian of the Library of Hell."

I recoil at the last bit and take a hesitant step away from her, "You're a demon?"

She looks taken aback, "Hardly! I'm a researcher! Though, I suppose that's not what you meant. I'm a Naga, my kind are a sort of serpentine humanoid. I've taken on a human form since I've been roaming around here for a while."

"But you're from hell, isn't everything in hell a demon?" I ask with a frown.

"Not at all, Demons only make up a fraction of the population of hell. Though they are some of the most troublesome and reckless of our people. Not all of them, mind you! Demons come in all kinds, just like most beings, they just have a bit more chaos and destruction in them than most." Her smile is blinding and pleased with herself, as if that explains everything.

I rub my neck, "Okay, why... why are you here then?"

"I am a researcher," she says emphatically, "I've been looking into the tears in the veil as long we've been aware of them. Unfortunately, I haven't been able to find a conclusive method for repairing them. I'm afraid that the only ones who can do that would be you and Samael, though, if his soul is in a similar state to yours, we have more work cut out for us than I expected. I doubt that you have the full power needed to repair the tears as you are, no offense."

I open my mouth to reply but she continues on, yet again, "Though, if we could heal the cracks in your soul, that'd be a good place to start. However, it's been over a thousand years and I am not familiar with how to affect souls, despite being able to see them."

"Wait," I almost shout.

She stops and looks at me, her eyes wide, "Was I rambling?" she asks, this time actually stopping.

I nod, "Yes, I... I might know what needs to happen, I'm just not sure how to make it happen."

Her face lights up, "Oh? How?"

"I just remembered something. It was something that Fate told me a long time ago, he said that an Eternal cannot usually define themselves with one word. That learning what you are made of is something you can find within yourself. Does- does that help?"

She frowns, "I'm not sure, that could mean any number of things. Most Eternals tend to just... pop up randomly. What they're 'made of' is usually something they find along the way as their powers develop. It's been so long since you first came about that I can't honestly say I know what you're made of."

"I might be able to find out, but I'd need to go back to the library and spend a good bit of time pouring through tomes. You're not exactly one to keep a log of your life... though I suppose Errill may know, but he's been in hibernation since before you disappeared. As for embracing what that is. I have no idea how one goes about that."

I deflate and run a hand through my hair, "What, what about an oracle? Do you think they'd know?"

She laughs, "They'd probably know exactly how you go about

doing it, however, whether or not they can actually give us a clue as to what that is would depend. An Oracle's power all comes from Fate, who predates even the Primals, and they control what Oracles can and cannot share with others. If this Oracle told you that you need to remember and embrace, that's likely all they can tell you, though perhaps they could tell another more."

I frown and toy with my hair, "Do you know... do you know where the final seal is?"

Sylvia frowns as well, her expression becoming drawn, "I... I do not."

Looking into her eyes I see uncertainty there, she may not know of the seal, but she knows something. "What is it? You're keeping something back,"

She shifts her weight and looks away from me, "I fear that the final seal lies not here, but beyond the veil. And I am uncertain how many allies you still have on the other side. Between your absence, the passage of time, and the lies being spread by Discord, it is hard to say who would stand by you if you return."

I frown, I'm worried I don't have any friends left, aside from the pleasant woman before me whom I'm uncertain can help much. I look up at her and put my hands on her shoulders, "Can you go back across the veil?"

"There is a tear not too far from here. It's easy to slip through if you know what you're looking for. As an expert on the magical workings of the world- "

I cut her off with a shake of my head, "Okay, good. I need you to go back and find if there are any people we *can* trust on that side."

"What? How would I do that? Anyone could say anything! I'm not the best at telling when people are lying, my Queen, I have never been good with people, they are often cruel and- "

"Syl," I snap, the nickname sliding off my tongue easily, "Enough. I need you to calm down and listen. There's a spell on me, an enchantment that prevents people who are untrustworthy from hearing my true name."

She frowns, but doesn't interrupt.

"I need you to go across and carefully ask about me, don't directly ask people what my name is, it'll be too suspicious. But ask about me, see if you can get them to say my name. If they are trustworthy, they'll call me Lilith, as you did. If they cannot be trusted, they'll call me Lillian. Can you do that?"

She frowns for a moment then looks back at the camp, "Come with me?" she whispers, clinging to my hands.

I shake my head, "No, I still need to find the second Seal. I'll find my way across once I have."

Sylvia closes her eyes then nods and comes in to hug me, "I will do as you say, my Queen, I swear."

I hug her too. The contact unexpectedly comforting, "Thank you, now you need to go before they come looking for me. Be safe."

She lets me go and doesn't argue as I dart back toward the camp, not looking back so I'm not tempted to forgo my plan and escape.

Ten

In Which a Beacon is Lit

Lilith

I raise the spoon to my mouth as Gavin hovers a few paces away. It's been almost a week since we left North River and he's barely said ten words to me. Though he's been quick enough to demand punishment whenever I do something he doesn't like.

I want to ignore him and his staring, but it's making my skin crawl as he drifts closer and I can't afford to let my guard down. The chains attaching my wrists clink as I set my spoon down and glare over at him, "What do you want?" I ask, unable to keep my annoyance out of my tone.

He frowns and comes closer, then sits on the log next to me, "I could free you from these, Lillian." he says, touching the chain.

"So take them off," I reply, holding my hands out to him, the clank of the chains has become a natural part of my movements.

"You just have to do something for me," he says, preening slightly like he's caught me in some sort of snare.

I glare harder and lower my hands, "What?"

"Apologize," he says simply, giving me a look that suggests he thinks I should know exactly what he wants me to apologize for.

"For?" I ask, giving him a puzzled.

He frowns now, "For betraying me! For choosing those, those nobles over me!"

I scoff and shake my head, "No."

"No? Well then you're going to stay locked up!" he stands up, "You're too proud to admit that you were wrong to want to stay there. As soon as they found you missing, they assumed the worst."

I glare up at him, "They didn't just find me missing though, did they? They found me and the very thing we'd been working to collect for the better part of three months missing. I was gone for a week before those posters came out, they clearly waited for me to come back. I honestly can't blame them for the conclusions they've come to. And at least they have the decency to be straightforward when I've done something that hurt them!" I shout the last bit, unable to contain my anger anymore.

He slaps my face, making my head snap to one side and causing my food to spill, "Then stay locked up, bitch. We can't afford to have a traitor roaming around camp."

All of my chains jingle as I straighten my shoulders, "Fine, you want an apology? I am sorry. I'm sorry that my wanting to stay somewhere that I'm appreciated was so offensive to you that you opted to drug, beat, and kidnap me rather than let me be happy. Sorry for not adhering flawlessly to your perception of me."

"I'm sorry for bursting that bubble of denial you'd been living in. But most of all, most of all, I'm sorry that I ever trusted you. So take your apology, your 'freedom', and your self-importance and shove them up your ass."

At that he hauls off and punches me, his fist landing hard on my jaw and sending me sprawling. I land in the dirt and gasp for breath as tears threaten, "Bitch," he spits, a few of the workers giving me sympathetic looks as they mill about their tasks.

I chuckle and climb to my feet, my voice cracks as I speak, "Figures, if you can't get me to cooperate, manipulate. If you can't manipulate, berate. If berate doesn't work, then it comes to fists." I stand up as tall as I can, which is still a good six inches shorter than him, but I manage to look down at him as I sneer.

"It must just piss you off that hitting me will not make me give in to your whims either; and you can't kill me. Not without angering your oh so important patron. So tell me, Gavin, what's your plan now? Cause if Tyler's torture isn't enough to break me, your pathetic attempts at pain aren't going to cut it."

He clenches his teeth and looks like he's going to say something. Then the Speaker appears, "Gavin, that's quite enough. I gave you permission to seek reconciliation, that has failed. Move on."

That proves my point and I grin wickedly at the shifter, "Run along, mutt, master's calling."

He launches himself toward me, but to my amazement, the Speaker moves with preternatural speed and cuts him off before he gets to me. "I said enough," they repeat, their voice actually taking a harder edge for a moment that has Gavin retreating.

Once he's gone, the Speaker turns to look at me and turns their head to one side, "Why do you reject a hand of friendship?"

"Because that hand has struck me," I reply flatly, "I won't accept aid from someone who's betrayed me."

"And you see his bringing you into our care as a betrayal?" they prompt.

I glare over at them, "Yes, I would consider drugging, kidnapping, torture, and manipulation all things that fall into betrayal."

They nod in a way that makes me feel like they think my senti-ments are childish, "Perhaps you're right. Though, if you no longer see him as a friend, and those from whom you were taken do not see you as a friend, where does that leave you, Miss Callam?"

I still at that, then meet their gaze, that usual blandness seems absent as they watch me, so I choose my words carefully, "That leaves me where I've always been," I say quietly, "Alone."

"And so you will face what is to come in that manner, alone?" they continue.

I grunt, "Do I have any choice? Your patron is insistent that my chains remain, Gavin's attempt at reconciliation failed, no one is coming to my aid. I am alone."

The distance in their gaze flickers for a moment when they say, "Perhaps, for one such as you, being alone is for the best."

I don't have time to question that sentiment before they turn and walk off, leaving me standing there awkwardly. I look up at the sky and sigh, realizing that I am alone, the whole time, my whole life. Alone.

***

The hired help is settling down for the night when a sharp cry fills the air. I turn my head to the side, trying to decipher why the sound is so familiar. The others go still at the sound. A moment later, another cry tears through the night, answering the first. I smile slightly at the tremors running through the men around me. More of the cries go up and my grin widens, I take a deep breath and when another call hits the air I reply with the same sound.

All the men jump and turn to me, but I've already schooled my features and stare blankly back at them. "A-aren't you scared?" one demands.

"Of howling in the night? Not in the slightest. There are plenty of strange animals in the woods, no need to fear them when I'm stuck with the worst beasts of all," I smile sweetly even as another howl fills the night.

A moment later, the howls turn to barking and the creatures

creating the noise come into view. At least into mine. There are only three of them, but they're big and snarling. By the way the men stumble back and wave their torches about, they're aware of the danger but not its location. One of them yelps when a creature brushes past them, they their torch brandished like a sword but doesn't turn around to where the threat now stands.

The creature has features reminiscent of a hound but also has a feline lean to them. Their large teeth and tongue are dripping with saliva, and their silver eyes glinting in the torchlight. I coo softly and hold my hands out to the beast; it sniffs my palms then licks them. Its tongue has a rough texture that drags against my skin, leaving a thick, sticky saliva behind.

I stare at my palm for a moment as the creature lays its head in my lap. The slobber makes my hand tingle, and it feels like my magic is being eaten away. I raise a brow at the beast and it rolls its tongue out at me. I smirk and let it lick my wrists. The effect on the cuffs' magic is immediate, the restraints on my magic dissipating quickly against the power of the creature.

I chuckle slightly and pet the beast's head. "What the fuck are you laughing about?" Gavin snarls, reaching toward me.

I look over at him and smile serenely, "Just a bunch of idiots jumping at shadows. There's three of them about, I'm surprised you can't see them." I point in front of Gavin where one animal is snarling at him.

He turns to look and yelps when the beast snaps at him, briefly becoming bright white and appearing before the humans.

"Fuck!" Tyler shouts, swiping his torch out as the other one appears and snaps at him.

The one with its head in my lap whimpers and licks at my hands. I pat its head and jerk my head at the others. It lets out a sigh, then darts through the shadows again.

A moment later, the Speaker is at my side, "Can you get rid

of them?" their voice doesn't have it's usual blissed out tone to it. Instead, they sound frantic and even frightened.

I blink at them, "Why would I get rid of them? They're not a threat to me."

Their eyes narrow then the snap, "We'll take one of the ankle shackles off during the day. You'll be able to walk freely, but the shocking feature will still work." The beasts continue to bark and one even bites one torch in half.

I eye the speaker for a long moment, then smirk, "And no more drugs in the food."

They hiss out a breath then clear their throat, "Half doses."

"Deal," I nod, holding my hand out to them.

They glare but shake my hand once. I smile and stand up.

All three of the beasts go still, standing just outside the men's range of motion, and look at me. I close my eyes for a moment and focus. I know these creatures are familiar and they seem to like me. When I open my eyes, I smirk and raise a hand to my lips, letting out a sharp whistle that has the beasts whimpering and backing off. I flick my wrist at them, waving them off.

The one that'd come up to me growls and takes a few steps forward, as if it's going to come to me. I shake my head and whistle again, the sharp note makes it recoil and then all three of them run off. I turn to the Speaker and smirk, "There. All gone."

They frown, "Fine," they turn to the others and raise their chin, "Get to sleep, we must keep moving." Then they disappear back to their tent.

Graves

We walk into the camp and the icy rain has left the ground muddy, all signs of our quarry washed away. I close my eyes and take a steadying breath, "Fan out and find the sigil, hopefully there's something stored in it that gives us a direction."

"The last one didn't," Damien grouses, even as he makes a circuit around the camp.

"It had more hope in it," I argue, beginning my circuit, "Ideally, that means she's realized someone is following the trail, hopefully she's leaving more information now."

Damien continues to grumble to himself, but keeps looking. I'm about at the end of my patience with him, he's always been a grumpy person, but his irritation with Lilith is beyond that. I'd thought he'd gotten over it based on his behavior at the ball, but I suppose after the stress of things going missing hasn't helped.

"Found it," Phil calls, I look up and see that he's next to a log that's lying near a tree, the tree looks dead and the log is rotting. But when I walk closer, I see the same sigil we've seen every time.

I sigh with relief and walk over, lowering my shields to get a read on the energies left behind. I place my hand against the bark and emotion washes over me. The first wave is concentration, that focus on creating the sigil. Then comes frustration, followed by a wave of fear, and finished with anger, but then it cuts off like she was interrupted. I pull my hand away with a sigh.

"Anything?" Phil asks, his eyes crinkling with concern.

"No direction or anything, it's almost like she got cut off before she could finish the message." I rub my neck and look up to the sky, "Better information would be nice at anytime now."

"How do we know that this isn't just her sending us on a wild goose chase?" Damien snaps, his voice harsh.

"Dem," Phil snaps, giving his brother a dark look.

I look over at the big man and see he's not looking at either of us, his eyes staring off into the distance like he's thinking hard about something.

"Do you really believe that?" I ask, crossing my arms as I

shamelessly read his emotions. The conflict of fear, hope, anger, and affection that hits me almost as me rolling my eyes. "Or are you trying to convince yourself that's what's going on so you don't have to admit how much you miss her?"

Damien spins to glare at me now, "What the fuck gave you that idea?"

I snort and shake my head, "Stubborn idiot."

"Don't act like you don't have any doubts about this whole thing," Damien snarls, taking a few steps toward me.

I walk up to him until we're almost nose to nose, "I am concerned, but not about what you think. I'm worried that when we finally find Lilith, she'll never forgive us for taking so long. That she'll hate us for doing what we've done to find her. But those are things *I* have done, I have no doubts that Lilith didn't steal from us. I have no doubts that Lilith is hoping that someone is coming for her. But I'm also not going to let my own fears prevent me from finding her."

He makes a snarling noise, "Well, whoopie for you, not all of us can separate our emotions as well as you can, *Sir*."

I don't think about my next action, not really, I just haul off and punch Damien in the jaw. I throw all my emotions into it, which leads to coating the fist in stone before it connects.

The blow sends Damien sprawling in the dirt and I shake the stones from my hand and say, "Keeping my emotions under control isn't the same as separating them. Get your shit together before with find Lilith; I won't be as nice if you're an ass to her directly."

Ignoring Damien, who's staring up at me like I've grown a second head, Phil asks, "Do we want to look around for more clues? Maybe she left another sigil somewhere else?"

"I doubt it," I shake my head again, "It seems unlikely that she would've bothered trying. I get the impression that even though she hopes someone is coming, she's not entirely convinced."

"So what do we do? If we don't find her soon, what little hope she has is going to fade out too."

"Is there a way for us to message her? Maybe not with the entire image showing up and all that, but a voice?" I ask, giving him a questioning look.

"Uh, unlikely. It's not in our skill sets," he gestures between himself and Damien, "And that kind of thing usually requires more finesse than your elemental magic allows for."

I groan and run a hand through my hair, grabbing the strands in my fists for a moment, "There's got to be a way."

A snapping twig has us all spinning toward the sound, I stare in shock as a dark, animal-like form slinks from the shadows. It's not the Chimera from before, even though it appears to have animal-like features. Its form blurs around the edges, making it hard to pin down what kind of animal it is. Phil steps between me and it, "Who the fuck are you?"

"Forgive my lack of a proper form, Lord of Panic," they speak in a deep voice but they say each word incredibly slowly, like they're having trouble forming them, "without the freedom my Lady provides me, I cannot hold a shape you would recognize."

"What do you mean?" Damien asks, getting between me and the creature as well.

They make a low noise that sounds like they're clearing their throat, then say, "I was asleep when their souls were lost to us. Without the Queen to come for me, I could not waken on my own. To do so would have caused mayhem, the likes of which none of you have witnessed."

Phil gasps and relaxes his stance, "Fuck, Errill? How are you awake now? I thought only the Queen could..." He trails off as the creature laughs, the sound grating and rough but no less amused.

"What's so funny?" Damien snaps, his voice a growl.

"My Mistress called for aid, and I *always* answer her call. I may be weak from so long asleep, I may be unstable without her care, but I will always find my way to her."

I clear my throat and step around the twins, deciding that we need to find Lilith more than I need to keep my peace about knowing the truth. "Could you carry a message to Lilith, then?"

Philip

I snap my head to stare at Graves. He asks Errill the question without hesitation. He knows who she is, does he know who he is? I go to ask but Errill shakes what I assume is his head, "No, I cannot pass a message to her."

"Then can you go find her?" Graves takes a step forward, his voice becoming insistent, "Tell her we're coming for her? Protect her until we can get there?"

Errill snorts and shakes his head again, "No,"

"Why the fuck not?" Damien snaps, "you care for her so much but you won't go fucking help her?"

Errill makes a derisive noise and shakes his head again, "I will not go Deimos, Lord of Dread, because were I to come upon those who've forced her to cry for help I could not contain my rage. And if Lilith is not at her full strength, then neither she nor I will be able to pull me back from that brink."

"What kind of Eternal can't control himself?" Damien sneers this time.

Errill lifts onto his hind legs now, his form growing vast and threatening, "I am *Primal* and there is not a soul in this realm who recalls the devastation I have wrought in lifetimes past. If I were unleashed on this world without Lilith to stay my hand, then it would not stop with those who harmed her. I would rampage through this pathetic world, tearing it to shreds and burning it to the ground until all that remains is she and I."

"There's got to be something," Graves says, stepping between the dark shadow and my brother.

Errill looks at Graves and settles on his feet again, "Show me the sigil she left,"

Graves rushes over to show Errill the carving in the wood, his hand reverently running across the marking as if he's trying to get another read on it. Errill draws close to it then pulls away and looks at Graves, who is still staring at the sigil.

"You wish to find her," Errill says slowly, "despite your fears, despite your doubts, you wish to find Lilith and protect her."

Graves looks at the behemoth and nods, "Yes, I need to save her, even if she hates me for what I've done in order to make it happen."

Errill looks over at Damien, myself, and finally back to Graves, "I might be able to share with you how I can track her, however it is not something I would do lightly. I would need to know your convictions. What would you sacrifice to see to our queen's happiness?"

"We're traipsing through the fucking woods following magical breadcrumbs, what more do you want?" Damien snaps.

I slap my brother upside the head, "Don't be a prick,"

"I'll lay down my life," Graves says, ignoring the two of us.

Errill chuckles and shakes his head, "One's life is easy to promise and even easier to part with, what will you *sacrifice* to see to her happiness?"

Graves pauses, his eyes staring deeply into the darkness that makes up Erril while Damien gets to his feet, grumbling slightly. I go to offer my advice when Graves finally raises a hand and stares into his own palm, fire erupts from the center and flickers in a small ball as Graves looks up at Erril.

"I will give anything to see Lilith safe and happy. I will fall on my sword, give up my title, my fortune, all of it. But that's not truly a sacrifice, is it? Those are things you say are easy to come by and part with." He looks at the flame in his hand for a few more moments, his expression grim as he thinks through his decision. "Lilith is everything to me."

"We can find her without his help," Damien snaps, "he's trying to make things harder than it needs to be."

Graves ignores Damien and looks up at the Primal. I swallow and shift on my feet, wondering what Errill is thinking is enough.

Samael closes his hand, the fire extinguishing with a sizzle. He meets Errill's gaze and says, "I will do whatever it takes. I may not be your rival in power, not as I am, but I will destroy whatever and whoever it takes to get to Lilith and see her happy and whole. Anyone who gets in my way will find only death at the end of my patience."

Errill chuckles again, "That will do, though I wonder what you'll think when you recall the last time you answered that question when I asked it. Come close so I may touch you."

Graves doesn't hesitate and steps up to Errill, who's leaned back and sitting on haunches like a massive dog.

"Samael, I share with you my link to our queen, that you may find her in my stead. While you see to her safety, I will see to my strength. When it is time, I will return and we shall rain destruction on those who dare lay their hands upon our queen, our Lilith."

There's a rush of magic that makes me stumble back and the ground shake. A moment later Errill is gone and Graves is standing in the clearing, looking straight north, his eyes wide.

"What is it?" I ask, looking the direction he is.

"I... I can see her. Well, it's like a beacon in the north, and I *know* it's her. We need to hurry though, the light is dim." He hoists his pack back onto his shoulders and starts walking, not bothering to see if we're behind him.

Eleven

In Which the Thief Is Saved

Philip

The sun is setting as we make our way through a deer trail. It's been about four days since we spoke to Errill and Graves is convinced that we need to go this way, but there's no sign that a large group of people has been through. Least of all, a group with a wagon and about ten people, according to the information we've gathered. I don't argue with him, though I have insisted on leading. We can't afford for him to get hurt or go missing, too.

What little light remains in the day gets brighter as the trees thin a bit. Another few paces and I pause when I hear sounds of movement ahead of us. I hold out an arm and Graves walks right into it, then glares at me, "She's in there," he says in a harsh whisper.

"Yeah, but we do not know what else is in there," I caution, "Usually you'd be more tactical about this."

Damien grunts, "Right, give me five, I'll scout." He shifts to his gargoyle form and takes to the sky without further discussion.

I watch him disappear into the darkness and let my arm fall away from Graves' chest. Graves gives me a dark look, "If delaying puts her in more danger-"

"I'll gladly let you beat the shit out of me," I agree, "But until such a time comes to pass, then we're going to be smart about it. I know you're getting antsy to find her, but if we rush in, we very well may put her in more danger rather than rescue her."

Graves looks back toward the sounds of movement and a few filtered conversations. I hear one voice that sounds eerie among the casual tones of the others, it's also moving closer to where we're hiding. I push Samael lower to the ground, using my gray cloak to help us blend in with the shadows.

"She is lying," the eerie voice says, it holds an almost deranged edge to it, "She knows something, something she is keeping from us, from you, master."

In the next breath, the voice speaks again, this time with a note of serenity that makes my skin crawl, "That may be so, but as I have told you, the seal is not our only goal. Let her lie, let her lead a merry chase, and when the time comes, you will see why we let her."

The deranged tone returns, "But master, the torturer, he, he has gone soft for her. And the shifter, he still wishes to bed her, we cannot let them."

"Enough!" that serenity breaks with ice cold ire, "You will do as you are told! If you cannot obey, then I will withdraw my blessing."

All goes silent for a few long moments, then that deranged voice, "As you say, as you say." The person marches away, back into the main part of the camp.

"What was that?" Samael asks, looking at me for some sort of direction.

"I don't know, but I didn't like the sound of it." I mutter, another sound from the camp makes me turn, this one sounds like arguing. As I'm trying to listen to the conversation, the flap of Damien's wings drown it out. I look up, Damien's silhouette momentarily blocking out the moon. Before my brother can say anything, a scream tears through the woods. Graves turns toward the sound and takes off at a run, straight through the camp.

"Fuck!" I shout, tearing off after Graves, but quickly getting intercepted by the other men in the group. Damien lands next to me and takes out one guard, "Graves," I say.

"After we deal with these." Damien snaps and I throw myself into the fight.

Lilith

I move silently through the camp, most of the hired hands won't go anywhere near me anymore. Apparently, glowing green eyes and a tendency to fight back is enough to scare them all away. I get toward the edge of the campsite and find a secluded spot to sit. I perch on the stump that's there and sigh. Letting my shoulders relax and allowing my eyes to fall closed, if only for a moment.

A snapping twig interrupts my slice of peace. My eyes snap open and immediately focus in on Tyler standing in front of me with a wild look in his eyes.

"What do you want?" I ask, trying to keep my tone antagonistic despite my growing appreciation for the man.

He looks around then comes up to me with a key in his hands, "You've got to get out of here."

"What?" I ask, staring as he crouches next to me and unlocks the chains binding my feet together.

"The Speaker is fed up, apparently they think yer leading us in circles. Whether or not ya are, they plan to kill ya to get the seal. I can't let them do that, yer a good lass and yer just trying to-" he cuts off abruptly and lurches forward, "Run," he gasps, his voice hoarse.

I look behind him and the Speaker is there with their arm

outstretched towards me, a wild look in their eyes as they stalk forward, "I warned them, I told them he was soft. I told them."

Their voice holds a deranged quality I've never heard from them before. I get to my feet, which are now free thanks to Tyler, and take a few tentative steps backward. I see a blade sticking out of Tyler's shoulder and wonder why it took him down so easily. Then I notice a semi-clear liquid sliding down the blade.

I swallow and take a few more steps back as they stalk forward and snatch the blade up, pulling it from Tyler's back with a sickening squelch. They point the blade at me, "And now you, you, you. You've been leading us in circles, round, and around and around, like we wouldn't figure it out. They say we can't kill you, that since you can handle the magic, it's better for you to keep it. But no, no, no, I won't let you ruin our lord's plans like that. My Lord doesn't know what's best for them, I do, I know we can do it. I can wear the seal, it will be grand."

As they continue to ramble, I keep stepping backward. I hear a strange noise from the other side of the camp. The Speaker hears it too and turns, that wild look still in their eyes. Once they're no longer looking, I take off at a run. The drugs and chains are still inhibiting my movements more than I'd like. I don't get far before I feel the bite of a blade in my calf.

I shriek and stumble, losing my balance and slamming into a tree. Turning, I glare at the small blade sticking out of my calf. I look up as the Speaker comes closer, "You think you're tricky, don't you?"

I grin wildly at them, "I know I'm tricky, it's you I'm worried about."

They cackle at that, then dart forward with unexpected speed with another blade in their hands. I turn and raise my arms just in time so that the blade embeds into the tree. But It still catches my arm and slices deeply into it. I scream again but maneuver so my feet are between the two of us and shove them back. They fall to the ground with a thump and I roll out of the way, trying to get to my feet.

Unfortunately, it becomes apparent that all of their blades are laced with some sort of poison cause I'm even more uncoordinated than I was before. I hit my knees again just in time for Speaker to recover and tackle me to the ground. They don't have another blade on them, thankfully, but they're grabbing for the one stuck in the tree. I push their hands away and barely manage to fend them off, but then they sneer and snatch up the chains that still bind my hands together.

I scream as they wrench my arms above my head and grab a hold of the blade. They yank the blade out and I scream again. The pain finally causes tears to fill my eyes and as my fighting becomes even weaker. I want to scream again and fight against the pain, but my limbs refuse to cooperate.

The Speaker, or whoever is in control right now, raises the blade above their head, cackling like a madman. I'm ready to embrace death as the blade descends towards my chest. From the ground beside us, a spike of earth shoots up and punctures the Speaker through the chest.

I yelp and my eyes widen as the Speaker looks down at the sharp stone now running all the way through them. They look back up at me and their mouth moves, though only a sickening gasp and a mouthful of blood come out.

The stone slides back toward the ground and I scramble backward, not wanting the weight of another person to crush me while I'm already weak. In my rush, I dislodge the blade in my calf and fall back over with another cry. I roll out from underneath my would-be killer when their body finally slumps to the ground. I swallow and stare at their body, with their wide, staring eyes looking just as crazed as before.

I hear movement to my right and turn, the tears in my eyes silhouetting my savior against the setting sun. Before I have time to process, they're moving toward me. As their features come into focus, I realize it's Samael. Relief floods me for a brief second, but then reality crashes back in and I remember I was on a wanted poster he'd signed, that I need to be sure before I can consider myself rescued.

I snatch up one dagger and shuffle backward, pointing it at the man in front of me. He stops and puts his hands up in surrender. "What's my name?" I demand, even as the world lurches under my feet.

Graves

Her question hits me like a sucker punch; the fear and hurt that washes from her makes it feel as if the world has dropped out from under me. Her hands are shaking as she holds up the blade, and I can see blood oozing from an injury near her shoulder. I've been expecting this reaction. Faced with the raw pain in her eyes, it is too much, tears fill my eyes and I hold my hands up in surrender, "Lilith, I'm here to help."

Relief floods her expression as she drops the knife, then falls back to the ground with a sob. I rush over to her and pull her to my chest, she makes a noise of pain but clings to my neck and sobs, "I thought-they showed-" every sentence cuts off as she cries, unable to get her thoughts together.

I press my face into her hair and cradle her against my chest. The tang of blood and dirt covers the scent of her aura, but having her in my arms helps settle some of my anxiety. She whimpers in pain as I try to pull her into my lap.

Instead of letting me support her, she pushes out of my hold. I try not to let the hurt show as she scoots away, her expression growing distant.

Now that we're separated I can see her wounds better, "Fuck," I hiss and rummage through my bag.

She continues to watch me with a wary gaze, her eyes glassy with tears. I find the bottles that Sarah sent with us and show her them.

I understand now why the seer insisted on both the potions and the seals. "Sarah sent these," I tell her, "She said you'd need them."

She nods and reaches for one bottle, but her hand shakes and I put my hand over hers as it closes over the top. "Lilith, can I open them for you?"

She stares at our hands, then at length says, "Yes,"

I sigh and pop the cork on the first one, then help her drink it and repeating the process with the other.

Once she's swallowed the last of the potions, she's looking better and the physical pain that she was radiating fades into a dull ache. "Better?" I ask.

"A bit," she says quietly, "That first one stopped the drugs, but the wounds are deep and will need a real healer."

I look over my shoulder and realize the sounds of combat have faded, "Sounds like the twins have gathered everyone up. We should head over there."

"Okay," she nods, keeping her eyes fixed on the ground and away from me.

I stand and offer her my hand, which she tentatively takes, but quickly releases once she's standing. She keeps her arms wrapped around herself as we move through the woods. It takes most of my self control not to try scooping her up and carrying her to safety.

When we near the clearing where the camp is set up, she stops, "I'm going to act like I knew the whole time."

My breath catches and I turn to look at her, "But- "

She holds up a still trembling hand, "They'll buckle faster if they think I knew all along it will throw them off and make it seem like we're more coordinated than we'd let on. Just... make it seem like everything is normal."

"But you're hurt, and you didn't-"

She glares at me, snapping with enough venom to make me recoil, "So fake it! We're booth able to manage that much, I'm sure."

That pain returns to her voice and I take a step back with my hands up, "All right,"

She nods and then steps into the clearing, moving with so much grace you'd almost think that she wasn't bleeding from a wound in her calf and shoulder. That urge to carry her returns, but I push it back. I know better than to make Lilith do what I want. I knew she'd be this upset, but it still stings far more than I expected. The rift between us feeling like a chasm that I'll never be able to bridge and tearing my heart in two.

Twelve

~

In Which Decisions are Made

Philip

When Lilith and Sam walk into the clearing, I almost cry with relief, she looks like shit, but she's alive and moving on her own. She walks up to the group of people we've got tied up around the campfire. Standing a few yards from the group, she lifts her head and looks down her nose at them, like they're so far beneath her that their very presence is an annoyance.

She looks them over, then gives Damien and I wary looks. I frown at the look, but walk up to her, "Lil, are you- "

"I'm fine," she levels me with a glare, "If you assholes had shown up sooner, I wouldn't look like shit. I need a bath, a healer, and a safe night's sleep. Not necessarily in that order."

"We can get all that once we've dealt with these," I gesture at our prisoners.

She turns to look at them again, to say her expression is full of disdain would be an understatement. "Everyone but Gavin were just hired to travel with us, they're innocent of that at least."

One man looks terrified as she comes to stand over him, a look in her eyes that I can only describe as vengeful. "I never truly got to deal with you," she says to him, a smile spreading across her face.

The man's eyes go wide and he tries to get his wrists free of his bindings. She looks over her shoulder at us, "This one had the audacity to slap my ass. I threatened to rip his hand off, think I should follow through?"

"No!" the man cries, actually shuffling away from her.

I walk up to her and drape my arm over her shoulders, she accepts the touch and leans against me, "No, need for you to dirty your hands with his blood," the prisoner looks relieved, "If you still want your pound of flesh let me do it."

I bare my fangs at the man, and he blanches.

Lilith laughs, the sound bubbling up almost like she's surprised by it; she shakes her head and looks up at me with a grin. "You're right, he's not worth the bloodstains he'd leave behind. Everyone but Gavin can be let go."

I grin down at her, then help Damien cut the binds on everyone except Gavin. They all scramble to their feet and bow to Lilith, "Thank you for your mercy,"

Lilith snorts, "Leave enough food for the four of us, then take the rest and get out of here. You've got an hour."

They scatter like she'd thrown a bomb into their midst and Lilith turns her attention to Gavin. "You," she says, her voice is silky, but I can hear the undercurrent of a threat, "Have a choice."

Gavin looks between the four of us, confusion on his face, "What the fuck? How? You, you thought that they weren't coming! You were devastated!"

Lilith laughs at that, the sound is haughty, but I can tell that there's some pain in it, "Acting, Gavin, *Acting.* You've seen how I work, what

I'm capable of, and you still can't fathom the idea that I could fake emotions?"

He looks flabbergasted, but Samael's tightened fists make me think maybe she wasn't acting those emotions. I look back at her and realize that there's a subtle sway to her stance and I can see the blood on her clothes, as well as the fucking shackles on her wrists.

I walk up and do the only thing I can think will help. Wrapping an arm around her shoulders and pull her back against my chest and take on some of her weight. "Lilith here was just trying to get as much info as she could. Weren't you?" I look down at her. She looks up at me and there's a hint of gratitude in her expression as she lets me take steady her and relaxes into my chest.

"Right," Lilith nods, "As I was saying, you have two choices. Either you answer our remaining questions and I'll kill you quickly. Or, you be resistant and I kill you slowly. Your call."

Gavin laughs, "Am I supposed to be afraid of you? Couldn't even save yourself, had to wait for these fucks to get here! Besides! Why would I give you anything if all you're going to do is kill me?"

Lilith goes unnaturally still and I swear the entire forest holds its breath when she finally steps out of my grasp. "Oh? You think I've been waiting to be rescued?"

"Well, yeah..." Gavin trails off as she walks up to him, his expression becomes worried, "Those shackles and that collar keep you from- "

He cuts off when she laughs loud and hard, "These shackles?" she asks, lifting one hand and gripping the metal contraption. There's a slight pop, and the device opens. She pulls it from her arm and drops it to the ground with the metallic clatter of chain. She repeats the process with the other one and Gavin's eyes get wider and wider as she moves.

"And this?" she touches a collar that I hadn't noticed before and there's another click and she pulls it away, dropping it on the ground as she leans over him. "Your little chains never held me back, *friend.*

You fuckers may have drugged me, you may have beaten me, but you never broke me. Now, are you going to answer my questions, or am I going to have to do this the hard way?"

The shifter bares his teeth at her, "Go to hell."

Lilith snorts and gives him a disdainful look, "You first."

Lilith

My hands are trembling as I stand in front of Gavin, trying to keep up the facade of being all right is taking its toll. Everything that's happened tonight has thrown me for a loop. I shake my head and crouch in front of Gavin again, "You know, Gavin, it didn't have to come to this," I whisper, "I would've defended you with my life... but you made two mistakes. The first is understandable. I put substantial effort into making sure it happens."

"And what's that?" he snaps, his eyes hard.

I lean close and smile wickedly, "You underestimated me. I am so much more than you've ever seen, than I've ever shown anyone. And I would've put all of it into defending you if you hadn't made your second and fatal mistake."

He scowls but straightens his shoulders as if trying to maintain a semblance of pride, "Oh?"

I lean close enough to whisper in his ear, "You betrayed me, Gavin, and now I am going to make you regret it. And the best part is it's barely going to cost me a drop of power."

He frowns as I lean back and place my hand on his head. I dive into his mind and skip through his early childhood, following to where we meet and getting any pertinent details from then forward. I'm not sure how far in I am when the first one happens, but it turns my stomach. A woman, no, a girl of about fifteen years old, is pinned beneath him, eyes wide with fear and black hair splayed around her.

I rush through it, my stomach recoiling as I find more and more instances. I don't even get to when he meets this so called Speaker before I have to pull away. Yanking my hand back, I stumble away, my stomach lurching as I look at him. He looks dazed.

"Lilith?" Phil asks, stepping up next to me with his hands outstretched.

"Don't!" I shout and hold my hand out to keep him at bay, "Don't touch me," I gasp the words, my skin crawling.

Phil stops, his eyes wide as I cover my mouth. A moment later, I vomit violently, my entire body feeling gross. Once the meager contents of my stomach are expelled, I turn back to Gavin with unrestrained rage.

"You're going to suffer," I say flatly.

He sneers at me, "You know it's your fault! All of those women... if you had just fucking accepted me, I wouldn't have- "

I slap him. His head lurches to the side as the crack of my palm hitting his face echoes around us. The second of contact is enough to set the spell into motion. Before he has time to recover from the impact, a scream rips from his throat and he falls to his side, shaking and struggling.

"Lil?" Phil whispers, "What did you do?" he looks at Gavin, then over my shoulder at Damien.

I pant for a moment as Gavin continues to scream and writhe next to us, "He's reliving every time he's hurt another person, and all the pain that I've experienced since being captured. Both the physical and emotional." I explain.

Damien makes a noise, "Did you get the info you wanted?"

I grunt and put a hand on my stomach as it lurches painfully, "And far more than I'd care to have gotten."

"Are you all right?" Phil coaxes, "Are you going to be sick again?"

I shudder, "I don't have much else to throw up," I look up at the caravan and see that most of the men have disappeared and taken the wagon with them. "They're quick," I murmur.

"We should probably leave too," Graves says from behind me, "Their employers likely know where they were camping out. The sooner we get to a new location, the better."

I nod, "Fine, but there's one thing I need to do."

Damien

Lilith leads us through the trees, back the way she and Samael came from. She pushes through a couple of bushes and we're standing over a corpse. She sighs and drags a hand down her face, "He needs a grave and burial."

I frown and walk up to the man, turning him over, I find a man in his mid-forties and with a dark hair. His eyes are wide and staring, he's been dead for a little while, possibly before we started attacking.

"Who is he?" Phil asks, finishing rolling the man onto his back.

"His name was Tyler, he uh..." she trails off as if not sure how to proceed, then she shrugs, "They hired him to torture me."

I jerk my hand away from the body and have half a mind to punch his face in, if he laid a single hand on Lilith he deserves to suffer.

Phil seems to have a similar thought as he snarls, "And you want to give him a fucking burial?"

She shrugs again, a pensive look crossing her features, "He may have had a hand in my physical injuries, but he did his best to protect me when he could. Made sure I was fed, kept the shittier men from getting too close. Tried to keep me from mouthing off, but you all know how well that goes." She offers us a wan smile.

"You want us to pay respects to a man who tortured you?" I demand, "I'm not- "

"Stop bitching," Samael says flatly, making all three of us turn to stare at him. "Give me a moment and I'll make a grave, then you can say your goodbyes."

He steps away from us and braces his feet. Lilith steps away from the body to give Samael enough room. Our boss takes a deep breath and a neat rectangle opens up in front of him. Lilith looks pleased and uses her shadows to lift the corpse and rest it in the grave. She kneels next to the pit and stares for a long moment at the body inside.

Sighing, Lilith lets her head hang and her shoulders slump, "Tyler, you may have been an asshole, but you died trying to save my life. I can't let that go unrecognized. Despite the danger of trying to help me, you still made sure I could eat, that nobody hurt me unless it was you. You could've gone a touch easier that first week, though."

"I know that you tried to keep me from getting hurt then, too, but I'm too damn stubborn for my own good. I'm so sorry that trying to help me got you killed. Here's to hoping that whatever afterlife you end up in, it's not the worst one. We both know you won't get a good one though," she chuckles humorlessly, then picks up a handful of dirt and drops it over the man.

She gets to her feet and nods at Boss, who takes a deep breath and the earth covers the body. We all sit in silence for a long moment, then Graves says, "Should we deal with the other one too?"

Lilith shakes her head, "No, neither he nor Gavin deserve this kind of respect. Let whatever comes across their corpses consume them.

As if on a deranged cue, Gavin shrieks from the campsite, the sound so gut-wrenching and pain-filled that it makes all but Lilith wince. Looking towards the camp, she rolls her eyes, "Always so dramatic, that one." She stands up and stretches, wincing in pain as the cut on her arm weeps blood, "Come along, the further away we go, the less of his screams we'll have to deal with."

Thirteen

In Which Feelings are Confessed

Damien

I watch Lilith's every move as we make our way through the trees. She has been raging through the brush for an hour, mumbling curses under her breath. She stumbles and sways, but when Graves reaches out to catch her, she slaps his hands away and glares at him.

"Lilith," he says, sounding desperate, "You need to rest, you're injured."

She turns to glare at him, her eyes taking on a frantic edge, "Now you care?"

I growl at that and stomp toward her, "What the fuck is that supposed to mean?"

She turns to look at me, her eyes glow with faint light as she lifts her chin, "Exactly what I said! I find it hard to believe you three care even a little. You didn't come to get me!"

I stalk forward and go to grab her, but she disappears into the darkness around us and reappears ten paces away.

"You think we didn't want to look for you?" Phil snaps.

"I don't give a fuck what you wanted. You DIDN'T come looking! I was in the city for a week, an entire week! I was kidnapped, missing, beaten, and dragged across the fucking countryside! You lot left me on my own!"

"We had no choice," Samael says, stepping toward her.

She scoffs and throws him a look that could kill a lesser soul, "There is always a choice."

He recoils at that, no doubt recalling when he used the same line on her, "Please, Lilith, you were in danger and we didn't... everything pointed..."

Her eyes narrow on him, "You didn't what?" she hisses, the flow in her eyes becoming bright enough to illuminate the clearing.

I growl at her, making her swing her gaze over to me, "We didn't know that you *didn't* steal the seal. Everything pointed to you doing it. From the fact that there's only so many people with the talent to unlock the safe, to the fact that you specifically asked to be alone shortly before it all went missing."

Her eyes darken and she spins to glare at Graves, "Is that your excuse? Really? Samael? That's what you told them?" she spits his name at him like it's poisonous.

He winces at that and holds his hands up, "I didn't know what to do, Lilith, I swear. I wanted to look for you, but I was afraid you'd end up in more danger. I needed a plan, I needed time."

"I didn't have any!" she screams and slaps a hand to her chest, "I didn't have any time!" a sob escapes this time, tears streaming down her cheeks.

Samael takes steps toward her but she backs up, "I didn't have any time, Samael. I didn't have a lick of it. I was drugged, chained, beaten, starved." She wraps her arms around herself as the tears continue to fall, "I stayed strong that first week, I thought... I was so certain you were coming to find me. After everything that happened at the Solstice, I had no doubts that you would be there soon. But then... then... they showed me those fucking posters. And I thought you'd abandoned me, turned on me, just like everyone else." she sobs and turns and walks away from us again.

I snarl and try to keep up with her, but then I hear a thump. I spin and Samael is on his knees, one hand held out as he says, "If you can't believe our words, believe my memories."

Lilith gasps and spins to face him, Phil and I already gaping at him like a couple of idiots. The look on his face holds nothing but conviction. I wonder if Errill was referring to this. Is losing *Lilith* the sacrifice that Samael needs to make?

Graves

When Lilith turns to face me, I can see the shock on her face. Her eyes are wide as she takes me in. I'm kneeling in fallen leaves, mud, and ice with one hand held out to her and the other holding my protection charm by its chain, letting it swing in the breeze. I don't know what to do. So I'm doing the only thing left, begging. She regards me with a guarded expression, "What did you say?" she murmurs.

"If you don't believe our words, believe my memories," I repeat and when she doesn't outright reject the idea, I press on, "I know I can't convince you to forgive me simply by asking; so look and see what I knew, what I saw, and make your judgment then. Regardless of what you decide, I'll accept it."

"Sam-" Phil says from somewhere behind me.

I don't turn, my eyes still fixed on Lilith as she continues to watch me. Her arms wrapped around herself and there's that subtle sway to her stance, like she's not quite steady on her feet. The silence stretches on and I can't handle it, "Please, Lilith," I beg, my voice cracking with the weight of my emotions.

She walks up to me then, that guarded expression still firmly in place. She takes the protection charm and lets it swing between us, "You're willingly opening yourself up to my power? You saw what I did to Gavin with just a touch."

I can't help but smile at that, "It was incredible."

Her brow furrows, as if she doubts that sentiment. Instead of questioning me more, she drops the pendant to the side and grips my hand. I focus on the day she disappeared, being woken by panicked voices. Screaming, searching through the house until we're all staring at the safe as it hangs open.

***

I rush over to it, not so concerned about the open door as I am about the snakes that appear to have pried it open. I stare at them, recognizing the coloring from Gavin. Trying not to lose my temper as I hear the twins barking orders in the background. Someone says something about "a lying thief," and a few other accusations are thrown around.

I ignore all of them and focus on the snakes, focus on who opened the safe. I get nothing. No direction on what to do, no gut instinct on where to go. All I feel is pain and a desperate need to find Lilith. So I turn and stride from the room, ignoring the protests around me and using magic to separate myself from the twins.

Unaware of anything but my goal, I make my way across the city. Slamming the door of Sarah's shop open, I yell, "Where is she?"

Sarah stands near the counter, a sad look in her eyes, "Who?"

I hiss out a breath, "Don't play coy, where the fuck is Lilith?"

"I don't know," she shakes her head.

"How do I find her?"

"I don't know,"

"Is she in danger?" I demand.

"Yes,"

I step up to the counter and let my magic crawl through the space, ice racing across the ground and up the walls, "Then give me one good reason I shouldn't tear this city apart to find her."

Sarah inhales, and her eyes widen, but I don't ask again. Her eyes become distant and glassy before she speaks, "Right now they see her worth as only being in possession of the seal. If you begin to hunt for her, they will try to use her against you."

Sarah levels me with a look full of sorrow, "And Lilith would rather die than let herself be used against you."

***

I'm thrown back into the present when Lilith pulls her hand from mine, I blink rapidly to clear the past from my mind, "There's more," I say, reaching toward her again.

She shakes her head and there are tears shining in her eyes, "Would you have really done that?"

"In a heartbeat," I vow, "I know you well enough to know that Sarah was right. If they tried to use you against us..." I shake my head, unable to even finish the sentence.

"In a heartbeat," she echoes.

I scowl at that, "No. Anyone who tries to use you dies, whether it's by your hand or ours."

"Agreed," Phil and Damien echo.

She smiles, then drops to her knees and hugs me. I wrap my arms around her and press my face into her hair. The contact makes the chaos of my mind settle for the first time since she went missing.

She sobs against my shoulder as the twins come to sit with us. They sit so she's protected by us in the middle of a small triangle. Abruptly, she pulls away and slaps my chest, "Don't you ever do that shit again! Do you hear me?"

"I hear you," I say with a nod, "but I'll do it again if it means keeping you alive."

"No!" she slaps my chest again and her eyes fill with tears, "I don't ever want to feel that alone again! I can't handle it!"

I rub her arms then cup her face in one hand, "Never. You are never alone; I will always come find you."

"Yeah," Phil agrees, "We'll always come find you, Lil. You're stuck with us assholes."

Lilith sniffles and grips my shirt, those tears spilling down her cheeks.

I pull her close and rest my forehead against hers, "I will always do whatever it takes to find you, all of us will. Sometimes that may include patience, deception, violence, whatever it takes. But you can be certain that no matter what information circulates, we will always be there."

"Always?" she mutters, her voice hoarse as her fingers curl into my shirt even tighter.

The fear in her voice breaks me in a way I can't quite explain, all I know is that I cannot stand it. I pull away and press a kiss to her forehead, "Every," a kiss to one eyelid, "Single," a kiss to the other eye, "Time."

When I look down at her, she's staring up at me with a frown and her confusion is bashing against my senses. Her mouth drops open just a touch and I can't resist, I pull her in again and feather a kiss across her lips. I pull away as quickly as I started and rest my forehead against hers again, "I will always find you, Lilith, no matter the lifetime."

Lilith

I'm not sure what surprises me more, the twins' soft touches on my hips, that Samael just kissed me like I'd break, or that this moment feels like it's been a long time coming. All I know is that too much has happened to me in the last two days. With all the pain, fear, confusion, and now this, I finally lose my control.

My meticulously assembled shields crumble like they never existed and my magic practically explodes out of my chest. Darkness coats the entire clearing, so thick and dark I can't see Samael in front of me. It crashes around us like a tidal wave of power. It feels uncontrolled but also like breathing for the first time after wearing a corset. I bury my face against Samael's shoulder and shudder with echoes of power as all three of them hold me tighter.

The magic retreats after a minute, but I don't bother with the walls again. There's no point. If these men would come find me through lifetimes, then trying to hide from them is stupid. The darkness abates as I pull my magic all the way back to me and I can see them again. I pull away to gage their reactions. I look at the twins first, too afraid to face Samael just yet.

Phil looks dazed, but there's a stupid grin on his face like he's won something.

I turn to Damien and when I meet his gaze he smirks, "About time, Hellion, those stupid walls were getting annoying," Despite his words there's still a flicker of concern in his eyes.

I stick my tongue out at him, then turn to Samael, who's staring at me still. "Uh," I look down, only to end up staring at his throat and chest, a blush races up my neck and I try to look away.

Graves catches my face and makes me look at him, "You've had that much magic the whole time?"

Fear creeps back in as my heart pounds out a terrified beat, "Mostly? I feel like I've gotten stronger since I touched the Seal, and the uh... experiences that I had while captive."

He chuckles then kisses me again, making my eyes blow wide, "You're amazing."

I laugh at that and hide my face against his shoulder, "That's what you have to say? Even after... that?"

"I could try for more," he says with a laugh, pulling me closer and pressing his face against my hair, "I'm just not sure I could ever do you justice."

I snort, "The ever thoughtful Lord Graves is at a loss for words? Should I be concerned?"

"Don't tease the poor man," Phil says, "He was begging you for forgiveness not five minutes ago."

"Won't be the last time," Damien says dryly.

I lift my head and glare over at him, "Neither of you apologized. Maybe I should make you beg too."

Before I can question the thought, Phil sits up onto his knees and takes my hand in his, "Lilith Callam, please forgive me for letting this idiot try to use wanted posters to protect you. I swear on my life that I will always come to find you and, while I may concede to his plans, I will call Samael an idiot when needed."

I go to argue but as if it's a contests Damien grabs my other hand and squeezes it until I worry my bones are going to grind together, "Hellion, I let my own doubts cloud my judgment and in doing so put you in harms way. I'm sorry."

I look between them, the intensity of their attention making me flush again, "Okay! You're forgiven."

Damien laughs and lets my hand go, "Good,"

I glare over at him and then yawn, everything finally catching up to me. My eyes drift closed and I sigh as I lean into Graves' hold, "I need sleep."

A moment later, I'm being picked up. I yelp and flail for a second before I'm turned and Damien grunts when I smack him, "Come on," he grumbles, "We'll get you tucked in."

I snort, "I'm not a child."

He grunts back but doesn't answer me. I look around to see Samael and Phil in the process of setting up bedrolls. "We should probably keep watch, just to be safe," I suggest.

"We will," Phil says, "but you need to rest."

"I can help!"

"Sure, tomorrow," Samael says, pulling a blanket up and over me, "You've had the shit beaten out of you repeatedly, you're going to sleep and get a full night's rest."

I pout, but don't resist as I am tucked in, the moment I'm settled I can't help but fall asleep.

Philip

I sit next to Lilith and Samael, both of them asleep. She'd passed out once we got her settled, but it'd been a fight to get Sam to rest as well. Once he'd laid down, they'd gravitated towards each other until their hands wound together. Now Lilith has their arms clutched to her chest. I wouldn't be surprised if, by the time they woke up, they were even more tangled together. The thought has me smiling slightly, I can't think of the last time I've seen them both properly rest.

I sit back and stare at the sky; the stars winking down at me as I contemplate everything that's happened today. Finding Lilith was just the start of the chaos, as usual. I close my eyes and let out a long breath. Damien comes up to sit on the other side of our long-time friends.

"What now?" He whispers, "Lilith's magic..." he trails off, then sighs, "It seemed close to what we remember, yeah?"

I nod, "Yeah, I bet having the seal with her is a contributing factor. But..."

"But?" he prompts.

"There's something that I hadn't thought about, at least not recently," I concede.

"Care to share?" he asks dryly.

I look down at the two of them and brush strands of hair from Lilith's face, "Immortal beings tend to gain power as they age,"

"Yeah? And?"

"And their souls have been aging for a thousand years, not to mention all the experience that would've added to their power as well." I look up at him and he's staring down at them now.

"Are you suggesting that they've just been gaining power this whole time? That what we saw today isn't even all of Lilith's power?" he asks quietly, his voice hoarse.

I grin, "Yeah, I'm willing to bet that she hasn't unlocked all that there is now. Not to mention that Sam is probably behind her since he hasn't experienced as much stress.

He sits back and huffs out a laugh, "So, once they've accepted themselves... they might legitimately be unstoppable."

"Especially together," I say, grinning over at him, "Just imagine... we've been looking for so long... I'm glad to have them back."

He nods, "Even if they don't remember yet, I'm happy too."

We both turn to look up at the stars and I ask, "Are you going to tell them?"

He scowls over at me, "Tell them what?"

I snort and look back at the sky, "I'll take that as a no."

I scowl, "No, what are you talking about?"

"How you feel? How you blame yourself? How you wish you'd behaved differently all those years ago? How much you actually care?"

"What good would it do?"

"I don't know," I admit, then shrug, "maybe help you get past that guilt you've been carrying for a thousand years?"

He grunts, "Maybe... but I think I will until they remember. If they don't remember *why* I feel that way, then they can't properly ease that guilt. What about you? You ever going to admit how you feel about Lilith?"

I hesitate for a moment, then look away, "Sam figured out the truth, but I don't intend to say anything to Lilith. Just like before."

He grunts, "I thought so. Don't be a hypocrite."

Deimos

I stare at my king with my mouth open, too shocked by his announcement to form a cohesive sentence for a moment. At last I shake my head, "What?"

He turns to give me a long look, like he's questioning if I'm daft or something, "I said, you are to be Lilith's personal guard. Errill is going into a hibernation state because, in his words, 'things are getting out of hand.' As to what that means, he's been unclear, but Lilith is also adamant that he go rest for a while."

"How the fuck does that translate to me being stuck watching her? She's perfectly capable!" I shout, throwing my arms around.

Samael looks at me for a long while, his silence abnormally unnerving as he observes my reaction. We sit in silence for a long moment, until he quirks a single brow, "Capable yes, however, given that she's still struggling with the after affects of... what happened. It has been decided that she needs to have a guard with her at all times until such a time that she feels safe enough to venture out on her own."

"So Errill is just abandoning her while she's like this?" I snap, not really listening to what he's saying, "Why me? She and Phobos get along, make him babysit."

"Enough!" Samael shouts, his voice becoming harsh, "I didn't bring you here to be berated. First of all, Phobos came to me asking that he be allowed to be her guard once he heard that Errill was going to be gone for a while. While I have no doubt about your brother's skills, a single Immortal does not have the capacity to provide the same protection as a Primal."

"Still doesn't answer why me," I shout and turn away to face the door, "I'm not the only Immortal in Hell."

"No," Samael agrees, "But you are the only one that Lilith, Errill, and myself agree are up to the task."

I stop just short of my hand touching the door and turn back to look at him, "What?"

He smiles at that, "You heard me just fine, but I'll elaborate. When posed the question of who she would prefer to work alongside Phobos in protecting her, Lilith said that you were the only Immortal she trusted with the task."

We stare at each other for a few minutes. Samael, as usual, is perfectly content to wait until I decide. I'm not sure what to say, most of my resistance was because I was certain Lilith hated my guts. I look up at my King, even more baffled than I was at first, "What?"

He chuckles at that, "I am not the person you should be asking, I've given you the information I have. Preparation for Errill's hibernation should be done by the end of the week, make up your mind by then." He turns back to his desk, dismissing me.

***

I storm through the castle, looking for Lilith, needing answers before I'm willing to make any sort of decision. Most of the staff scatters when I pass them, knowing better than to get in my way. I finally get to the butler's office and he looks up at me with a confused expression, "Yes?" he asks.

"Where are Lilith and Phobos?" I snap, not bothering with a preamble.

The old demon snorts, "I take it you've been given the news. Last I heard, Lady Lilith wished for sweets and they'd gone to the kitchen to procure them."

I growl at him, ignoring the comment of being given news. As I get halfway to the kitchen, I wonder how many people in the palace know about the change. I shake the question as I slam my way into the kitchen.

I stop short at what greets me. There's flour and baking supplies all over the place, and Phobos is chasing a flour covered Lilith around the room. "What the fuck?" I shout, startling them both.

Lilith slides to a stop just short of slamming into me. Phobos skids to a stop before barreling into her, but wraps an arm around her waist and pulls her back against his chest, "We were making cookies," Phobos says with a grin, "Want some?"

"No! And that's not what I fucking meant!" I glare down at Lilith, "Why do you want me to help Phobos guard you?"

"Oh, that," Phobos says, actually pulling her closer and looking down at her like he's trying to protect her but also waiting for her answer.

She doesn't look up at him, instead her eyes are fixed on my face, "You are the only person whose abilities compliment Phobos's in a way that covers all angles. Additionally, you two are the only ones available who, together, even remotely stand a chance against the beings that have hunted me in the past."

I growl at her, "You don't even like me? Why the fuck would you want me to be responsible for your safety?"

Lilith raises an eyebrow at me, the action reflecting Samael's in an eerie way, "I don't recall ever saying I disliked you, found you impertinent and rude, maybe. But I can also be impertinent and rude, so that's not really that big a deal. That's not the important part though, it's that I trust you."

"I trust that once you give your word, you're going to keep me safe to the best of your ability. There's no doubt in my mind that when you make that decision, nothing will sway you from it."

I open and close my mouth a few times; I want to argue with her, to tell her it's pointless and storm away. But the conviction in her eyes, the soft way she's regarding me, that she's so certain I'll agree, it takes all the wind out of my sails.

When I don't immediately reject the idea, she smiles, and it melts the last bit of resistance in me. I truly can't deny her anything, and every time she grins at me, I wonder why I ever thought I could. I drop my shoulders and sigh, then laugh at myself and look back up at her, "All right, if you're so sure."

She grins, her entire face lighting up, then she disappears from

Phobos's grasp and reappears before me, practically jumping into my arms and hugging me, "Thank you, Deimos! I knew you'd accept."

Fourteen

In Which the Tribe is Found

Lilith

I wake with a start, all my senses going on high alert. My magic stretches out and seems to find nothing. I look around and see that all three of the guys have fallen asleep, Phil is on one side of me, Samael on the other, and Damien looks like he fell asleep while on watch, his back propped up against a nearby tree.

A sense of unease continues to coil over me as I look around. I hear a twig snap and get to my feet, using shadows to shake the others awake as I scan the clearing. My eyes flick across the tree line and I spread my magic around my feet, trying to find where the threat is coming from.

"Whu-?" Damien grunts, then seems to wake all the way and growls, "Shit,"

Phil rolls over and is on his feet in a second, "Crap, do you hear that?"

"I heard movement," I admit, "But I'm not sure where, I can't seem to track it. Which is annoying as hell, it's like..." I trail off.

"It's like whatever is hiding the village is hiding them," Graves says where he's still sitting at my side, he stands up and looks around, "We're not here to hurt anybody. We're looking for the- "

"The Children of the Lost Gods," Phil cuts him off.

Graves shoots Phil a look, but doesn't argue as we wait a tense moment.

There's another snap, a few shuffled steps from somewhere, then a well-armed man appears with a rifle pointed at my chest. "Hands up and come quietly, you know of our people so you can speak to our leaders, but that doesn't mean we'll trust you."

Damien growls, "Why the fuck should we do that? So you can fucking shoot us?"

"Damien," Phil snaps, "We need their help."

The angrier twin makes another noise, but I cut in, "Enough," I raise my hands and step toward the man, "We'll cooperate, we just want you to hear us out."

Damien makes that noise again, "Hellion," he growls, making a grab for my arm.

I turn to glare at him, "Enough, Damien, like Phil said, we need their help. To get it we have to cooperate, if you aren't going to behave, you can stay out here."

He growls at me again, then sighs, "Fine! Fine," he throws his hands up in a gesture of surrender too, but keeps a glare fixed on the strangers.

I roll my eyes as the others all put their hands up. More people swarm out of the trees. We're handled roughly as they bind our wrists and half lead, half drag us deeper into the woods.

Philip

The guards lead us through the trees and into a clearing that I swear wasn't there before, perhaps this is what Lilith detected. I don't have long to question what I'm looking at before we're shoved to the ground in front of a handful of people. One is a burly man with his arms crossed and glaring down at us, another stands with his hands clasped behind his back and is listening to something the bigger one is saying.

There are five guards gathered, adding to the ranks of the ten who brought us in. And tucked behind the rest is an older man leaning heavily on a walking staff, his head is turned to one side as he regards us, but he says nothing.

We're shoved to the ground and the middle man steps forward, the way he carries himself, suggesting he's in charge. "Strip them, make sure they don't have any weapons on them."

They start with Damien, taking a blade and cutting his shirt away, repeating the process with all three of us. When they turn toward Lilith, Damien snarls, "Don't fucking touch her."

I hiss and bare my teeth, my eyes fixated on the guard who is standing a few steps away from her. He looks at the three of us, then down at Lilith, who smiles sweetly up at him, "Wanna risk it?" she taunts.

He shakes his head and stakes a step back, holding his hands up in surrender. Lilith chuckles, then, with an impressive maneuver, pulls her shirt off to pool at her wrists. It leaves her pale skin exposed save for a bodice that's laced together over her breasts. "There, saved you the trouble." She says to the man.

The man, who I assume is the chief, snorts, and steps close, "Are you afraid of a waif and a few tied up fools?" he looks down at us now that he can see disarmed and crosses his arms over his chest.

"Says the man who wouldn't approach until we were as vulnerable as possible," Damien grumbles, his voice dark.

The man spins to glare at my brother, "I am the leader here, I cannot witlessly put myself in danger. Even if I do not believe you four pose any genuine threat."

Lilith snorts and rolls her eyes, she looks over at me and smirks. The chief stalks closer and snaps, "Got something to say, bitch?"

She gives him a sickeningly sweet smile, "If I have something to say, I'll say it. You can be certain of that, chief."

He scowls then glances at me, his eyes catch on my chest and I tense, wondering what the fuck has drawn his attention in. He comes closer and looks at the tattoos on my chest. "You, you're one of them."

I frown and try to ask what he's on about when he hisses, "Traitor."

I recoil as if struck, even as Damien growls, "Excuse me?"

He looks over at my brother and his brow furrows further, "You're the other! Traitors, you two were supposed to be our gods' closest guards, and when they disappeared, you abandoned them and us!"

The words hit like a cannon; I suspected any mortal followers that remained would feel that way, but to hear it drives the point home. I drop my head, old fears rising and tearing my heart open. Damien makes a growling noise, but before anything else can happen, Lilith speaks up, "Watch your fucking mouth!"

The chief spins to stare at her, though it's clear to see that he isn't intimidated by a small, semi-naked woman. "Excuse me?" he snaps.

Lilith's eyes narrow, "I said, watch your mouth. You don't know the first thing about them or what they've been through. You have no right to pass judgment on them."

"I am the leader of our people! The keeper of our histories and I know that- "

"That a thousand years ago, these two made the decision that the best thing they could do was go seek out the souls of their dearest friends?" Lilith cuts him off, her voice sharp and angry, "That the people you claim to worship, whom you know nothing about, were into mortal forms and that these two men have been searching for them this whole time? That they've been stuck looking for their friends and losing them over and over again? Is that what you know?"

The chief looks bewildered for a moment before drawing back and snapping, "How dare you accuse me? You wretched," he pulls his hand back as if to strike her.

Unfortunately for him, Lilith's patience is at its end. She disappears into the shadows before he can bring his hand down and then reappears behind him with her hands on her hips. He stumbles forward when he sees that she's gone. He turns and stares his eyes wide, "What? How?" he says the second word like a demand.

"Lilith," Samael says, his voice warning.

Lilith cuts her eyes to Sam and crosses her arms, "I know we were trying to be cooperative, but I can't," she closes her eyes and exhales through her nose, "I can't stand by and watch this idiot so blatantly insult my friends. Especially when he knows nothing about their situation!"

The chief looks from Lilith to Samael, then to Damien and me. His eyes grow wary and I wonder if he's made the connection that none of us is as helpless as we look. He takes a half step away from her, which puts him closer to his men, then points at her, "You watch your tongue!"

Sam sighs, "She did warn you," he looks up at Lilith with clear warmth in his eyes, "She if she has something to say, she'll say it."

The Chief makes a disgusted noise then shouts, "Seize her!"

A handful of guards move forward but Damien roars, "Touch her and it's your head!"

Lilith ignores the guards and the chief and comes to crouch in front of me, she puts a hand on my shoulder and presses her forehead to mine, "Don't let what he said get to you."

I don't argue with her, but I can't find any hope in myself at the moment. She pulls away and gives me a sympathetic look, wiping away a tear from my face, she leans forward and whispers in my ear, "You're acting like we're still missing rather than right in front of you."

I tense at that and look up; she leans back and grins at me, then winks. My heart kicks into overdrive, if she's figured out the truth and hasn't run screaming, maybe we're closer to success than I'd thought. The chief turns to us and raises his hand again when his guards don't reach for her.

Before he can get close to her, she turns to look at him. The darkness around us comes alive as Lilith's magic wraps the chief in tendrils of shadows, holding the man in place and shrouding him in darkness. "I said we were being nice," she says as she stands up, "We tried to cooperate and instead of giving us any sort of mercy, you have the audacity to accuse and attack us? I don't think so."

The ropes that are binding the three of us snap, freeing us from the confines. I rush to get to my feet and wrap my arms around Lilith, needing to have her in my arms and know that she is here. As I pull her close, she leans into my hold and lets her magic wrap around me, the comforting presence settles my nerves.

"We're looking for something," Lilith continues, "And you can either help us find what we're looking for or we'll go through you to get it."

"Lilith," Samael says as he gets to his feet.

Graves

Lilith shoots me a wary glance, but when I nod, she sighs and lets the chieftain go. Phil is hanging onto her like she's the only thing anchoring him to this world, once she lets the chieftain go, she turns and hugs him. The big blond man dwarfs her slimmer frame, but it's clear that he is hiding in her arms. Damien walks up behind the chief, which has the guards scattering like ants. I sigh and look at the chief again, "We need help to find something. Our tools led us here, and we're pretty sure you have it."

"What are you looking for?" the Chief says warily, edging away from us.

Phil lifts his head and looks over at Damien, who gives his brother a sympathetic look. A moment later Phil detaches himself from Lilith, he looks steadier but keeps an arm around her waist as the two of them walk over to us.

"It's the second seal," Damien says to the Chief.

The man looks taken aback, "Why should I give it to you?"

Lilith hisses and reaches a shadow out toward the man. I hold my hand out in front of her and she gives me a dark look, "Your hand, Lilith,"

She sighs then holds her hand out, the first seal hanging from her wrist, "You're going to give it to us because we already have the first seal," I explain.

The Chief walks up and reaches for her wrist, making Damien growl, "I just wish to verify the authenticity of it."

Damien sighs and relaxes as Lilith holds her hand out to the Chief. He grabs her wrist and turns it, inspecting the engraving on the surface. An uneasy feeling creeps up on me and I grab his wrist, "Enough,"

He glares at me but lets her go, "I suppose we can let you attempt to retrieve the seal."

"Attempt?" Lilith asks, her tone bordering on venomous.

"Yes," he straightens his shirt, "Having the first seal doesn't automatically qualify to have the second."

"So what does qualify one to have it?" I ask, before Lilith can lose her temper again.

The Chief looks smug as he says, "There are trials that one must pass to get it, if you can pass the trials, then you can have it."

Lilith groans and leans against Phil, who holds her tighter, "Fucking hell, I don't have energy for this," she complains.

I sigh, "We need time to rest and prepare before we can do anything remotely considered trials. Where can we rest?"

"You expect me to let you stay inside our borders? When you've openly threatened us?" The chief snaps, trying to retake control.

I want to tell the sniveling man to go fuck himself. Instead, I keep my mouth shut and glare as I think of a way to get the help we need.

I'm contemplating murder again when Lilith sighs and looks over at me, "Graves, let's just go find a place to make camp. I'm not inclined to trust them to leave us alone, and my fucking stab wounds are acting up."

I sigh and drag a hand across my face, "All right, maybe we can purchase the services of your healer tomorrow."

The Chief looks as if he's going to argue with me but goes silent when the older man from their group approaches, "It would be my honor to offer my assistance to the Bearer of the First Seal."

The chief turns back as if to argue, but Lilith cuts him off this time, "I'd appreciate it. Yesterday, someone attacked and poisoned me, and although we've neutralized the poison, it has left me rather weak.

The man bows so low I'm surprised he doesn't fall over, "If this is you in a weakened state, my lady, then I thank you for your restraint."

Lilith smirks and tosses her hair over her shoulder as she turns away from the Chief, "At least someone around here knows how to be respectful. We'll be back after sunrise."

The Chief glances to me as if for approval but the Healer replies, "That will be fine. If I may take a look at your wounds before you leave, it will give me the time to prepare the appropriate poultices."

Lilith bites her lip at that uncertainty in her eyes.

Damien comes up behind her and glowers at the Healer, "Do anything shifty and I'll take your head off."

Lilith sighs at that and tips her head back to look at him, "You need a new threat, Demon."

He looks down at her and makes a face, I think it's intended to be a grin but it looks too feral for that, "But it works."

She shakes her head and walks up to the healer, "it's the one here on my shoulder and another on my calf. Made by the same blade and poison, so I'm hoping we don't need more than one poultice. I'm not taking my trousers off in front of the entire tribe."

"I wouldn't ask you to, my Lady," He steps closer and raises a hand as if to touch her. She flinches away, and he stops as the three of us step forward.

His eyes flick up to hers and he says, "I can examine without touching you, but it will not be as thorough. I can see from here that they are deep. I may be able to instruct one of your companions on how to clean and dress the wounds, however there are still risks."

"Can't you heal them with magic?" Phil asks, coming closer to Lilith with one hand outstretched.

"Not without touch, they're too deep." Lilith murmurs, that contemplative look on her face.

I step up next to her and brush her hair back before leaning close and whispering into her ear, "I think it would be best if you allowed the healer to properly check the wounds, but it's your choice."

She looks up at me, her eyes shining with equal parts fear and trust. The twins close in around her as well, silently offering support. I smile softly, tucking the strands of hair behind her ear, "We won't let anything happen to you."

A small smile tips the corner of her lips at that, then she turns to the healer, who is still waiting for her answer. "You can touch to inspect the wounds, I'd rather do this correctly."

He nods, "Thank you,"

Fifteen

In Which the Thief is Tended To

Lilith

I brace myself as the Healer steps closer and gently prods the scab that's crusted over the wound on my shoulder. He makes a soft tutting noise, "Did you clean this at all?"

"No," I say quietly, "I uh..." I glance at Graves, and without another word, he picks up the explanation.

"There was a misunderstanding which lead to the wounds being a bit neglected. We'd planned to clean them when we made camp tonight."

The Healer makes that tutting noise again, "I fear infection may have already taken root, there's an additional warmth to the area."

"Fuck," Damien growls whispers, "We should've gotten to it sooner,"

"I wouldn't have let you," I quip, "I'm pretty tough, I don't foresee a minor infection being enough to put me down for the count. The wounds themselves certainly didn't."

Damien grunts not sounding amused at all, "I think you could be at death's door and still spitting and fighting like a hellcat."

I roll my eyes but the healer prods the wound again and I wince, "Okay, that is rather tender."

The healer nods, "I will need to use magic…" he meets my gaze, "I'm concerned that letting it sit overnight may cause it to take a turn for the worst. I understand if you are hesitant, but I would prefer not to take the risk."

I bite the inside of my cheek, chewing softly as I think. I don't know if I want to be alone with a stranger, even a healer.

As if sensing my concerns, the man glances behind me, "One or all of your men may also accompany us, it would help to have extra hands to help with cleaning the injuries."

I'm about to retort that they're not mine, but then I remember the multiple, albeit chaste, kisses from the night before, and a blush hits my cheeks. "That would help," I say instead.

He smiles, "Excellent, this way." He walks off and I frown as I realize that the guys have closed ranks around me. Samael on my left, Phil on my right, and Damien at my back. Instead of feeling trapped like I may have at one point, their presence is comforting.

We're led to a small hut where the healer gestures for us to enter, "Here we are," we step inside and the scent of herbs washes over us. I look around, my eyes adjusting to the darkness in a blink.

"Do you not have an apprentice?" Phil asks.

"I do, however they are currently with child, and I shan't disturb her whilst she's in a delicate state. If one of you is able to help in some way, that would be appreciated."

The three men exchange a look over my head, I want to snap at them for having silent conversations. But some conclusion is come to and Samael says, "I can clean the wounds," he glances down at me, "that okay?"

I glance at Damien and Phil, then back at Graves, "I trust you," I say.

The smile that earns me makes my heart stutter. Before I have too much time to linger on that, the Healer hands me a cloth skirt, "Here you go dear, so you can expose your wounds without sacrificing too much modesty."

I smile gratefully and pull the skirt on, not bothering to turn my back as I swap the tattered breeches for the fresh skirt. I reach for the laces on my bodice to take it off as well and wince as the movement pulls on the cuts, "Fuck," I hiss, dropping my arms.

The healer gives me a sympathetic look, "We'll have to cut it off. Would you like me to numb the area?"

I scowl as I'm handed a loose-fitting shirt and Samael takes a blade to the bodice, "What?"

"I can use my magic to mitigate the amount of pain you feel, it does inhibit your ability to move the limbs, but it will help with the pain."

"How much of an effect?" I ask, frowning as I sit on the cot he directs me to.

"It varies. On a scale of one to ten, how badly does it hurt?" he asks.

I frown and glance at Samael, "Uh, three?"

The Healer blinks at me a few times then says, "Ah," he glances at the wound on my arm, "How?"

Phil scoffs, "It might be better to ask how much of an affect she's willing to have on her mobility."

"Yeah," I agree, "That'd be easier for me to answer."

The healer frowns, looking between the four of us like we're all insane. Finally he sighs, "Ten would be completely paralyzed, no motion what so ever. One would be like when you lay on a limb too long and it falls asleep."

I grunt, "Three, I don't want to feel the limb, but I need to have the freedom to move."

"We'll protect you," Phil says.

"Yeah, and who'll protect you?" I snap, glaring up at him.

He holds his hands up in surrender and takes a step back. Sam chuckles and the Healer passes a hand over my arm. The difference is immediate; the limb feels disconnected from the rest of me. "Lie down," Samael says, supporting my back as I do so.

"I can help with the herbs," Phil says brusquely, walking away with the healer before anyone can argue.

"What was that about?" I ask, bracing as Graves pulls a cloth out of a basin of water.

"Blood," Damien says, sitting on my other side and glaring down at me.

"Oh," I breathe.

Graves presses the damp cloth against my skin and I wince, the pressure feeling strange despite the numbness of the limb. "Will he be all right in here?" I look at Damien for an answer.

"That's what you're worried about?" Damien growls.

"Uh, yeah?" I ask, looking over at the big man, "I mean, I don't want him losing his composure or anything, besides I'm in no state to actually take on a vampire right now."

I'm not sure what about it is the wrong thing to say, but no sooner have the words left my mouth Damien is on his feet, partially shifted. I jerk back at the sudden motion, making Graves' pressure on the wound increase and causing me to cry out.

"You're a reckless fool!" Damien shouts, throwing one of his hands out to the side, "you were almost killed less than a day ago and have the audacity to, to act so flippant about the whole thing?"

"Damien," Phil says, standing behind Graves with a serious look on his face.

Graves continues to work on my wound, and I try not to flinch at every prod of the tender skin. Even though the pain is gone, it still feels strange. "What?" Damien snarls at his brother, his eyes frantic.

"Get yourself under control, she's not to blame here." Philip says trying to ease whatever is eating at his brother.

Damien makes a rude noise then stomps up to his brother, "Don't act like you don't feel the same! She let these fucking injuries go untreated because she was too proud!"

Before he can start shouting again Philip grabs his brother and shoves him out of the room. I try to sit up to go after them but Phil turns and pins me with a look, "Stay there, Princess, let Samael take care of you. I'll deal with my idiot brother."

I lie back down, startled at the sharpness in Phil's tone as he storms after Damien.

Damien

I storm out of the healer's hut and try to slam it, but Phil catches it and says something to the Hellion before following me out. Heading into the woods nearby, I slam my fist against a tree, the wood dents, creaks, then falls over with a thump. I can't even find it in myself to care that it's dead now. Phil walks up behind me, "Feel better?" he asks dryly.

I spin to glare at him, "How are you so calm? She could've died! She still could! And you're acting like, like, it's all fine despite the danger she's put herself in!"

He crosses his arms over his chest and gives me a long look, "But she's fine, the healer will take care of the infection, and we both know that there isn't much that can keep her down."

"If she were herself, she's still fucking mortal! A fragile, weak, HUMAN!" I roar the last word, unable to keep all my fear and anger in check.

"So that means you're allowed to take your fears out on her?" he asks sharply, taking a threatening step toward me, "She hasn't done anything wrong. She was kidnapped and abused for nearly a month. But she's still grinning, she's still fighting. She's stronger than you're giving her credit for. I could've sworn we got over this when you figured out she's actually our queen."

"You're ignoring the fact that she's still mortal!" I shout.

Instead of reacting to my accusation he just grins, "She's figured it out."

I still at that, my eyes going wide, "What do you mean?"

His grin widens, "I mean exactly what I just said. She's figured *it* out, Dem, she knows the truth. She more or less told me today when the Chief started throwing accusations. I get that you're scared but this, this is the closest things have ever gotten. Lilith knows that she holds the queen's soul, and I bet she's connected that Samael is the king. Though I'm not completely certain about that."

"She's still vulnerable," I assert, other fears coming to the forefront as I'm reminded of what will probably happen once she remembers everything.

"Yeah, but I'd bet that right now she's more emotionally vulnerable than physically. You saw how much magic she showed in that clearing. Taking your anger and fear out on her isn't going to help her. We've got to be supportive and stand with her, with them."

I bare my teeth, "Just because I lose my temper doesn't mean I'm not with them."

"Yeah, but pushing her away and acting like a prick isn't going to help." He snaps, "Get yourself together and stop living in the past. They are here now, they're strong enough to handle the knowledge of what they are. And as soon as we can help them figure out how to finish mending that last bit of their souls, they can fix the veil."

I close my eyes and press the heels of my palms against them, "It could all still fall apart. If... if I tell them what happened, how we got here, they would have every right to hate me for it. And I don't know if I can handle it."

I hear him approach and he places a hand on my shoulder, "I still don't know what it is you think you did, but I don't think that they'll flat out reject you for it."

"You don't know that."

"And you don't know what they would, so stop beating yourself up, stop expecting the worst and just... be there. Be here."

I breathe out a heavy sigh and look away, "Fine, I'll do my best. I'm going to go cool off." I turn and walk away before he can argue with me further.

Philip

I watch Damien walk away, my heart breaking for him. He's been living with a guilt so heavy it's crushed his spirit, but he won't do what it takes to lift the burden. I'm half tempted to tell them he's blaming himself for this, but it'd violate his trust and I don't want to risk it. I just hope that when the time comes I'm right, that they don't reject him or push him away. Though, at this rate, he'll do that without telling them the truth.

I'm not able to linger in my thoughts long before I hear something loud and large crashing through the forest. I half expect Damien to be storming back to me with another point to make, instead Parsley leaps out of the brush and lands in front of me.

All three of their heads focus on me, their eyes narrow to slits before I'm hit with an onslaught of emotion and a few words. "*Mama! Mama! Hurt! Find!*"

I hold up my hands, keeping myself between the chimera and the tents behind me. Their voices become a cacophony as they glare at me, "Mama!"

I scowl and address the beast in the Old Tongue, "I know where your Mama is, but she's hurt. You need to be gentle."

They roar at me, which causes a commotion behind me. I walk backwards toward the healer's hut; I need to get them inside and with Lilith before they cause too much chaos.

"Come along," I gesture at them, "I'll take you to her."

They growl softly, then stalk after me as I move back. The tribesmen behind me scream and scatter when they spot the beast. Its owl and serpent heads, watching them curiously as their lion head focuses on me. They keep very quiet as we move around the building; I push the door open and lead them in.

"What is go-" Graves cuts off before he can finish the sentence as Parsley moves the rest of the way into the building, "Oh, it's back."

"Yeah," I agree.

Parsley's serpent head must spot Lilith behind me because they try to launch forward as they scream "MAMA!" into my mind.

"*No!*" I shout in the Old Tongue, cutting between them, "Mama is hurt, you have to be gentle."

Parsley whimpers and drops to their stomach before beginning to crawl forward.

I breathe out a sigh and turn to look at Lilith and Samael, "They're uh,"

"Looking for me," Lilith completes, "I've encountered a couple demons and monsters since I was taken, this isn't the first that's been friendly."

I nod, "Yeah, they're looking for you. This is..." I look at the chimera then back to her, "This is the Queen's pet, Parsley. Each head has a name too, but they're a little flustered now and I don't think they're operating independently enough to react appropriately."

She nods and I step aside so Parsley can creep up to her, still making those soft whimpering sounds. They ignore Graves at first, and he ignores them, continuing his process of cleaning out Lilith's wounds. Lilith holds one hand out to the enormous beast and makes a soft noise, "Hi sweetie,"

Parsley whimpers again and gets up to her then lays their serpent head across her middle, then the owl turns to survey the room as the lion licks her face and hands. She pets them and coos sweetly, telling them it's all right. It only takes a couple moment before the chimera's whimpers turn to purr.

I lean against the door of the building and watch in slight amazement. Graves finishes cleaning Lilith's wounds as the healer finishes up with the herbs, all while Parsley keeps vigil next to Lilith.

Graves stands up and says, "The wounds are clean, all you, healer."

The healer eyes Lilith and Parsley then looks at me, "Will the beast let me tend to her?"

I shrug, "That beast is more intelligent than they appear. I suggest you tell them what you're doing and see what happens. If they get too defensive, I'll do what I can."

Lilith hums something under her breath then pats Thyme, the serpent's eyes open, and she smiles, "The healer needs to tend my wounds, sweetheart, you be nice to him, okay?"

The chimera looks over at the healer who's hovering nearby; they look back at Lilith and hiss. She shakes her head, "No, nice."

I clear my throat and provide the word for nice in the Old Tongue.

Lilith grins over at me, then repeats the word to Parsley, patting their head again as the Healer approaches cautiously. I smile as the healer is able to tend to the wounds, and the massive animal doesn't tear his arms off when Lilith winces and jerks at the discomfort.

Graves

I stare at the door to the Healer's tent, the older man having left us once he'd tended Lilith's wounds. She's sound asleep on the bed beside me, the massive chimera's heads all resting on some portion of her. I smile slightly at how relaxed she seems with the colossal beast laying across her.

It's been a few hours since she's fallen asleep, but I can't bring myself to sleep. Phil left about an hour ago to go retrieve the rest of our supplies. Leaving me, and Parsley, to watch over Lilith alone. I tilt my head back against the wall and close my eyes.

I can't shake an intense sense of urgency even as I try to get my mind to relax. Even though we're so close to the end. We're still too far. Too far from what? I can't be sure. I open my eyes again and Phil is standing in the doorway, he looks somewhat amused, "What?" My voice is quiet and rough, as if I was asleep.

"Nothing, just looks like you passed out for a bit," he brings in our bags and sets them down next to me, "You can get some proper sleep, I'll keep an eye on both of you."

I grunt and sit up, stretching and rolling my shoulders, "Are you sure?"

He waves dismissively, "Yeah, I'm sure. I only need a couple hours of sleep as it is."

I nod and look around, trying to decide where I'm going to lie down. I look back and he's staring at Lilith with longing, that deep current of love for her seeping into the surrounding air. "You should tell her," I state, I know I'd kissed her, and she seemed pleased with that, but if she knew the extent of his feelings, would her opinion change?

He sighs and turns to look at me, putting Lilith and Parsley behind him, the look in his eyes is long-suffering, like this is the thousandth time we've had this talk, even though it's only the second, "You've made the connection that Lilith is the Queen, and that you're the King?"

I scoff at that, "Of course I have, though I don't understand why you've waited so long to confirm that."

He sighs and takes a seat, "Generally, when we've outright told you two who you are, things have gotten out of hand in a volatile way. This is the first time that either of you have figured it out and not gone mad with the knowledge in the space of a few hours. So, forgive my hesitance."

"Okay, what does this have to do with my thoughts on your feelings?" I ask with a frown.

"Knowing you, you're weighing how much and how long I've cared for Lilith against your own affection for her. But you're probably leaving out two key things in your mental equations."

"And that would be?" I ask, crossing my arms to give him what I hope is a superior and not desperate look.

He grins now but there's an undercurrent of disappointment in his emotions too, "Your affection for her is older than mine, you just don't recall it, as is her affection for you. And most importantly, prior to the incident, the two of you were married. So don't forget to factor those things in."

I turn my head to regard him, staring at his tight grin as I decide to pry again. Ignoring any guilt that tries to come up from tapping into his emotions. He's pushed his affection back, locking it up and away, but the act doesn't seem to strain him much, as if he's familiar with having to push them aside.

His smile falters and I refocus on him, "How long have you just hidden how you feel?"

He looks startled at that, "I..." he trails off and looks away now, his expression growing grim.

"Damien does it too, doesn't he? You both push how you feel aside... because of me?" I ask, glancing at Lilith again.

He clears his throat then shrugs, "You took us in when we were essentially unruly kids with chips on our shoulders. We'll do a lot for you."

"And you've always done that? Always kept your feelings to yourself for my sake?" I pry, confusion taking root. Why would they do that? Why not at least say something, communicate their feelings? Or just be up front about it? It's not like everyone ascribes to the idea of a single partner, especially not the longer lived beings.

"Of course," he says with a harsh laugh, "I'd always rather hide what I feel than risk losing you two. I'm fairly sure Damien feels the same. In the past, you were always protective of her, and after... certain events, it became even more so. Seemed the safest way to stay close was to remain faithful friends."

"That's bullshit," I snap as an anger that's somewhat foreign rises in me. How dare he blame me for his hiding, how dare he try to make it my fault, I have never, not once told them or suggest that I'd be jealous of their interest. In fact, I'm pretty sure that, on more than one occasion, I've made it clear that I'm aware and comfortable with it. "Don't blame me for your fear."

His eyes snap over to me and a scowl covers his face, "What?"

"You heard me," I reply, "Don't use me as an excuse to keep your feelings to yourself. For one, Immortals and other long-lived beings rarely stick to one partner at a time. Two, Lilith is not someone who'd change how she treats you if she did know. And, if we're as close to our old selves as you keep saying, then I can guarantee that I would not stand in the way of my friends' or my love's happiness."

"But Clarissa-" he starts, like what that bitch did means anything in this situation.

"Clarissa *lied* to me," I interrupt, "She was seeing someone without my knowledge and then up and left me when it was convenient. This is not the same."

His mouth drops open as he stares at me, I wait to see if he'll reply, when he doesn't, I sigh. "Well, now you know how I feel. So, whenever you decide to stop being an idiot, let me know." I unroll my bedroll and turn over, ignoring the immortal now staring at my back.

Philip

I stare at Graves as he grunts and curls up with his back to me. I'm not sure how long I sit like that, but what he said strikes a cord. Maybe I should take my own advice, we should all stop trying to hide from the truth. It's not like I was ever good at keeping secrets. It makes me wonder if Samael knew all along. I chuckle and shake my head, of course he would've known. He wasn't shy about reading our emotions back then. It's only Lilith's influence that kept him from doing so as much.

Just thinking her name draws my attention back to Lilith. I look over at her, and she's curled up against the rough bed like it's the softest thing she's ever felt. That she's been so abused, again, makes my heart ache and I wish I could take it all away from her. I close my eyes, wrangling my anger back. I open my eyes and see her sleeping peacefully. As I admire her, I think back to the very first time I fell in love with her.

***

I turn the corner of the dark hallway and pause in surprise at the petite woman standing in the hall with what looks like a bucket in her hands. Her raven hair is braided today, and the dress she's wearing is a pastel blue. She's struggling with the bucket as she tries to hoist it up to the partially open door. "Lilith?" I ask in a low voice, not wanting to startle her.

She startles anyway; the bucket teetering and sloshing a portion of its contents onto her head. I rush to her side and steady it before more spills out. I look down and she's glaring up at me with a slight pout on her lips and water dripping down her face. It's the most adorable thing I think I've ever seen. "Sorry," I rush as I take the bucket from her grasp, "I didn't intend to startle you."

She huffs out a breath and wipes the water from her face, "Are you going to take my bucket from me?" she demands with crossed arms.

I look at the bucket in question, which is full of water and what looks like a sort of mud at the bottom, "Depends, who's the unfortunate soul you're setting this up for?"

She looks me over with narrowed eyes for a moment then taps her foot impatiently, "Deimos was an ass again; He's entitled to his opinion of me, but I shan't stand by whilst he treats me like shit. I've tried ignoring him, I've tried avoiding him, none of that has worked, so it looks like I've got to switch tactics."

*I laugh, "Then I am **not** taking your bucket, my brother deserves any and all pranks you see fit to inflict upon him." I lift the bucket and arrange it so it's balanced to fall inward when someone opens the door.*

"I have a rope," she says, holding up a cord, "I wasn't sure if it'd be all right to drop on him."

"He'll be fine, he's hardheaded." I assure her, then I pause and turn my head, "He's coming."

She squeaks, it's adorable, then grabs my wrist and drags me to the end of the hall, "Shhh," she hisses at me then looks back at the door.

I frown as something occurs to me, "Couldn't you have used your magic to place the bucket?"

She chuckles then grins up at me, "One, that's not as much fun as setting it up with my own hands. Two, if I'd done that you wouldn't have been able to help and take some of the blame," she winks.

I can't stop the laugh that escapes, just as Dem pushes the door open and the bucket falls with a satisfying splash.

"Phobos!" Deimos roars, he marches down the hallway and turns the corner, finding Lilith and I standing there laughing like a couple of idiots.

"Wasn't me," I say, putting my hands up in surrender.

His eyes flick to Lilith, who's doubled over, her arms wrapped around herself as she laughs, "You look like a damp hell pup!"

He growls and takes a few steps toward her, but she squeals and darts behind me, "Phobos! Save me!"

I don't think twice about her request; her shout makes me grin and I wrap an arm around her waist. Then, with a quick thought, we phase through the stone and outside the building.

Sixteen

In Which the Trials are Set Forth

Philip

The sun has only crested the horizon when the Chief comes to the healer's tent and barges in. Parsley stands and roars in the door's direction, but Lilith's hand darts out and soothes the beast.

"What's the meaning of this?" the healer demands, his eyes wary as he looks at the leader of the tribe.

"Our visitors wished to undertake the trials. I'm here to administer them." The chief looks down his nose at us as if the logic is obvious.

"The seal bearer is recovering, she'll need a few days at least." The healer says.

"Then perhaps she isn't worthy," he says, giving Lilith a look that's full of contempt.

Lilith's eyes flash with green and Graves stands, "I'll undertake the Trials. Lilith does need her rest, but we can't afford to wait."

The chief sneers, "You are not the bearer of the seal, you cannot undertake the trials."

I step up next to Graves and glare at the chief, "That's absurd, she's clearly injured and needs time."

"Slow down," Samael says, grabbing Lilith by the waist and pulling her against him, "Lilith, give me your wrist."

"Samael," she hisses, her voice low, "I am not going to let this-"

"Trust me," he whispers, kissing her cheek.

She sighs and sets her wrist in his hand and he looks up at the Chief, "There, I'm now bearing the seal. Let me take on the trials."

The chief opens his mouth as if to argue, but the healer laughs, "He has fulfilled the request. He does bear the seal, just because it remains on her wrist is beside the point."

"I could pick her up," I offer, coming up next to them, "Then you could let me do it."

The chief glares at me, then snaps, "No! I'll let the lord-ling do it, not you, Traitor."

I hiss at him, making him take a step back.

Lilith snags my shirt, halting my progress, then snaps at the chief, "Get on with it then, what're these trials?"

The chieftain sneers at her, "There are two main things which must take place. First, you must face our strongest warrior in combat to prove your power. Then, there's a maze you must traverse where the seal is waiting. Once you are in possession of the seal, we'll show you where there was once a gate between realms."

Samael shifts his weight, eying the man in front of him for a long moment before squaring his shoulders, "Very well, give me ten minutes to prepare and I will meet you in the square for this combat."

The chief huffs out a breath and turns on his heel to leave the room. Lilith grabs Sam's shirt, "Be careful," she says, staring at the door, "I don't trust him."

Damien grunts and gestures at the healer, "Are you sure that's information you're willing to be saying aloud?" he asks.

The healer bows his head for a moment, then when he lifts his head, he looks at us and says, "I am afraid that I share your sentiments. For some months now, the Chief has become more and more volatile. While I understand, to an extent, his hostility toward your little troupe. I cannot bring myself to condone his behavior toward you all. I will attend the combat, to help ensure that all remains fair."

"Someone ought to stay with Lilith," Damien says, giving her a look.

She scowls up at him, "Parsley can stay with me. Both of you need to be with Graves."

He bares his teeth at her and stalks in her direction, "You can barely stand."

As always, Lilith doesn't back down from his hostility, "Yeah, but if things go wrong at the fight, you need to be with Graves. I can defend myself well enough and if anything goes too awry, I can just hide in the shadows."

Damien grunts and growls again, before he can reply though, Graves snaps, "Damien, enough! Lilith is capable, and I'm in agreement. I think you need to be with me, not her. Parsley is sufficient protection."

With a snarl, my brother turns on his heel and stalks from the room again. Lilith crosses her arms and stares after him, "Is it just me, or is he getting grumpier?" she demands.

I huff out a breath and shake my head, "I think he might be, this is all getting to him at this point. Come on, Boss, let's get this over with."

Graves

Sometimes I wonder if Damien is actively trying to push Lilith away, as Phil and I follow the gargoyle out into the square, I try to reach for his emotions. Before I can get far, Phil smacks my arm, "I may have let you get away with reading my emotions, but Damien is not going to be so forgiving."

I turn to glare at him, "What makes you think that I'm trying to read him?"

Phil just smirks, "I know the face you make when you're concentrating, it's not much of a change, but I've been reading your expressions for an incredibly long time."

I sigh and shake my head, not bothering to rebuke him. We walk right up to the square to find Damien glaring down the Chief. There is another man waiting as well. He's enormous, almost a head taller than me, with a shoulder width to rival Damien's. Phil and I exchange a look and Damien crosses his arms. "I can see why she wanted us with you," He mutters.

I snort and shed the leather coat I'm wearing, "This won't be too bad, I've taken on bigger and meaner, I'm sure."

"Not in this lifetime," Damien grumbles.

I drag a hand through my hair, the wayward strands standing up as I do so. "If there's one thing I've noticed since we've been searching for Lilith," I say as I draw my sword and step into the ring, "it's that sometimes the polite way isn't an available option."

Phil lets out a low whistle, like he's impressed with my statement. The warrior steps into the circle, taking a massive ax from the hands of the man next to the ring, "Come fight me, Lordling."

Damien chuckles now, leaning back on his heels, "Oh, this is gonna be good."

The Chief scowls at Damien and snaps, "What are you so amused about? Your friend is about to fight Orville, our best warrior- "

"Aye," Damien says with a nod, "That he is."

Behind me, Phil laughs aloud, "I hope for his sake that Graves doesn't lose his cool. We'd hate to deprive your entire tribe from his protection."

"Enough," I snap, readying my sword and looking at Orville, "Let's get this over with."

The warrior rolls his shoulders, stretching and flexing his arms as he stalks into the ring. I stand steady, my sword in front of me in a neutral, defensive position. I scan him from head to toe, searching for weaknesses.

As he flexes, I see that his left arm has lower mobility. His left leg also seems weaker, the most subtle of limps pointing to his knees being the weakness there. He grabs his ax with both hands as he comes to stand in the center of the ring.

I remain on my side of the circle and wait; the healer steps up to the edge of the circle and raises his hands above his head. "By the sacred traditions set forth by our gods, we test this man. May his strength be tested against the strongest of us, to prove him worthy to stand before the altar of our gods."

Once the healer steps out of the ring, my opponent rushes at me with a battle cry. I roll my eyes at the stereotypical decision. It's a simple matter of dodging to the side, letting ice form under my boots to allow for an easier slide. Orville stumbles, nearly falling over the edge of the ring.

I use a gust of wind to upset his balance, but it doesn't work. I make it around the circle so I'm on the far side of the ring from Orville before he recovers from his attack.

His eyes narrow on me and he snaps, "Going to run like a coward? Not going to fucking fight me? Pathetic, just like your little bitch."

Damien snarls, taking a step forward, but Phil grabs his shoulders and stops him.

The dark smile that spreads across my face makes Orville hesitate, "You're lucky you got me, big guy. She'd have handed you your ass before you knew what happened."

He puffs out his chest and stalks toward me, "Big talk for a man who keeps running away."

I grin and send a shot of earth at the man with enough force that it makes him stumble away. As he steps back, ice forms under his feet and he slides again. I dart forward, the ice disappearing as I bring my sword up and under his defenses. He shouts and gets his ax down in time to block the blow, but it's clear that he's unable to redirect the force by the way he winces.

I move behind him and land a blow to the back of his knee, the joint buckles under the pressure and he falls forward. He drops his ax to catch himself, and I lay my blade against his throat. "What you call running, I call assessing. Also, Lilith would've taken you down without you ever laying eyes on her."

He grunts and looks up at the chief, "Sir?" he asks.

The Chief nods, his expression severe.

I wonder what in the world he's asking about when a dagger appears in one of his hands. I hiss as the blade comes back, aiming for my thigh.

"Foul!" Phil shouts.

Before I have a chance to disarm him, Orville is on his feet again, coming at me with the dagger. His eyes have taken on a manic glow, and I let my magic check his emotions. All he's got going through his mind is rage and violence. I scoot back and try not to let him close. Now he truly has me on the run, somehow his movements are twice as fast as they were before. I keep my distance, trying to identify how best to subdue him.

"Sam!" Damien shouts, "He's been hexed, I can smell it."

"Crap," I mutter, unable to gain any ground as I keep myself out my harm's way.

"Enough!" the healer shouts, "Nolan, stop this madness! He bested Orville."

"He bested Orville in a weakened state, if he cannot handle him like this, then he is not worthy," Nolan shouts, pride in his eyes.

The healer goes to shout again, but I tune them all out. If I'm going to stop Orville, I need to keep myself focused on his movements. I'd rather not have to kill the man, since he is the strongest protector of this village. I don't step back this time, bringing my sword up to block the blow.

The force of the blow jars my arms, and I clench my teeth against the pain. I tap my magic again and use the wind to push him back. It lets me put space between us as Orville tumbles back. I go to point my blade at him, but he's on his feet again with uncanny speed.

I dance back and block another blow. I've tuned everything else out and I realize that I've either got to completely immobilize the man or I need to kill him. The second option makes my gut twist, I can't deprive these people of their protector, even if he is trying to kill me. I curse under my breath, moving to my right, I drop my blade to my side. Distantly, I hear Phil shout my name, but I ignore him as I stab the blade into the ground. Using a surge of magic, I raise the earth around us and create a cage around Orville.

I catch Orville's hands outside the stone cage, keeping him from hurting himself or anyone else. He screams in rage and I spin on the Chieftain, "Stop whatever you've done to him, now."

"I've done nothing," he says haughtily, but not meeting my gaze.

I stalk forward, my blade pointed at him, "I've been kind by not killing him, but if you do not break whatever enchantment you've put on him, I'll have to put him down for the safety of the innocents here."

Nolan scowls at me and at length sighs, "Very well, I suppose you've shown yourself well enough." He waves his hand in front of Orville's face and the other man snaps out of whatever spell had been on him.

Orville's body deflates, and he breathes out a heavy breath. The healer rushes over to him and starts checking his vitals. I sheath my sword and look at Nolan, "Now, take me to this maze. I don't have time for your games."

He sneers but doesn't comment as he waves me forward and the three of us go with him.

Seventeen

In Which the Second Seal Is Secured

Lilith

I pace in the healer's tent, something making me antsy. I just cannot figure out what is upsetting me so much. Samael left a few hours ago to undertake the trials the tribe has, but from what I understand, the time he's been gone is expected. It's not been more than an hour or two, but I cannot resist the incessant need to move.

The door opens, and the healer is standing there, his eyes go wide, "Miss Callam, you really should be resting," he takes a few steps toward me but I dance away.

"Something is wrong," I say flatly, "Any word on Lord Graves?"

He shakes his head, "No, the trials can take quite a long time, it's only been a couple hours."

I groan and run a hand down my face, "Can you go fetch one of the twins for me?"

He nods, "Yes, I can do that but, please, sit down. It won't do for you to open your wound again, even with the healing, the tissue is still tender."

I grunt and do as I'm asked, plopping onto the bed and looking away, "Fine."

I hear the door open and close again, my seated position only lasts ten seconds before I'm up again and pacing. Rubbing my chest, I stop when I realize that the charm on my wrist is warm, unexpectedly so. I stare at it for a long second, then wrap my other hand around my wrist and focus.

The charm heats against my skin and I feel it sort of tug me along, pulling on my chest and leading me out the door. I let the charm lead me, my clasped hands held a few inches in front of me as I weave through the small town. That warmth growing stronger as I move closer to the center of the space. I come to a halt when I see the Chieftain walking in my direction.

The man looks me over and sneers, "Well, well, what are you doing here? Aren't you supposed to be resting, *Highness*?"

I scowl at that, the unease in my chest increasing tenfold. Why would he call me by an honorific, even in taunt? I turn my head to one side and look him over, his eyes are humorless and dark as he glares at me. He shifts his weight under my stare and the glint of metal makes me pause, the charm on my wrist warms again and I glare.

"What's that?" I point at his throat.

He scoffs and tries to turn away, "It's a symbol of my station, no concern of yours, thief."

Again, we've said nothing of my being a thief, he knows more than he's letting on. I scowl as the charm heats further and I lift my chin, "You're lying."

He snorts and turns away, "Think what you will, I do not owe you an explanation. Your lover is still in the trial, you should go back to the healer and wait for him."

That warmth spreads up my arm with ire chasing after it. I clench my jaw and slide the knife Damien gave me from its sheath at my hip. In a single step, I slide into the shadows and reappear in front of the chief, my blade at his throat.

His eyes widen in surprise and he casts around for a second then lifts his chin, "You dare raise a blade to me?"

"Give me the seal," I reply, the charm on my wrist heating to a near painful degree.

He laughs, but there's an unhinged note to it that reminds me of the Speaker. The comparison has me hesitating, wondering if we're in more shit than I thought we were. "The seal? It's in the maze, remember?" he taunts, stepping closer to the blade.

I take a half step back, not seeing a reason to harm the man. Apparently, that moment of hesitation is all it takes, a shard of stone launches from the ground and pierces my stomach. I look down in horror, blood gushes from the wound. I take a stumbling step back, my body trying to kick into shock and protect me.

I don't let the shock take me, instead I wave my hand and shadows wrap around the Chief's neck. I sway on my feet then bare my teeth, even as I can feel the heavy blood-flow fucking with me, "I've wanted to kill you since the second you insulted my family."

I twist my hand and snap his neck with the shadows, the crack of bone satisfying. Stumbling forward, and snatch the seal from his throat even as I release his body and let it collapse to the ground. I turn toward the entrance to the maze, using a combination of magic and willpower, I rush in that direction, I need to get the seal to Samael.

Philip

Damien looks at the entry to the maze with a dark glare, "This whole thing isn't sitting right with me." He announces.

I snort, "Does anything sit well with you?"

He rolls his eyes, "They shouldn't be keeping it from us like this, I don't understand why they're being difficult about it."

"Why are you difficult about things?" I ask, raising an eyebrow at him.

"What does that have to do with anything?" He snaps.

"Exactly, them being stubborn isn't something that bothers explaining. Sam will be out before too long and we can fucking mo- " I stop short and turn back toward the encampment, "Do you smell that?" I ask.

He frowns but inhales deeply and his eyes go wide, "Blood," he whispers, "It smells like..."

"Lilith," I breathe, my feet taking me toward the smell before my mind can fully grasp the ramifications of being able to smell this much blood.

Damien is hot on my heels as I take off at a run. We're a few houses from the middle of the camp when we find her. Lilith is sitting on the ground with Parsley at her side, the beast is whimpering and trying to help her stand, but there's a trail of blood leading to them that suggests she doesn't have much left.

I run to her side and tear my shirt off as I look her over. Blood is dripping from a wound on her side, it's deep and seems to go all the way through her. She falls into my arms as I press my shirt to her wound.

"What happened?" Damien demands.

"Chief... Seal... Power..." she gasps between each word, but then lifts one of her hands and is clutching a pendant, "Samael," She breathes the last word, her hand dropping into her lap.

Damien grabs her hand and is kneeling next to me, he peels the pendant from her grasp and stares at it, "It's the seal," he whispers.

I look at it, then at Lilith, "We need to stabilize her, she's lost so much blood."

A scream goes up somewhere nearby and a moment later, the

word 'murdered' filters to me. Damien and I exchange a look, "Go," I breathe, "You need to get that to Samael, quickly. I'll look after Lilith."

He looks down at her, his expression clouding.

"GO!" I yell and with that he gets up and launches into the air.

I look back at Lilith, her head has lolled back and her eyes are cracked open, but I don't think she's conscious. Looking at Parsley, who's whimpering and nudging Lilith's hand, I command, "Parsley, guard." As I hear footsteps approaching our position.

The beast looks hesitant, but I repeat the order and they get up and post up between us and the encampment. I stare at Lilith, hopelessness creeping in because I'm not sure what the fuck to do, she's lost so much blood. The bleeding isn't very intense at the moment, but I'm afraid it's because there isn't enough blood to spill. I shift her weight and her mouth falls open, my eyes catch on her teeth and I feel like the biggest idiot in the world.

"Lilith," I say, shifting her weight so her head is next to my shoulder, "Lilith I need, I need you to bite me, Princess. Please,"

She groans and rests her face on my shoulder, but that she's reacting at all is a good sign. I grab the knife in her hand and bring it to my shoulder, "I hope this works," I drag the blade across my shoulder and blood wells up. When Lilith doesn't react, I drop the blade and wipe at the blood, then smear it along her lips and gums. "Come on baby, I need your instincts to kick in." I shift Lilith so the tip of her nose is in the blood on my shoulder.

The wound has healed up, but there's enough blood on the surface that it should awaken that power, hopefully. "Pho- Phil," Lilith says, her voice trailing off as her face falls against me again.

"Yeah, it's me, I've got you. Come on," I prompt, wiping another round of blood on her tongue.

She groans and licks her lips. The blood disappears and she falls still again. I hiss and try to shift her weight, only for her eyes to snap open. I go still in response, usually when she's accessing her powers, her eyes glow bright green. But this power, it's one she inherited from the dark, hidden things in the world. So her eyes become black as the darkest night.

I swallow and turn my head, exposing my throat to the predator now sitting in my lap. Next to us Parsley is roaring and attacking the villagers that dare get close. I swallow again when Lilith doesn't move, "Take whatever you need, Lilith. As always, I'm yours."

She makes a noise that's somewhere between a growl and a purr, then strikes. Her little fangs sink into the soft skin of my throat and pain spears through me. One, two, three heartbeats later, the pain fades away as her venom takes hold, making everything feel sort of fuzzy and numb.

She sinks one hand into my hair and yanks my head further to the side, exposing more of my throat to her. She pulls away for a second only to strike again, the second dose of venom makes that fuzziness worse and a moment later darkness closes in.

Graves

I stand at a junction in the maze. I've been in here for hours and it's feeling like I'm going in circles. Or worse, the maze is shifting around me, keeping me trapped. The thought makes my magic flare, a burst of wind rushing through the tunnels and whipping around me. I close my eyes and take a deep breath, maybe it is a circle, maybe this place is a trap unless you have a way to break it. I take a few more corners, then glare at another junction. It looks identical to the last.

I groan and drag a hand down my face, a feeling crawling up my spine that tells me there's trouble. "I don't have time for this," I mutter, glancing the way of I think the entrance is, "Something is coming."

I look back at the walls in front of me and when I hear Damien shouting for me. Straining my senses, I try to hear what he's saying, but he's just repeating my name. I sigh and when I catch the panic in his tone, I shout, "FUCK THIS!" I extend my arms to the side, causing the stone walls around me to collapse, hitting the ground and merging together until the maze is destroyed.

Moments later Damien appears in front of me, "Damn, that was impressive," he says then shakes his head and holds out a necklace, "The chieftain had it, Lil got it from him."

"Why didn't she bring it? What's going on?" I demand, though I still snatch the necklace from him and put it on. The metal heats where it hits my skin, by nothing else changes.

"She was hurt," he explains.

"And you left her?" I demand and turn to glare at him.

"No, Phil was with her, we've got to hurry though. I don't know how long she's got." He takes to the skies without me and I grunt in annoyance.

I shake off my ire at the gargoyle and take off at a run toward the village. As I get closer, I feel the pull of heavy emotions, anger, fear, violence. I hear shouting as I burst from the trees and find Damien trying to fend off a handful of villagers with Parsley. Lilith and Philip lying on the ground next to them.

I take in the scene and run forward to Lilith and Phil. Lilith is curled over Phil, her face buried against his neck and her hands tangled in his hair. I take a moment to process what I'm looking at, Phil isn't moving, but Lilith is. "Lilith," I breathe.

Her head snaps up to look at me, her eyes are pitch black, seeming to absorb the light shining into them. She bares her teeth at me, they're stained with blood and I realize that Phil's bleeding from a wound on his neck. "Lilith," I say again, "We need to get out of here."

She hisses at me, shifting her position so that she's crouched over Phil instead of laying on him. A shout from Damien has me turning, he's trying not to harm the villagers, they're shouting something about the Chieftain. I try to approach Lilith and she hisses again.

"Damien!" I shout, "She's behaving like a vampire guarding a kill."

The gargoyle turns and his eyes narrow, "Fucking hell, hold them off." He points at the villagers and we swap places. I send a burst of wind at the first row of people, sending them off balance. Another gust sends them sliding back. I lift one hand and the ground beneath them becomes sandy, making them fall and stumble.

"Dammit hellion! We don't have fucking time for this!"

I turn to see that Damien's approached her far closer than I would have. She's standing now, shadows curling around her hands as she prepares to strike. He takes another step. She darts forward. Her hands come forward toward his chest. He catches both of her hands to redirect them up and away from his vitals. Lilith slams into the gargoyle with enough force to daze her for a second, then she bares her teeth and makes a bite for him.

In my distraction I've let the villagers get too close and a blade nicks my arm, "Shit!" I shout, turning and using ice to shove them away from me.

A second later, something slams into the villager and shadows spear through them from multiple angles. I stumble back. Turning, I see Lilith standing up now, her eyes on the now dead villager.

"Fuck!" Damien has Phill in his arms, "She's drained him pretty badly, I'll have to carry him to get out of here."

"If we even can," I say as I realize that Lilith's now drinking the blood of the villager who hit me, and all the others have backed off with horrified expressions on their faces. "She's not responsive."

"She was pretty badly injured, the fact that she's moving is pretty impressive." He mutters, "Maybe we can bait her away from them some how?"

"No need," Lilith's voice is rough as she stands and turns to us, her lips and chin covered in blood. Thankfully, her eyes have returned to their usual green. "We need to go," she says, her eyes flicking to the villagers, "I don't know how many are, but the Chief was working for Discord."

My eyes scan Lilith for injuries, and I see that there's a massive tear in her shirt, revealing an expanse of unblemished skin, and her clothes are soaked in blood. A villager moves closer and Parsley roars in his face, jumping between Lilith and the threat.

"Come on then," I nod, "Damien, get Phil." I hold a hand out to Lilith, "Shall we?"

Her answering grin is macabre with her face covered in blood, instead of taking my hand she darts around me and disappears into the trees. Leaving Damien and I to chase after her.

Eighteen

In Which the Veil Is Crossed

Lilith

I try to ignore the fact that I'm covered in blood, and that most of it isn't even mine. I spring through the woods as fast as I can, Parsley bounds a few yards ahead, their various heads swiveling to watch from all directions. I can hear Damien and Samael somewhere behind me. I didn't give them much time to follow, but that Damien is carrying Phil will greatly slow them down. Shaking myself, I try to ignore the pang of concern for the vampire; I know with certainty that being drained like that won't have killed him, but I'm not sure how long it'll be before he recovers.

Parsley slides to a stop and roars, their lion head preening as they circle a small clearing. I stand next to the chimera and put a hand on their shoulder. Damien and Samael stumble out of the trees a couple of seconds later. "What the fuck?" Damien snaps, "We do not have time to- "

"There's something here," Samael cuts, "It's strange, I can feel... emotions coming from the ground. That doesn't make any sense."

I frown and walk around the clearing, Damien sets Phil down and is checking his brother over as I make my second circuit. "It's perfect." I mutter.

"What?" Damien snaps, "Nothing is perfect! Phil is down for the count, we're in the middle of a forest being stalked by a village of cultists, and you're covered in fucking blood."

"No," I wave him away, "The circle is perfect, look." I point to the treeline, one has a flat plane facing the inside of the circle, like it's grown up against a wall.

Samael goes to the tree in question and places a hand on it, "What in the world?" he asks quietly, then jerks his hand back abruptly, "Shit, that's got a powerful magical residue."

"Great," Damien snarls, "So helpful, we've not got time for this. We need to keep moving."

Shaking my head, I make my way to the middle of the circle. There's another circle carved into the ground. I crouch down and pick at the moss; it peels away with ease and reveals that there's a symbol carved into the front. "Damien," I say, "Come look at this."

He growls but stalks over and stops short, his eyes going wide, "What the fuck? How'd you..." he trails off, then looks at Parsley, then at me, "It's a waygate." He says, as if that's supposed to explain everything.

"What the hell is a waygate?" I ask with a frown, I've heard the term a few times but I've never gotten a proper explanation on what they are.

"It's a door between planes," Phil says, making us all jump and turn toward him. He's propped himself up but looks like shit, "It's how people used to travel between here and Hell, or the other planes."

"It used to be a way home," I mutter, running my hand along the inscription.

"What?" Samael asks, "How is that a way home?"

"Not the manor," Phil says, "It's a way back to Hell."

"Which means we can open it," Samael says brightly.

"No, you can't. Neither of you have figured out what the fuck you are, so your souls aren't whole." Damien snaps, "We're stuck, so if we don't get moving soon, then we're going to get our asses kicked by a bunch of psychotic zealots."

"Wait," I stand up, "We are whole." I lift my wrist, "The seals hold the last piece, right?"

"Yeah, and?" Damien snaps.

"And our entire souls are here," Samael says, turning to me with a grin, "Which means..."

I walk up to him with an answering grin, "I can find it in our memories."

"You don't remember though," Damien snaps, "That's the entire problem! You two have all your pieces but you're not whole, you don't remember and you can't open the gates until you do."

Samael comes up to me and cups my face, both of us ignoring Damien's bitching, "Who do you think remembers best?"

"You were the king, I figure you're our best bet. But... it'll be dangerous, I don't know what digging around in repressed memories is going to do."

He gives me a soft kiss, "I trust you."

I grin and close my eyes, reaching up to hold his hand against my face, "Try to stay calm," I don't give him any more time before I'm diving through his memories.

Samael

I stand in front of the circular gate, staring up at the massive struc-ture with its daunting energy. Next to me, Fate stands with his hands on his hips, "What are we doing here?" I ask the Primal.

He looks over at me and smiles slightly, "It is time for you step into your proper role. We're here so I can show you the most important action you're responsible for."

I frown, "What role? What action? You're not making sense."

"When do I ever?" the Primal grins at me, the expression making me frown, but he turns back to the gate and says, "The Primal council has voted that you be the King of Hell, among those duties you are also custodian of the waygates in this realm."

I shake my head, "Uh, no, I don't think that's a good idea. I'm destructive and dangerous, I can't fucking lead."

"We didn't ask," Fate replies, pointing to a spot a dozen feet in front of him, "You will be king and custodian, as has long been your destiny. You may even find that you've grown past simply being destruction. Now, come here and I will show you how to operate the gates."

I go to protest again. But I'm interrupted when a woman materializes on the far side of the clearing and skips to Fate's side. She's draped in light blue fabric that seems to dance around her. I can't say I've ever seen her before, but she carries a sort of energy with her that makes me take a few steps forward.

She launches herself at the Primal, who catches her in his arms, "Fate! You've been hiding from me."

Fate chuckles and tucks a strand of black hair behind the woman's ear, "Hardly, little shadow, I've been busy with council matters. Where is Aggression?"

"I am here, brother," another Primal rounds the corner, this one is not so human looking as Fate, they've taken on a hybrid sort of form that looks part wolf and part man.

"I asked you to keep Lilith away from the gates, especially today," Fate says with a frown.

"You try stopping her," Aggression grouses, though the look he gives Lilith is full of affection. In fact, the three of them seem close.

Fate sets Lilith on her feet and scowls down at her, "Lilith, what did I say?"

She drops her shoulders and seems to shrink in on herself, "That you were appointing the new king and to stay out of trouble while you were gone," she looks up at Fate with big eyes and says, "I just wanted to meet the king too."

Her eyes flick over and meet mine, they glow green, and the small smile tugging at her lips tells me she's entirely up to trouble.

Fate crosses his arms and continues to scowl at her, "You can't cute your way out of this one, even my daughter must obey the commands of the Council. And as commanded, only council members and the rulers of hell may know how to operate the gates. So, off with you."

Lilith lets out a dramatic sigh and throws her hands in the air, "Fine! I'll go, but let it be known that my feelings are deeply hurt."

"And why is that?" Fate asks, raising one eyebrow at her.

She crosses her arms, "That you don't trust me to keep a secret. I wouldn't tell anyone how to open the gates if I knew."

"I wouldn't mind if-" I start, but Fate shoots me a dark look.

I close my mouth and a second later Lilith is standing in front of me, a mischievous grin spread across her face, "You'd let me know? If you're King that means you can tell the council that it's fine."

Before I can reply, Fate covers her entire face with his hand, "No. And you don't encourage her." He snaps at me, then pulls Lilith away, "I know you'd keep the secret, it's more the fact that you'd use it that bothers me. Now go home."

She pouts up at him, but doesn't argue as Aggression herds her back toward the palace that overlooks us. Once they're out of sight, Fate turns back to me, "Apologies, Lilith is independent and mischievous. She'd find far too many ways to exploit being able to travel between realms. Let me show you how it's done, then you may go."

He steps up next to me in the center of the spell circle, which is carved into the stone below us. He holds out one arm and slices down, creating a cut that wells up with blood. The Primal's blood is golden, pure energy pouring off of it enough that it's dizzying. Fate turns his arm and the blood drips into the center of the circle, "I offer my blood as tribute to the Veil, may my power fuel its strength. I offer myself that my magic may be the conduit by which the way opens. Upon these ley lines, I beseech thee, open to the realm of humanity."

The blood on the ground lights up, then sizzles and burns. A moment later, the circle before us explodes with light and, on the other side, awaits a forest, not unlike the one we're currently standing in. "And so you've been taught."

Philip

I watch with my heart in my throat as Lilith and Samael go extremely still. I can feel Lilith's magic swirling around us, and based on the way his eyes are moving behind the closed lids, Samael is deep in memories. I know there's still a risk if he recalls something too difficult for a human mind to comprehend. But that's not something I can do anything about.

Damien paces a few feet away, glaring over at the two of them every so often, "This is a bad idea," he says to me.

"It's the best one we've got though," I answer, "It's kind of terrifying, yeah, but we can't afford not to try. If we can get across the veil, we may find more allies who can help them remember who they are."

"And if we don't?" he shouts, "What if we cross over and find that fucking Discord has screwed everything up? What if we get there and all those people we once considered allies are now enemies? What then?"

I go to reply, but I'm cut off when Lilith speaks, "If that happens, we'll do the same thing we usually do when people betray us. Make them pay."

Damien spins around and she's got her hands on her hips, giving us a look that leaves no room for argument. Samael is standing next to her looking amused, then smiles over at me, "Surely you didn't think the answer would be anything less than that?"

I stammer for a moment, then Damien snaps, "Awfully cocky for someone who's still in danger of dying."

Lilith saunters up to my brother and glares up at him, "Awfully angry for someone who's close to a long-term goal. But we'll get into the reasons for that *after* we get through the waygate." She turns on a heel and faces Samael again, who's now standing in the center of the gate with his dagger drawn.

"Do you think one person will be enough?" Lilith asks, "I doubt our blood currently holds the amount of power needed to operate this thing."

"True," Samael says, "All of us should contribute a couple drops of blood, it'll be our best bet."

I walk up, but Lilith puts a hand on my chest, "Phil will sit this one out."

"But-" I start, but she looks up at me, her eyes imploring.

"Phil, I almost drained you dry, you barely have enough blood to keep yourself upright; let alone getting a waygate open. So do me a favor and listen to me."

I frown down at her, but relent without further argument, she's right that I'm in no condition to help. I nod and she pats my chest before walking over to Graves and taking the dagger from him. She slices a thin line down her arm and lets the blood drip onto the center of the circle. Damien grumbles but does the same, his blood is close to black as it drips to mix with the bright crimson of Lilith's.

Samael takes the blade from Damien and ushers them aside to stand over the circle, as he draws the blade down his arm he says, "I offer my blood as tribute to the Veil, may my power fuel its strength. I offer myself that my magic may be the conduit by which the way opens. Upon these ley lines I beseech thee, open to the realm of hell."

As he finishes the incantation, a portal shimmers into existence in front of us. A roughly circular shape spreads from an epicenter, but its edges are trembling and the image on the other side flickers.

Lilith looks concerned, then grabs my arm and shoves me toward the opening, "Hurry, it's unstable."

I try to say that she should go first, but her grip is stronger than I expect and she's propelled me into the opening before she grabs Damien and does the same. I stumble through and trip, landing face first in the dirt with Damien following a moment later. The portal is closing, but Samael falls through, catching himself just before he face plants in the dirt. Just as the portal looks too small for anyone to fit through, Lilith fades into a shadow, darts through the tiny space and reappears, looking none the worse for wear.

The portal fades from existence and Lilith is standing over the three of us with a smirk, "There, we're not being chased anymore."

Damien gets to his feet and scowls at her, "Yeah, but where the fuck are we?" he gestures out around us. I frown as I realize we're more or less in the middle of nowhere. It's not the forest near the palace. I can't detect the magic of the wards, and nothing has any echo of familiarity.

"Shit," I mutter, "This isn't good."

Nineteen

In Which The Gargoyle is Lost

Damien

I look over at Phil as he stares at the barren landscape around us, too. It's not a forest like we left behind, in fact, it doesn't even look like a proper waygate location, and I can't detect any ley line energy. It's like the portal didn't open to the right spot at all. Gods only know where the hell we ended up.

Lilith's smug expression falls as she looks around to, uncertainty in her eyes. Phil mutters under his breath and all I catch is 'Isn't good', I laugh aloud drawing all of their attention to me.

"Not good?" I ask but continue shouting before anyone replies, "Not good is an understatement! We're fucked! We don't know where we are, they're still not whole, you're half dead, and this entire thing is going to blow up in our faces before we know it!"

"But we're safe from-" Lilith starts, but cuts off as something shimmers to my right. A second later, the fucking chimera walks through what must be a tear in the veil. Lilith stares at the chimera as it comes up to her and nuzzles into her cheek.

"Safe?" I ask, glaring at her, "The veil is torn, it's just a matter of time before people can come through in either direction, waygate or not."

"Damien," Phil says, giving me a dark look, "Calm down."

"No! You're acting like everything is fine! Like we aren't in the middle of hell, with two mortals, grave wounds, and no clue who is an ally or enemy. We are fucked. There's not a damn thing that we can do about it!" I turn and stalk a few paces away, needing to get space from their collective stare.

I'm only a couple paces away when I hear someone following me, I spin to yell at them but stop short when I find Lilith looking up at me with an expression that's unnervingly familiar.

"What is really wrong?" She murmurs, her tone soothing, like she's talking to a wild animal.

I glare down at her, a quick look at Graves and Phil tell me they're also waiting to know what I'll say. I have no intention of answering.

When I remain silent for a few minutes, Lilith turns her head to the side and regards me with a thoughtful expression, "You know," she says slowly, "There are times, when you yell at me, when it feels like you've done it before. Oh, I know you've yelled at me plenty, but this... this feeling is different. Like, the reason behind your yelling is different from it has been before."

I scowl down at her, not understanding what she's getting at.

Lilith just continues to stare up at me for a long while, everyone else watching in silence.

Eventually I snap, "Maybe it's different cause before I was yelling cause I didn't trust you, now I'm yelling cause you're being an idiot."

She doesn't rise to the bait, replying gently, "Maybe it's because you're afraid of something and too much a coward to admit it," then she turns away, "We should see if we can find a road. If we're not sure where we've ended up orienting ourselves is first priority."

For some reason, that dismissal is more infuriating than if she'd yelled back. I want to scream at her for it, how dare she just dismiss my anger? I don't though, I just clench my fists as Phil looks at me with a scrunched brow and Samael with his signature raised one. I ignore them both as they both fall in line to follow Lilith.

I growl and follow them too; we get a few paces and I can't take it. "I'll scout from the sky. I'll catch up," Not giving them time to reply before I take to the skies.

Graves

I watch Damien fly away with a frown, Lilith is right, he's running from something. I just can't figure out what in the world would cause him to shift his attitude like this. Again. Lilith keeps walking away from where he took off, her eyes focusing on something in the distance that I can't see. Phil and I walk alongside her and it feels like we're all waiting for something. I glance over at my friend and he shrugs and shakes his head. It seems he's as baffled by the tension as I am.

Lilith comes to an abrupt halt then, to my surprise, drops to her knees. We kneel next to her and my first thought is that one of her wounds has opened up. But then she sobs and her entire frame shakes as she wails, "I don't understand. Why does it hurt so much? It's like my soul is being torn into pieces."

She lifts her face to look at Phil, like he has an answer, and he just shakes his head, looking helpless and lost. Snapping her head in my direction, I can see the plea in her eyes, begging me to have an explanation for what's going on.

I open myself up to her emotions, and I'm hit with what I can only describe as an unfathomable pain. There's no way the pain is exclusive to this lifetime, I don't know why I'm so certain of that, but I can't imagine that pain like this is something humans experience. I shake my head, not having an answer for her, but I open my arms and she throws herself into my embrace.

"Talk to us," I murmur into her hair, "Tell us what you're feeling, what you're thinking."

Phil comes up and sits next to me, his hand coming up to rub her back as I rock back and forth, cooing and stroking her hair.

"Every time... every time he's lost his temper since you saved me, it's like it's not the first time." She gasps and sobs, "He's, he's running away, pulling away and I don't know why. But every time he snaps at me, or tries to make me angry, it feels like it's happened before, dozens of times, hundreds of times. I don't know how much more I can take, it's like he doesn't believe in me... like he's going to *abandon* me, just like everyone other than you."

I hold her tighter and press a kiss to her hair, "I don't know."

Phil clears his throat and both Lilith and I look up at him, he looks somewhat abashed but says, "I can't say for certain, since he's never actually told me the specifics, but Damien blames himself for what brought us here. Whatever got you guys killed and taken from us in the first place. I don't know what he thinks he did, but he's confident that when you remember, you'll hate him," His eyes flick to me, "Both of you."

"What? That doesn't..." Lilith scoffs as she wipes at her eyes and sits up to stare at Philip, "Hate him? How does that make any sense? He's been searching for us for a thousand years! He's one of Samael's best friends and I lo-" she cuts off and looks at me, her entire face going red.

I chuckle and cup her cheek so she's looking at me, "No need to be embarrassed, I'm well aware," I kiss her forehead, "You are free to love as many people as you want, I just hope to be counted among them."

Her face remains red, but she grabs my shirt and meets my gaze, her emerald stare more intense than usual, "Of course I love you," she kisses me fiercely.

After she pulls away, I see Phil has dropped his hand from her back and is looking away like he's trying to give us space. Lilith isn't having it, she reaches over and grabs the front of his shirt too. She pulls him in close and says, "I love you too. So don't you run from me."

His eyes widen in surprise and then he grins at her, "Wouldn't dream of it, Princess," then kisses her.

A snapping twig causes them to break apart and Lilith is on her feet a second later, a slim form comes out from the brush and stands staring at the three of us. They're humanoid looking, but their features are very flat and their eyes have slitted pupils. A closer look reveals that their face is covered in small scales that flow down their neck and seem to cover their entire body.

To my surprise, Lilith jumps to her feet, "Sylvia! You're here!"

The reptilian woman's face lights up and she comes forward to hug Lilith, "My queen, you made it safely! I felt a portal open and had hoped."

Lilith laughs, "I'm so glad you were close by." She pulls away from the woman and says, "Unfortunately, it's not all good news. I was badly injured and got carried away feeding from Phobos. We need somewhere safe to stay, to recover, and to plan our next steps."

Sylvia looks at the three of us and frowns, "Where is Deimos? Has something happened to him?"

Phil clears his throat, "Dem is scouting, I'll send a signal up to him once we're tucked away safely."

The woman nods, "Yes, yes, my den is nearby," She turns and takes off into the brush.

Lilith reaches back and snags Phil's and my hands, dragging us both along.

Damien

I'm only flying for a few minutes before I spot a road. I wasn't able to see it at because of the density of the trees, but once I'm directly overhead, I land and look around. There's still nothing familiar around, and worry is creeping in. That we appear to be in the middle of nowhere, when the forest gate has always been near the palace, it all feels wrong. I shake my head, the gates could've shifted over time, not to mention who even knows if the palace is still where it ought to be.

I'm about to take off again, hoping that if I follow the road, I'll find a semblance of a direction to take. I spread my wings and take a deep breath, but a noise to my right makes me turn.

Standing on the road is a young girl, she looks human except for her eyes, which are a strange shade of yellow. We stare at each other for a moment, then she says, "Are you here to help?"

I frown, "Help with what?"

"My brother," she says, pointing off the path.

I take a few steps toward her and she skitters toward the edge of the road, still pointing. Looking past her, there's nothing I can see from where I'm standing. "I don't see anything," I tell her.

"But my brother," she sobs, reaching out to grab my hand and tug me towards the woods. Her eyes filling with tears and making my heart squeeze.

I glance over my shoulder, into the trees where I know the others are still making their way around. They won't blame me for helping a couple kids, they'd probably be more upset if I didn't. With a sigh, I let myself be pulled off the road and into the trees.

The moment my foot hits the brush, the world shimmers and then everything changes. The forest opens up into a large clearing. There is what can only be described as a sacrificial circle carved into the dirt. I can see bones of a few different demons strewn about the corners. Another figure, which looks similar to the girl, is kneeling in the center of the circle.

I jerk my hand out of the girl's and rush to the boy's side. He looks pretty beat up and battered, with bruises on his face and throat. I reach for the ropes that are wrapped around him and freeze. The ropes are untied, and as soon as my hand touches them, they leap up and coil around my wrists.

"Fuck!" I shout, trying to pull back, but it's too late. The ropes transform from cord to chain in an instant, a heartbeat later I feel my strength being sapped.

The boy laughs, his features shifting from that of a child to one of the many snake-like demons who inhabit the plane. "That wasss too eassy!" he laughs, "Good job sissster!"

The other demon comes up, also laughing as her features shift too. "I didn't expect it to be quite that easy, Master said that the traitorsss were dangerousss and that we should be careful. But this one blundered right into our trap!" she laughs as more ropes wrap around me and turn to chains.

"You know who I am," I accuse.

They laugh, "Of course we do," they speak in unison, "Master told us that today was the day! The traitors return and we're going to take you to him!"

I snarl and try to break out of the chains, only for them to tighten with every move I make. "You'll regret this!" I shout.

They laugh, one leaning in close with a too-wide smile, "Perhaps, but I doubt you'll live to make it happen."

I snarl and snap at them, my teeth clicking close to their face. They laugh again and skip around me, "Time to call, master!" they sing to each other.

They sing in one of the demon languages I am not familiar with. The hissing sounds blending together in a way that makes my eyes droop. As their song reaches a crescendo, there's a flash and a pop. A figure appears a few paces in front of me, the heavy magic in the air makes my nose itch and as they turn to look at me, I inhale with a hiss.

Duke Martin Hurst stands over me with an amused expression on his face, "My, my, I hadn't expected one of you to stumble over to the road this quickly. Though, I suppose it is to be expected of you, Deimos, given your propensity to run from things that scare you. You'd think that an Immortal of Dread wouldn't be such a coward, but alas." He shrugs and turns to the demon children.

"Did we do good?" The girl asks, bouncing on her toes.

"Yes, you did," He pats her on the head, "now it's time to move him to the fortress, and be sure to leave a trail."

"But master-" the boy starts.

"Do as you are told," Hurst snaps, "He is bait to bring the others to us, we must make it easy for them to follow us."

I growl and try to break free, but the chains tighten and a jolt of magic hits making my body numb and a moment later I collapse, unable to resist the power of an Eternal on my own.

Twenty

In Which the Thief Runs Off, Again

Philip

Sylvia leads us through the trees for half an hour, finally stopping outside a large fallen tree. She walks up to one side and presses her hands against it, magic seeps from her palms and a door appears. She pulls the door open and ushers us all inside; I bring up the rear and she closes the door behind me.

The space is much larger than it appears at first, looking like it goes down deep into the ground. Sylvia is a burrowing type of demon, known for their tendency toward knowledge and hoarding. Some consider them dragons, though they're certainly not the same creatures. Over all it looks like a library, shelves in every corner, books on every surface. Honestly, it reminds me of what her quarters looked like before. I smile slightly at the familiarity, but Sylvia walks up to Lilith with tears in her eyes.

"We're safe here," she says, "Unfortunately, Lilith, I could not find many allies to your cause. In the last few centuries, Discord has been spreading lies through the realm. Most of what he says is that you and King Samael are traitors, usurpers, liars. All the people I've been able to coax into saying your name have said Lillian. I fear that too many are compromised to be of any assistance."

Lilith frowns at the demoness then goes over and hugs her, "It's all right Syl, I knew it wasn't likely, I'd just hoped things were different."

I step up next to them, running my hand down Lilith's back to comfort both her and myself. She looks up at me and I look at Sylvia, "Can you get a map? We need to know where we are in relation to everything, and right now we're rather turned around."

Sylvia nods and darts off into the recesses of her home. Lilith looks at me, "You should let Damien know where we are."

"You're right, give me a moment." I step out of Sylvia's den and take a deep breath. I raise my hand to my lips and whistle twice, two quick notes that mimic the sound of a screech owl. After a second, I let off another note, knowing that Damien can identify where we are based on scent. Hopefully he comes back soon, so Lilith can talk to the idiot before we have too much on our hands.

I turn back into the den and Samael is leaning over a table with a map on it, scanning the surface with his brow creased in concentration. Sylvia has Lilith sitting down on a bench, poking and prodding her mid-section and tutting. "The injury is healed over, but still tender, and the muscles are probably weak. Though they are stable and you should be well enough to at least find some way to heal further." She looks over at me with a frown as well, "As for you, based on my understanding of the severity of your blood loss, I'm surprised you are in a walking state."

I shrug then smile, "Lucky I guess,"

"Try lying," Graves says, slapping me on the back and making me stumble.

I glare over at him and Lil chuckles and pats the bench next to her, "Come sit, you need to rest too. Did you signal Damien?"

I do as I'm told and sit down next to her, "Yeah, he knows we're in a safe spot, and will track us by scent."

"Doesn't that mean we're open to being tracked by anything that can scent us?" Samael asks, frowning down at the two of us.

Sylvia hums, "Perhaps, but I have wards around the house, so only those who mean no harm can cross it. Though we may have enemies on our doorstep when we attempt to leave." She hums again and looks all of us over. "You need to rest, but I fear we do not have the time for it."

"Agreed," Lilith says, "We may have escaped the tribesmen, but we're now neck deep in enemy territory."

"What do we do then?" I ask, "We can't afford to go traipsing through the forest without knowing what we're doing and half of us aren't in any condition to fight."

"Unfortunately," Sam adds, "I can't reliably say that I'll be able to fight anything that comes our way on my own."

Sylvia hums again, standing up and pacing for a moment, "I have an idea," she says, looking up at us while twiddling her thumbs.

"But?" Samael prompts, crossing his arms and giving her his signature raised eyebrow.

"It will be exceedingly risky. There are two demons nearby, they are powerful enchanters and tend to keep a wide variety of elixirs on their property. They'll occasionally negotiate to trade for them, however they're equally likely to just try to kill someone. If the two of us try to haggle with them, Lilith can try to sneak in and steal the potions."

"How would we know what the potions do?" I ask, "It's not like demons are going to label and have full restoration potions just sitting around, right?"

"Actually," Sylvia says, "I know for a fact that they keep them.

They are powerful but not immortal, if they are badly harmed, they need a way to heal themselves and daren't rely on time."

"And I can identify what the potion is intended for by reading its history," Lilith says with a grin, "Besides, something like that it likely hidden in a safer spot."

I drag a hand down my face, "Okay, I guess that makes sense. But I don't like it."

Sam sighs as well, "Me either, but it seems our best bet aside from waiting until you both recover."

"Can we at least wait until Damien gets back?" I ask, looking hopefully at Lilith, "I don't want to go into that without all of us there in case something goes wrong."

She frowns for a moment then nods, "Yeah, when he gets here we'll tell him the plan and head out," She yawns and leans against my side.

I smile and put my arm around her.

Graves

I stand by the only window in Sylvia's den, staring out into the forest with my arms crossed. It's only been a few minutes since we made our plan and Lilith has dozed off curled against Phil, who quickly followed.

Nothing seems amiss; Sylvia is trustworthy, we have a plan to get Lilith and Phil back in fighting shape, and the librarian scrounged up a suitable map to get us to the palace when we're done. However, I can't shake the feeling that something is terribly wrong.

As I stare at the forest, Sylvia approaches, "My lord?" she whispers.

"Hmm?" I ask, turning to look at her fully.

"I don't wish to disturb Lilith and Phobos, but it has been a half hour since Phobos sent up the signal for Deimos. I fear that something has gone awry." She whispers, stealing a glance over her shoulder.

I look past her and both of them still appear to be asleep, "What do you propose we do then? You don't strike me as the fighting type, no offense, and I am uncertain of how I measure up to the opponents we may face."

She shifts her weight and nods, "I agree. I am willing to donate a portion of my blood to Phobos's recovery, but Lilith has reached the limit of her vampiric abilities," she hums, and starts pacing in front of me.

"I can't exactly donate my blood to the cause, it'll lower my ability to assist."

"We could hunt something," she suggests, "but there aren't many creatures in the area."

Lilith makes a distressed noise, then sits up with a shout, waking Phil as well. Sylvia and I rush to their sides and Lilith looks up at me with tears streaming down her face.

"I-I," she shakes her head and wraps her arms around herself.

"Nightmare," Phil says quietly, pulling her into his lap and wrapping her in his arms.

She nods and hides her face against his shoulder, "I hate chains," she murmurs.

Phil pets her hair and looks around, "Damien isn't back?" he asks.

Lilith tenses and looks up, "Did he leave?" she demands.

"He hasn't come back," I clarify before she can panic further, "Sylvia and I are concerned that something may have happened to him. We were in the process of discussing what to do when you woke."

Phil frowns, "How long has it been?"

"About half an hour," Syl says, coming to sit next to them and looking perplexed.

"Then we need to move with the plan so we can go find him," Lilith says succinctly, "I know we wanted to wait for him, but we can't afford that anymore. Also, if he was nearby, it's possible that the demon enchanters are the ones who got him."

Sylvia makes a distressed noise, "If that's the case, then we certainly need to hurry. Deimos's temper has often caused problems in the past, if he encountered them, he's likely in trouble."

Lilith stands at that, "Then let's go, maybe we'll meet him on our way," she says it with a hopeful smile, but the look in her eyes tells me she is not optimistic.

***

Sylvia leads us through the woods and to a narrow road, she looks around, wringing her hands, and looks back at us, "We must be careful, they like to prey on unsuspecting travelers. If we play into their traps, then we won't be able to negotiate."

We all nod and move silently down the road. As we move further along, Sylvia becomes more and more agitated. We stop near a footpath into the trees and the Demoness looks down right terrified, "This is troubling," she says looking back at us, "we haven't encountered them or anything any of their traps."

"What do you think it means? They're busy?" Lilith asks hurriedly, "We need to hurry then."

Sylvia shakes her head, "No, my queen, if they were preoccupied we would've encountered one of their traps. If we haven't encountered any, then..."

"They're too far away for them to be active," I mutter, "Even the most powerful spells would need to have the caster nearby in order to maintain their power. Especially if they're elaborate and meant to capture highly sentient beings."

"Precisely," she nods.

The color drains from Lilith's face, before any of us have time to react, she darts off into the trees.

"Fuck!" Phil shouts, taking off after her.

I groan and look at Sylvia, "Do you have any combat skills?"

She shakes her head, "Basic self defense,"

"Then go home and prep for at least one person to be hurt. I'll bring them back," I run off before she can reply.

It's not far into the forest that I find them. A wide clearing is so filled with magic I can taste it on the air, Lilith is standing in the center and there are shadows swirling around her feet.

Philip is a few feet away from her, his hands up in a nonthreatening posture. "Lilith, slow down."

She spins and glares at him, "We shouldn't have let him go off on his own! He's reckless in the best of situations, but he was furious when he left!"

"Lil," Phil says, "he is the best suited to scouting."

"You two are lucky that the enchanters aren't here," I snap, getting both of their attention, "And squabbling over what we should've done isn't going to fix anything. I sent Sylvia home, let's go find those elixirs and then we can plan."

Lilith makes a noise that I could nearly be called a growl, then stalks toward the building on the far side of the clearing, muttering under her breath the whole way. Phil looks abashed as we follow her and looks over at me, "Sorry,"

I shrug, "Just be careful, we can't afford for anyone else to get into hot water. If these enchanters took Damien somewhere, it's likely that they know who he is."

We get to the cabin, and Lilith is violently tearing it apart. She's thrown over two beds and knocked over a bookshelf, her shadows yanking open cabinets and picking up bottles before setting them on a table in the center. We stand at the doorway and stare at the carnage she wreaks before turning to the table.

"Planning on helping?" she snaps, her eyes flashing green for a moment.

"I'm not dumb enough to get between you and the outlet for your ire," I reply, unable to keep myself from smirking, "I'll wait here until you're done."

She bares her teeth at me, her recently acquired fangs glinting, "Asshole,"

I nod and smirk, "Usually, but that doesn't negate the fact that it's true. Did you find the ones that'll help restore you two?" I gesture to the table.

She rolls her eyes and waves her hand over the various bottles. She stops over one that's a putrid green color and winces, "ew," she mutters before moving on. Toward the middle of the row she stops again and picks up a bottle, it's a bright red color and moves more like a syrup than a potion.

"Here," she says and pops the cork, then chugs it.

"Lil!" Philip jumps forward, trying to snag the bottle from her, but it's too late.

My eyes widen as Lilith glows slightly, the light starts off red then shifts to a green that mimics her magic. A few seconds after she swallows the last of the potion, the glow stops and she sets it down. "Oh damn, I feel... amazing," she grins up at me and glows again, though this seems intentional.

I frown as she picks up another bottle and hands it to Phil, then gets on her toes and kisses his cheek, "Catch up when you can," then she disappears into the shadows.

"Fuck!" I shout, trying to track her, but she's already gone.

Lilith

Once, when I was small, I told my mother than the shadows were my friends. That they'd hold me, guide me, and protect me no matter what. She'd laughed at the idea, chalking it up to childish musings. Until the day she tried to sell me to a flesh trader and the shadows did just as I'd said they would. That was the first of many times that someone betrayed and then abandoned me. One of these days I might say fuck it and close myself off from anyone else who could possibly hurt me. But not today.

As I leap through the deep shadows of the forest, I can't help but recall that feeling of comfort and calm that still lives in those memories. A rational part of me is screaming that running off on my own is a terrible idea. That I should not go head-first into a trap without a solid plan. But, a louder part of me demands that I hurry, that if there are any delays, then the situation will get worse. We don't have time for a plan.

I don't think of where I'm going as I toss myself from shadow to shadow, each patch of darkness catching me gently and passing me to the next. I let the darkness call to me, let it lead me through the trees and to my target. As I near my goal, I feel the energy in the air shift. The comfort of the darkness flees, and I'm left with a sense of defeat as I look up at the massive building before me.

It's an enormous estate, but something tells me it isn't the Palace that the others were referring to. This looks more like a fortress, with massive walls and battlements with guards patrolling. Vines appear to be growing from the foundations, snaking their way up along the walls until there are only a couple spaces where I can glimpse dark gray stone. I stand there on the edge of the property. I can see a faint shimmer of magic on the walls, telling me that there's more than stone protecting the place.

I see the gates are well guarded and well fortified; I know that despite my powers, I won't make it through there. Another scan and I spot a section of the outer wall which looks weakened, even the creeping vines more sparse in that section. I jump from my perch in the trees and land on the soft leaves.

Skirting through the darkness, I approach the section and see that, sure enough, there's a gap behind it. A quick jump through the shadows has me enclosed by the vines that protect the space. The gap is small, but my magic confirms it goes all the way through. Silently praying, I leap through the crack and emerge on the opposite side.

As I reappear, I see that the entire courtyard is illuminated with bright torches and patrols, who also have torches. "Fuck," I mutter, they clearly know that light makes my magic finicky, confirming that this is very much a trap.

I press myself against the wall, using as much shadow as I dare to hide myself. A patrol turns the corner, the two men talking, "Do you really think they'll come? The prisoner seemed pretty certain that they're not going to come anywhere near here."

"Master Discord swears they're coming, not sure how he's so confident, though. It seems like they're too smart for that."

"I dunno, Master's pretty adamant. I guess we'll see."

The first man snorts, "Like they'll tell us if they do, we'd have to catch them to find out, I'm sure."

They move out of earshot and I'm left wondering if I should turn back and return to Graves and Phil. A sick feeling hits my stomach, the first man said that their prisoner is sure we're not coming. Damien is sure that we're not coming for him. I look up to the sky, the dwindling light making everything seem more gray than colorful.

I close my eyes and press myself more fully against the wall, "I know this is reckless, I know this is probably a trap, but Blessed Fate let this be the right choice."

I open my eyes and darkness has fallen more fully, a cloud covering the moon and throwing the courtyard into heavy shadows. I smile and fight the urge to laugh, trap or not, I'm going in.

***

It's not long before I find an entry point, it's not well hidden, which just reinforces my concerns. I take a deep breath before I slide through the shadows; the darkness welcoming me with the barest caress of resistance from the magical shield surrounding the place.

I reappear inside the building, these halls are also well lit in a way that seems contradictory to the rest of the space. There are lighting fixtures that don't match the rest, making it so every available space has light. I shake my head, I can't stare at the architecture, I need to keep moving.

I move down the halls, keeping my shadows stretched out through the space to get a feel for what surrounds me. The lights are too bright to use the darkness for concealment.

Carefully pushing a door open, I'm immediately greeted with a flash of bright light and a searing pain. I fall forward; the pain sending me to my knees and another flash of light preventing me from using my magic for protection. I fall to my side and gasp for breath, more light continuing every couple of seconds.

Mere moments later I feel cold metal snap around my throat, the weight is familiar, just like the one I took off two days ago. I feel my magic being chased away, this enchantment far stronger than the last. A sharp tug pulls me to my knees and forcing me face to face with someone I never expected. Duke Martin Hurst stands in front of me, looking all too pleased with himself.

"You are so predictable, dear Lillian," he tuts at me. "And to think, Deimos was so certain you'd never come to his aid. It's as if he doesn't remember how hopelessly protective you are, especially of your men. Though you're the one who still doesn't remember, aren't you?"

I glare up at him, "Am I supposed to find that amusing?"

"Not necessarily, although I find it particularly pleasing. It's so amusing to me, seeing that you would so willingly risk your life for this man, even when you're ill equipped to do so. Come along, let's go find your daring beau."

Twenty-One

In Which The Palace is Infiltrated

Graves

I don't bother staring after Lilith before I turn to Phil, "Drink that, I'm going to try tracking her."

He tips the potion back and I step outside the small hut. I look up and Errill's beacon is in the distance, the dark column giving me a straight direction to Lilith. I just hope we can catch up with her, I can tell that she's using shadows to speed up her movement and it'll make it all the harder.

Phil joins me and frowns at the trees, "Is she using the shadows?"

"Yeah, we need to hurry. She's bound to run in there without a plan and get herself into trouble," I say with a scowl.

"Agreed," he bounces on his toes, "I feel a lot better, those potions were something else. Let's go." He starts off into the trees and back toward the road.

"Has she always been this fucking reckless?" I ask when we get to the road.

He snorts, "There was a time she was way worse. Believe it or not, being close to you made her more thoughtful and calculated."

We're jogging down the road, which has gone silent since Lilith ran off. It makes the hairs on the back of my neck prickle. The sounds of the forest are gone, no bugs, no animal calls, nothing. I pause on the road and look around, trying to find what is setting all of my instincts on high alert, "Do you sense something else here?" I ask when Phil pauses next to me.

"Parsley did run off when we crossed the veil. They might've come back." He says, clapping me on the shoulder and ushering me forward, "We need to hurry, as long as we're not attacked, we'll be fine."

"Alright," I nod, then resume our jog.

We're about to breach the edge of the forest when a deeper darkness settles over us. Sliding to a halt, Phil grunts and looks around, "This isn't Parsley. But I can't tell what or who it is."

I snort, "No kidding,"

Out of the darkness stalks a half-human looking creature with wolfish characteristics marring their features. My eyes widen in surprise as their name springs to my lips, "Aggression."

The big creature chuckles, "So you've begun to remember, good." He stalks around us, his darkness blanketing us and making the world look like we're viewing it from underwater.

"What are you doing?" Phil asks, his eyes wary.

"I am shrouding you in darkness so you may approach our enemies without being observed. It will not block direct visual, simply magical detection."

"That helps, thank you," I nod. "Will you be joining us?"

"No, Lilith's soul remains fractured," he shakes his head as he comes to stand before us, "Were I to engage in the combat before that is repaired I could not guarantee anyone's safety, even hers."

"Can you patrol the area?" I ask, monitoring the marker leading to Lilith, "I wouldn't want any responsible parties getting away, not when there's so much at stake."

Aggression chuckles and rises on his hind legs, "It would be my pleasure, King Samael, it would be my pleasure."

I nod then look over at Philip, "Ready?"

My best friend nods at me, "Ready as I'll ever be, let's go save our dumbasses."

Philip

Graves and I crouch behind a copse of trees, we've followed Lilith's trail she left and are now staring at the familiar palace. My home for so long, overrun with enemies and guards with bright touches that will make it a pain in the ass for Lilith to remain hidden. I run a hand through my hair and sigh, "There are dozens of them, and Fate only knows where the hells Lilith got off to."

"If there's anything I know about her, it's likely run in headlong and recklessly," he stares up at the sky above the palace and his expression falters, "We have to go in, now."

I snap my head over to look at him again as he gets up and starts walking to the gates. I grab his shoulder and try to pull him back, "What the fuck?"

He doesn't look away as he says, "You heard me, we have to go. The beacon that Errill gave me keeps flickering, if we don't go then gods know what may happen to her," he smiles wickedly, "So we're going to go in ready for a fight, there's not much other option."

I can't help the grin that spreads across my face, "Lead on, Boss, I've always followed you. I plan on continuing to do so until the end," I draw both my weapons and gesture to the gates.

The wicked smile turns violent as he draws his own weapons, "Come along then."

We stalk right up to the gates and as we get close, all the guards point their weapons at us. One man steps up from the others and points a gun at my chest, "No entry, get back."

I point a gun back and go to reply, but beside me Graves's gun goes off first, the bullet going right between the guard's eyes. "I will only say this once," he says, I look over and his gun is aimed at the next man, "Either get the fuck out of my way or die."

I have to keep my surprise stifled as the men all exchange worried glances, when they hesitate the gun fires again, taking down the next one, "Last chance," my king snaps, his voice dropping lower.

The men in front of us drop their weapons and scatter. I lower my weapon and chuckle, "Damn, that was unexpected."

He grunts and gives me a look, "I'd really rather not end up with too many dead. It seems, counter productive. However, I'm also not looking to take longer than necessary."

"I doubt they'll be the last two tonight," I explain as we walk up to the doors of the fortress. The other human guards are dragging their friends away from us as we approach, "We may not have any choice in the matter."

"Maybe, but until then..." he trails off as he looks up again and scowls, "Shit, Lilith's magic flickered again. Hurry," he takes off at a sprint through the palace, not bothering to look back and see if I'm following.

Graves

Phil and I turn a corner, the pillar of energy from Lilith flickering in my peripheral as we slide to a stop in a massive room. To call the place cavernous seems like an understatement, but the size of it isn't my biggest concern. What does concern me is the hundred creatures occupying the space, they've all turned to stare at us as we stare back at them.

Beside me, Phil shifts his weight, "Lesser demons, looks like a couple stronger ones in the back," he whispers, like he's trying to hide that observation from the swarm in front of us.

One of the larger demons in the back lets out a cackling laugh, "You know, I didn't believe them before, how in the world could what amounts to a small force of demons take on the King of Hell and his Lord of Panic? But you aren't the king, not truly anyway."

Phil opens his mouth like he's going to argue with the demon, but they cut him off, "Attack!"

"Fuck," Phil says, dropping the shields that usually prevent people from panicking.

As soon as his full presence is let free of the barriers, handfuls of the demons screech and try to flee. I ignore them and take aim not having time to debate the best course of action.

The demons still try to get to me, despite the waves of Phil's magic, making many of their brethren flee in the other direction. A quick slash of my blade decapitates two of the smaller ones that look like animals. Another one breaks around Phil's magic and makes a mad dash at me, screaming with a sword above its head. I bury a bullet between its eyes and move away, dodging and stabbing as more of them make their way toward me.

Phil's magic slips and more of the demons get to him. A moment later, his glamors drop, revealing the deathly pallor of his skin, bright red eyes, and vicious fangs. He discards his weapons for his claws, tearing through demons and tossing their bodies aside.

I keep my movements fluid as I weave through the onslaught of enemies. Slicing through a group of five, I take stock of my surroundings. I'm not sure when or how it happened, Phil and I are now separated by most of the room and the stronger demons are making their way towards me. As I turn to face them, a smaller demon launches itself at me, throwing me off balance and dragging me to the ground.

Phil screams my name, his voice carrying over the demons cackling in my ears. I try to shove them off, using ice and air to move them around and end their lives. Every time one goes down or tossed aside, another takes their place, until I'm pinned by the little beasts. I continue to struggle as the one who'd taunted us in the first place stands over me.

The demon looks me over and laughs, "Oh, this is going to be sweet. I'll be a legend! The demon who killed the King of Hell." I expect him to run me through with the sword in his hand, instead he tosses it aside, "it's going to feel good to crush your beating heart."

I struggle again, the urge to tear the whole place apart hits me like a freight train, but I can't risk- my train of thought dies, replaced by a voice in my head, or maybe a memory, *"You are a king by merit, but you are eternal by birth. You are an Eternal of judgment, tactics, and destruction. You must trust your instincts, your birthright, and all will fall into place."*

I close my eyes, the word 'trust' echoing around my head like a chant. When I open my eyes, the demon is leering down at me, his hands having morphed into claws that look wicked sharp. Just as the demon thrusts his hand forward, the sound of Lilith screaming pierces the air, and it's like everything slows to a crawl.

Warmth spreads through my chest and I swear all my thoughts speed up at once. I'm blasted with memories and thoughts and feelings that pile together. I'm barely able to keep myself, my mind, from fracturing under the torrent of information. The warmth grows stronger as things stand out in the remaining jumble of thoughts and connections.

I know that scream. Lilith is in danger and, if the tone is any indication, someone's triggered a flashback or panic attack. I made a promise to Lilith that I will keep her safe no matter the cost. I'm reminded of something Lilith told me in more than one lifetime. I think about so many possibilities and so many outcomes that I know what I want or need to do when faced with the choice. So, as the demon's claws scrape my chest, I stop thinking.

Twenty-Two

In Which Truths Are Learned

Lilith

Martin pulls my collar taut, dragging me through the compound. Walls and sconces pass by in a blur, whatever is dampening my magic, making all my thoughts jumbled. We get to a large chamber with a throne. I try to track where the exits are, but my vision remains blurry. Hurst drags me to the dais, just before the throne, and shoves me to the ground. He looks me over before making a tsking noise in the back of his throat, "Such a pity, having you on your knees like this, Lillian."

I don't raise my eyes to look at him, don't acknowledge his obvious baiting of my attention. He makes an annoyed noise then stands, "You know, since I've got you here. I think I'll reiterate my original offer, though I know you don't remember it."

I twitch at that and raise my head, eyes narrowing on him, "What?"

He smiles, the expression too wide on his face, "Oh, that caught your attention. Yes, my original offer, I gave you a choice all those years ago. See, you and Samael had gotten into a tiff and I gave you a choice. Leave him, abandon him, and join me. If you agreed and co-operated, then I'd leave you alone, but if you at any point tried to go back on our agreement…" he drags a finger across his throat, "dead in a heartbeat."

"What makes you think I'd take that offer now if I didn't back then?" I ask, looking down at the ground.

He taps his chin and grins, "Oh, I don't know. Maybe because when you needed him most, he put a bounty on your head? Or, perhaps how from the very beginning, he planned on using your powers and just sending you on your way."

"Things change," I reply, though the pang of those truths still stings through me.

"Do they?" He asks with a wry smile, "Do things, do people, truly change that much? Surely you've started to remember more, you've seen things that you did in your first life. Things that you still do now, that you've done again in this life. So tell me, do you truly believe things have changed enough? Or is it just wishful thinking?"

I don't rise to the bait, keeping my head down.

He's silent for a long moment. When he speaks again, I can hear the sneer in his voice, "I was so surprised, you know, that first night you turned up. I was amazed that Graves dared to show his face at my home, given the way he and Clarissa always clash. However, when you walked up beside him, I thought it was too good to be true."

"What was too good to be true?" I ask, still not looking up.

"That the key to my goals was being walked into my home like a sweet little treat. I wanted so dearly to trick you to my side that night. Then Clarissa had to go make a fool of herself, so I had no choice but to send you away.

"I suppose it ended up even better in the end. You not only retrieved the seal, you were delivered into my hands so easily. I wonder, are you still holding hope that Samael will come? Or do you realize that once he's able to restore himself, he's going to leave you behind, like everyone else?"

I swallow and close my eyes, choosing not to answer even as I hear him approach.

"Look at me Lilith, look in my eyes and answer me." He says as he yanks my jaw and forces me to look up at him, "Do you really think that you're worth the effort it will take to come get you?"

Pain lances through me, and like a perverse echo I'm bombarded with memories of being rejected, of being left behind. The onslaught of is far greater than what I can recall, like dozens of lifetimes of pain suddenly surfaced and are trying to drown me. I can't recall *who* left me, only that I'm abandoned, over, and over again. I cry out and try to pull my head out of his grip, but he doesn't relent.

"Let me go!" I shout, trying to shake my head away and struggling against the chains tying me to the ground.

He laughs and shoves me away, making me fall to the side as he stands straighter and sneers at me, "You've been left behind before, repeatedly, people leaving you when they no longer have use of you. What do you think makes them so special? Hmm?"

I close my eyes as tears roll down my face, "They've come before," I whisper.

"Why would they come for you? What even are you? You're just a tool," He grips my hair and yank my head back.

I yelp and my eyes snap open, "Let me go! I'm not just a tool! I'm not-"

"You're not anything!" he yells, cutting off my protest, "At least not anything useful. A thief? A lady? An urchin? A mage? You don't even know, don't even remember."

Tears are streaming down my face, my mouth opening and closing as pain seeps into my soul. It's like I can feel the fractures getting wider, fissures opening up in the parts of me I thought healed. "No," I whimper, not sure what I'm denying, "No."

He releases me with a laugh and lets me drop to the ground, "Pitiful," he waves at the guards, "Bring me the prisoner."

***

I lie on the ground, trying to keep my head level as I wait, knowing that Phil and Samael are on their way. I have to hold on to that hope, despite the fractures that Hurst opened up. A door on the side of the room slams open; two men have Damien suspended between them. All parties are bloodied and bruised. I can barely recognize him as they throw him at our feet. "Damien!" I cry, trying to pull away and move toward the injured gargoyle.

Discord laughs, "My oh my," they yank me forward by my hair, straining my arms as the chains pull taut, "Here's the one you came to find, quite sweet of you. Even though he was convinced you wouldn't, that you hate him enough to leave him behind. Which is so amusing, considering no one has more unrequited feelings for you, dear Lillian, than this man here."

"Damien," I sob as I tremble, "you, you should have stayed with us. We're stronger together."

The big man raises his head to look at me, one eye is swollen shut but healing, "I don't deserve to have your concern, Lilith, I've done so many things to hurt you in this life and others. I, I'll always come to rescue you, I owe you that much."

I shake my head as best I can, Discord's tight hold on my hair preventing much motion, "Stop this, stop blaming yourself for something that happened a thousand years ago! I don't know what the fuck it is you're trying to atone for, but stop."

Discord laughs, "After all this time, you still haven't found the balls to tell her? Pathetic," They throw me aside and stalk down to Damien's side, "Tell me, Lord of Dread, what is Lilith Callam to you?"

Damien looks up at me, his eye healing enough that both are fixed on me, even as I pull myself up from the ground. I meet his gaze and we just stare at each other; it feels like a million things are going unsaid and the longer he stares, the more it hurts. As if all the years of silence and fear are suddenly too much for me to bear. I look away.

"Still too much a coward," Discord says with maniacal laugh, "too much the coward to admit that she's here because of you. Because you asked for something that Samael wouldn't give you; that she fought for you to have without knowing what it was you wanted. She didn't even question you, she was quarreling with the man she loved for you when you had asked to *leave her.*"

The evil laugh that follows makes my entire being shudder, the charm on my wrist warms until it's burning, and I can't contain the pain, the rage, the sorrow, the memories that crowd into me. It rips through me until all I can do is scream.

Deimos

I press my ear to the door as I shamelessly listen to the conversation Lilith and Samael are having. Neither of them has bothered to shield the room, which makes sense given that usually there's no need to. I can't catch everything that's being said, only snippets of words here and there as they raise their voices.

I strain my attention, Lilith's voice cuts through the air, "Damn it! Samael, you can't do this! Deimos is one of your closest friends and confidants! You can't just outright deny what he's asking for regardless of how it makes you feel, or what you think you read in his feelings."

"Lilith! I'm not trying to-" Samael shouts back.

"No!" Lilith's voice becomes shrill, cutting him off, in the next few words, her voice shifts and seems to come from every shadow at once, "You cannot make decisions for him, Samael! If you don't stop this stubbornness, then I'll fucking do it myself!"

Everything goes silent for a moment, my heart caught in my throat, before Samael speaks again. His voice isn't loud, but carries, leading me to suspect he knows him here, "Very well, you know I would never stop you from doing what you wish. If you truly desire to give Deimos what he's asked for, then I'll allow you to take over arrangements. In truth, it is likely wise for you to take the lead on it."

"If that's how it's going to be," Lilith says, her voice clipped, "What has he asked for?"

I'm frozen in place as Samael answers her, "He asked to be removed from your guard squad."

My stomach drops, nausea hitting me like a tidal wave as my brain catches up to the reality of what his statement means; Lilith has been fighting on my behalf with no idea what I've asked for. And to hear him say it aloud, I realize that the idea seems absurd now, so stupid and dense to have even considered, let alone asked for.

The silence from before was pleasant compared to the overwhelming sense of despair that fills the air now. Shadows become oppressive as they darken with power until the silence breaks as a single, keening note echoes through the entire palace. The note cuts off. I hear scuffled movement and another brief cry. The horror that'd locked me in place a moment ago releases me and I shove my way through the door.

I have to fix this, set it right, before something worse happens. Though I fear that I've already fucked it up, even thinking about being apart from Lilith is enough to hurt her. To go so far to ask for it? I may as well be a fucking traitor. I rush up to the thrones and stare in horror; standing over Lilith and Samael's bodies is fucking Discord. They look up when they see me, a maniacal grin on their face, "Ah hahaha, you're too late, they're gone!"

***

The scream that tears from Lilith cuts through me like a knife, so familiar to a sound I've heard once before. My own failures, my shame, hit with enough force to knock the wind out of me. My forehead hits the stone floor and Hurst laughs, their voice echoing around the room. "Such a pain, such a failure, poor Deimos destined to torment the woman he loves. Though, can you truly say you love her after all you've done?"

Lilith's scream becomes sobs and I try to lift my head, only for the guards to slam my face back into the stone. "Shut up," I grit out, trying to reclaim my dignity and get to my knees.

"No," Hurst sing-songs, "I don't think I will! Your desire to leave her side gave me the opening I needed! They're too caught up in their argument, in her pain, for either of them to notice me. The only problem," they go quiet for a moment.

I look up and see that they've wrenched Lilith's head back and have a blade pressed to her face, "The only problem is that instead of dying like they were supposed to, their souls went and ran off into the aether. Sure, they got broken up by the whole dying thing... but it still. Wasn't. Enough." They punctuate each word with a slice to Lilith's cheeks.

A loud boom draws Discord's attention, they release Lilith and take a few steps in that direction with a puzzled look on their face. Lilith lifts her head to look at me, her eyes meet mine and tears are streaming down her face, the pain that I see there makes my heart ache. I can't believe I'd been so stupid, I hate that even after all this time I'm still hurting her.

So, as our eyes meet, I finally let out the words that have held inside me for over a millennium, "Lilith, I'm so sorry. I'm sorry for being so stupid and selfish that I even thought that leaving your side would be the right thing to do. I'm sorry that instead of telling you every day how much you light up my world, I ran from it. I'm sorry that I've brought us here. There's only one thing I'm not sorry for..."

Her brow furrows, another boom causing Discord to make their way across the room further, still distracted from us, even as the guards beside me shift nervously.

"I'm not sorry for loving you, I have never been sorry for loving you. Dozens of lifetimes, a thousand years, countless moments and I have never, not once, regretted how much I care for you. Only the mistakes I've made for fear of it."

More tears fill her eyes and she stammers, "B-but, I still don't remember, I still don't know how to embrace what I am. Am I really her? Maybe, maybe I'm not really the queen, I'm nothing like her."

"You think that matters?" I scoff and get to my knees, "Do you really think I, or anyone, expect you to be the same person you were a thousand years ago? Do you think that the passage of lifetimes and years is truly enough to change a soul so irrevocably that the people who love them won't recognize them?"

"Then... what am I? Who is Lilith?" She begs, her expression so genuinely confused that it breaks my heart.

"Anything. Light and dark, mischievous and serious, optimistic and realistic, a queen and a beggar, a woman and an Eternal. You are free to be anything and everything you want. And no matter what, you'll always have us too. Samael, Phobos, Myself, we will always be there; looking out for you, protecting you, loving you."

Another cacophonous crash comes from somewhere else in the building and I turn my head to see what the hell is going on.

Twenty-Three

In Which Discord Falls

Lilith

I stare at Damien as his words echo around in my head, *"You are free to be anything and everything... you'll always have us too. Looking out for you, protecting you, loving you."* he turns away when there's another boom somewhere in the distance, but I can't take my eyes off him.

Other memories join his words, echoes bouncing around and reminding me how many people care. How, even though I'm ridiculous and sassy and cause many problems, they've always come to my aid. Always stood by my side, no matter how insane. Maybe he is right.

Maybe I am anything. Maybe there's no reason not to be? Who said I had to be one thing? Getting into trouble while simultaneously fixing other problems. Needing saving while also being formidable myself.

I close my eyes and let my head drop, taking deep breaths and steadying the pounding in my chest. If I can be anything, it's my decision. It's *always* been my decision, what I truly am, and I'm done letting anyone else decide for me. A question that's plagued me for my entire existence has always been in my hands.

I don't notice right away; but when the charm on my wrist becomes searing hot, I look down at it in surprise. It's glowing red, like it's been in a fire, and the heat races up my arm like a jolt of electricity. Pain races with it and I scream again, the sound ripping out of me involuntarily, like years of rage and pain and aggression finally being released.

After the initial pain, my thoughts become a vortex of memories. Snippets of lives lived, of smiles and laughter, of tears and screams. Memories bombard me until it feels as if my brain may explode, a vastness of experience and knowledge filling my mind past the point of breaking. The heat from the seal spreads, burning me from the inside out, drawing forth another scream. I'm distantly aware of another crash and a voice calling my name.

Then, when the searing pain has become all-encompassing, it goes from burning to soothing and mending. It becomes the warmth of a hug, the soft caress of sunlight, peace. I swear I can feel cracks and pieces of me, my soul, sliding into place and fusing back together. The memories settle and a sense of self-satisfaction seeps through me. I no longer feel an like an impostor, no longer feel as if my life is not my own.

As everything in me finally quiets, I collapse to the ground, my body weak from the onslaught. I hear a surprised noise and lift my head, Deimos is looking at me with awe and I offer him a wan smile. It's then that I see the shadows seeping from my feet and wince, too early to let all that out. I pull the magic back, locking down till I'd almost pass as mundane.

Another crash sounds somewhere in the distance, but then Hurst is at my side. He grabs me by the hair and drags me to my knees, "Are you done with your theatrics? Such a bold thing you were, fighting against my people every step of the way. But look at you now, reduced to nothing more than a pathetic, crying mess."

Another booming crash in the distance and a familiar energy fills the surrounding air. Samael's magic further bolsters my resolve as my own powers replenish themselves. I can't help the grin that spreads across my face, which makes my enemy hesitate, "What?" they demand, yanking my hair back further and giving my head a shake.

My grin widens and a laugh bubbles out of me, even to my ears it sounds unhinged and wild, but I don't care. "Oh, you poor thing," I croon, "You call yourself Discord, claim the title of Eternal, proudly hold yourself as above all those you meet. But you are no such thing. You are nothing but a petty tyrant. A power hungry coward who is afraid to accept that the world is not yours to dominate or control. Desperately hoping that ending independence and freedom will somehow give you the power to rule."

Their eyes widen, their smug satisfaction melting away for fear and terror. "H-how? When?" they stammer, releasing my hair and taking a few steps back.

I laugh again, a deep belly laugh that has me doubling over for a moment. Then I raise my head and meet their gaze head on, letting my magic loose and allowing it to spread around us, "You sought to torment me, but in doing so gave me the key. Now, you are going to pay for all the pain you've inflicted on me and mine." The chains binding my wrists and ankles disintegrate as I get to my feet. I smirk at them and make a shooing motion with my hand, "Run, Cowardice, and pray that I am not the one to catch you."

The color drains from their face and they do as they were told, turning tail and running away from me. I laugh as they go, then half skip half hop down the stairs. The guards holding my dear Deimos try to block my path, but a quick flick of my wrist sends them sprawling as I get to the Immortal's side. He goes to stand, but I put a hand on his shoulder and lean close, "You and I, darling, are going to have a nice long chat when we're done here."

He opens his mouth to say something, but I grab the back of his head and kiss him fiercely. He grunts in surprise, then returns the kiss, hands grabbing out for me. I dance away before he can pull me to his side and wink at him. "Come along, love, we've family to find and prey to catch."

Samael

The blast of power I release sends demons sprawling, the pillars around us cracking from the force. The demon who'd had his claws at my chest is in a twisted heap before me, limbs bent at weird angles and bone jutting from the breaks. I take stock of myself, noting that the bruising is already gone and I can *finally* feel the weight of my wings again. Looking over my shoulder, I verify the wings are, in fact, where they should be. I smile as I spread my wings and give them an experimental flap, the resulting gust sends the demons sliding across the ground.

I turn and Phobos is standing a few paces away, his eyes wide with a demon's throat in his grasp. I cock an eyebrow at him and just wait, letting the immortal catch up with this fresh development. A few seconds later, a wide grin spreads across his face, flashing fangs, "Welcome back, Boss."

I snort at that and shake my head, "I wasn't gone,"

He snaps the neck of the demon he's holding and tosses the corpse aside, "For me, you were. Regardless, there's not really another good phrasing for it."

I shrug and flex my wings again, "I suppose. We need to keep moving, Lilith screaming like that is bound to be bad."

"Right," he nods as one demon who's recovered their senses tries to charge at us. He plucks the being from the ground as if picking up an unruly child and sinks his fangs into its neck, blood spraying from the wound and across his face.

My lip curls at the unnecessarily bloody display, even as more of the demons get their shit together and start attacking us. I turn to face them and grunt, my magic shoots out in all directions and the ones who're hostile die immediately. The others scatter and make their way down a hallway away from us, conveniently, the direction they're headed is also the way to the beacon that tells me where Lilith is.

Phobos and I follow the scattering demons; whenever one darts down a hallway I collapse the passage, preventing any more from sneaking up on us. Together, we keep moving toward the beacon of darkness that is Lilith. We get a ways away from the ambush when Phobos says, "So, why haven't we just killed all of them?"

"There's no need for a massacre," I reply, "These beings aren't all guilty by association."

He grunts, "Maybe, but it'd help me feel better," He snatches up another demon that gets too close and tosses them through a doorway, "you're the boss though."

I collapse the passage and shake my head, but don't bother to correct him. Ahead of us, the remaining demons burst through a door, all of them screaming, "Master! Master!"

No sooner have they passed the threshold than shadows shoot up from the ground, shooting through their chests and cutting off their cries. "Speak of the devil," Lilith's voice carries from somewhere inside, "I'd bet that's the family."

Phobos darts into the room, and I smirk when I hear a delighted squeal and a thump. I join the others in the room and find Phobos with Lilith wrapped around him, kissing him like she'll die without him. Deimos is kneeling a little way away from them, looking shocked as hell, even as Phobos groans and pulls Lilith closer.

I chuckle and Lilith tugs Phobos's head back to look at me,

"Sammy!" she cries, disappearing from Phobos's arms and reappearing in mine.

I instinctively catch her, pulling her close even as she wraps around me. I smile down at her, "Hello, Love, I see you're back in one piece."

"Same to you," she grins then pulls me close for a kiss, when we part she brushes a hair from my face, "Have all the explosions been your doing?"

"Of course," I glance behind her where Deimos is still kneeling, there's two bodies near him, but otherwise the room seems empty, "Where, pray tell, is Discord?"

She snorts and shakes her head, "You mean Cowardice? I told them to run, and they did."

I sigh and raise an eyebrow at her, "Sweetheart, they've been instrumental in not only our suffering but that of your other loves, and you just let them go?"

She pouts up at me, "It's no fun if we don't get to chase them down, once they realized I was whole, they were all too happy to run away. Besides, I am tracking them, and it's not like they'll get far. Also, there's someone else who deserves a chance to get their pound of flesh, and now that I'm whole they're-" she cuts off as an echoing roar sounds from somewhere in the distance.

"What?" Deimos turns to look out the window, looking confused as he finally gets to his feet.

Lilith's grin becomes feral, and she laughs, throwing her head back, "See, told you they wouldn't get far." A moment later, shadows cover all of us and blots out all senses.

When we reappear, we're outside somewhere, Lilith detaches herself from me and I let her slide to the ground. A quick look around shows that we're in a field of flowers, a few yards away is a massive dark shape that seems to have something pinned underneath it. As we watch, the creature solidifies into Aggression, a feral gleam in his eyes.

After a few moments, he finally looks like a solid being rather than a nebulous shadow. Fur covers the majority of his body and his face has a pointed muzzle like a wolf, but his body shifted to be more like a man with longer limbs. Lilith squeals in delight and skips to his side, "Aggie!" she cries as she throws her arms around his neck and nuzzling against it, completely ignoring the wailing from Aggression's captive.

"Aggie?" Phobos and Deimos echo.

I cross my arms and smirk, "You know him as Errill; Aggie is a shortening of an older name of his."

The Primal in question turns to look at us and bares his fangs, Lilith cuts off his line of sight and kisses the end of his snout, "Don't growl at them,"

Another cry from Cowardice draws Lilith's attention and in a heartbeat all her playful smiles disappear, "You didn't run fast enough," she states.

I walk up next to her and hum in surprise, "Not a form I would've expected Discord to take," I bend over and stare at Duke Hurst, "That does explain why Clarissa has been so involved and begs the question of how long they've knowing my identity."

"Too long, and stop calling them Discord. They're nothing but Cowardice," Lilith spits, her voice losing even more of its gentleness and gaining a dangerous edge I know all too well.

I wrap an arm around her shoulders and pull her against my chest, "Darling, you can't kill them."

"Aggie," Lilith commands, and the Primal in question flexes his claws into their chest.

"Lilith," I caution and lean close to her ear, "Remember the laws. I know that they didn't abide by them, but if we don't uphold them ourselves, we're no better than them."

She makes a soft hissing noise, but doesn't reply. I gently rub her arms and hum softly, Aggie releases the pressure on Cowardice's chest, but does not release them. Behind me, I hear the twins move closer. "They cannot go unpunished," Lilith says at length.

"I never said they would, simply that the punishment cannot be death. I can think of a particularly fitting punishment, would you like to hear it?"

She hums and turns her head to look up at me, I kiss her cheek, "What'd be more fitting than forcing them to relieve what they've put us through? I know you're particularly fond of that sort of restitution, your stunt with Gavin is still fresh in my mind."

She frowns for a moment, "Will you handle the others?"

I chuckle, "Of course, I'll always handle the other Primals and Eternals for you. There is nothing they can do to you."

She hums again, "Very well, but it will be all four of us, not just you and I, and it'll be consecutive, not concurrent."

I nod, "Of course, my love,"

"No!" Cowardice screams and flails, "You cannot do this! I am an Eternal! You can't punish me like this!"

I snap my wings out, kicking up debris and letting my magic flare up around us, "You killed our bodies and shattered our souls! You should be grateful that I'm keeping her from destroying you entirely!"

They whimper and try to retreat, seeming smaller, "You can't," they repeat, whimpering like a wounded puppy.

I hear wing beats in the distance and Lilith looks in that direction, "It seems Fate is on his way," she murmurs, she looks up at me, "Should we wait for him?"

"Yes!" Cowardice shouts and struggles under Aggression's hold.

Aggression growls, his claws digging into their chest, "Do not expect Fate to treat you kindly, after all you have done to his daughter," He looks up at us, "We wait for Fate, none can dispute his judgment."

Deimos

Lilith turns in Samael's arms once Errill declares we wait for Fate.

She looks up at Samael with such open admiration it's almost sickening, though I'm not surprised, it's always been like that with them. Phil- Phobos, walks up to one side of them and clears his throat, "Lil, are you... okay?" he whispers.

She turns to him and gives my brother the same dopey look, "Of course, I'm excellent, in fact. Aside from the pending judgment for the craven behind me, everything is perfect. I no longer feel like an impostor in my skin. My magic and my soul are intact, and to top it all off, everyone I love is with me in once place."

My throat tightens and old fear rears its head, forcing me to look away from the three of them, only to meet the silver gaze of Errill.

The Primal meets my stare then rolls his eyes with a sigh, "My queen," he says in that low, slow voice of his, "Your Fool is still wallowing in doubt and fear, perhaps you should address that while we wait."

I don't look back at her, even when I hear a soft noise and can sense her standing close.

"Deimos," she says quietly, "Speak." The word is equal parts command and request, and who am I to deny her anything?

"I didn't wish to intrude," I manage through the lump in my throat, "I'm simply awaiting my judgment."

Lilith sighs, "Oh Deimos, how much clearer must I be?" she places a hand on my chest and my attention snaps to her, the touch is soft and reassuring and my hand comes up to hold hers against me.

When I don't reply right away, she sighs again and cups my face with her other hand, "There is no judgment coming for you, my love, you have more than atoned for the misstep you made all those years ago. I hold no resentment or anger toward you, but you must let go of what you feel toward yourself."

I swallow again, tears gathering in my eyes, "I don't deserve your forgiveness, or to be by your side." I sob, even as I hold her hand tighter and lean my face into her touch.

Cowardice makes a noise of annoyance, or perhaps protest, and a moment later they're covered in stone from the mouth down, their nose and eyes uncovered but all else encased.

Lilith doesn't react to our captive's sudden change of confinement, "How about you let me decide if you deserve those things? I love you, you big idiot, and that has never changed,"

I open my mouth to question her, only to be hit with memories from her perspective; love, adoration, and trust are present in every one. Even before my foolish request, she loved me, and through it all still does. I sob again and drop to my knees, just about dragging her with me. She coos and runs a hand through my hair as I press my face against her stomach.

I don't know how many minutes pass when there's a heavy thump as Fate lands next to us. I look up and find the silver-haired man standing next to Errill looking somewhat amused. Fate looks at the lot of us and slowly smiles, "Ah, it is good to see you all hale and whole. Pray forgive me for the events that led to today, there are things even I cannot control."

Lilith hums and combs her fingers through my hair, "You'd go a long way to repayment if you allow me to kill Cowardice."

Fate gives her a look that makes everyone else take a step back, but she stands her ground. After a moment he sighs, "You know I cannot, daughter, it is unwise to kill Eternals. However, aside from that, you may proceed with any sentencing you wish."

Lilith frowns and looks down at me, "What do you think, demon, shall I make Cowardice relive the pain they've caused us?"

I swallow and glance over at the others who are all awaiting my reply, "I don't know, will they relive it in the same manner we have? Every moment and everything?"

A wild smile spreads across her face, "Of course, they will live four thousand years in our shoes, seeing through our eyes. First you, then

Phobos, then Samael, and finally myself. I would include Aggie, but given that he was hibernating, there is not much to experience."

I look over at the being in question, they're glaring at me and attempting to move their mouth, anger clear in their gaze. I look back at Lilith and nod, "Yes, that seems appropriate."

She hums and puts her hand on the top of my head, her fingers woven into my hair, and she takes a deep breath. My life flashes before my eyes, not sitting on any one moment long enough for me to experience them fully, but enough for me to understand that she's pulling my memories.

After a few moments, she pulls away and turns to Samael and Phobos, "Come here, Phobos, you're next."

Phobos comes right to her side and wraps her in a hug, she snorts and places her hand on his scalp as well. After repeating the process with Samael, she walks up to the stone tomb that encases Cowardice. "Fate has put your sentence in my hands, and you have heard my verdict. Have you anything else to say before I enact it?"

"Don't give them the-" Errill starts, but Lilith cuts him off with a swipe of her hand.

Samael removes the stones covering their mouth and they spit out at Lilith, "I have nothing to say to you! I'm not a coward! I'm-" they cut off when Lilith plants her hand in the center of their face.

Everything is eerily silent for a long minute. I get to my feet and walk closer to the group, Phobos puts an arm around my shoulders as we all wait, even Fate seems to hold his breath.

When Lilith finally steps back, she shakes her head and sways. Errill gets to her first, shifting into a human shape and catching her in his arms, "Love?" he asks quietly as her eyes flutter for a moment.

Her eyes open and she smiles lazily up at him, "It's done."

"Very well," Fate says with a slight bow, "While I do trust you to look out for their wellbeing until the end of their sentence, I won't impose such a task upon you. Farewell," He snaps his fingers and both he and Cowardice disappear.

Lilith sighs with relief and looks over at us all, "Sammy, can we go home? I'm awfully tired."

Samael chuckles and comes to her side, "Of course, my love, I think we could all use rest."

"All together?" she says hopefully, her voice cracking ever so slightly.

I clear my throat, "All together."

"Forever," Phobos adds.

Lilith smiles at that, "Good, you idiots are stuck with me now."

Twenty-Four

In Which It All Comes to an End

Samael

Once Fate disappears with Cowardice, Errill picks Lilith up and walks over to the group. "So, now what?" Phobos asks, shifting his weight.

I pat my friend on the back, "First, I should go start mending the Veil. It'll take time, but now that Lilith and I are back to ourselves, it's a simple matter."

"Those who made it across will need to be returned, or terminated," Errill says as Lilith yawns and snuggles against his chest.

"Yes, it'd be wise to return to Hellgate and inform the residents there of these developments," I agree.

Lilith perks up at that, "Who did you get to be in charge of Aegis while you were gone?"

"The Evans' family." Deimos says, lingering near Lilith and Errill. "They're the best suited to the task, given their collective skills."

"I intend to leave Aegis in their care now," I state as we begin the short walk back to the palace.

"I would like to see everyone," Lilith says, not fighting Errill as he carries her. "I also think it would be wisest if we were to continue to live on the material plane while we hunt down those who made it across. Then we can return here and reestablish our authority."

I nod, "That does sound like the best option. Once we cross back over, I can begin the rites; I need to be on the Material plane to do them."

Lilith yawns, "Can we go home? I want bacon."

Deimos chuckles, "Don't you always want bacon?"

"A trait she picked up from you, brother." Phobos laughs, slapping Dem on the shoulder.

I chuckle, "Come on, I'm sure Cook will be more than happy to make you come bacon."

"Woo!" she throws her hands up, knocking Errill off balance and making him growl down at her.

She just beams up at him and the Primal sighs, shaking his head as we enter the fortress, making our way to the gate in its depths.

Marie

Sarah is sitting at the counter, staring down into a cup of tea and looking somewhat dazed. "Is something wrong?" I ask her for the fifth time.

She shakes her head, "No, just that it I have not seen anything to do with Lilith and Samael in days."

"So something may be wrong," I argue, "If you haven't seen anything."

My sister looks over at me and her eyes have glazed over, "The King and Queen have come; their Souls Healed and more. Careful now, sister dear, there are friends at the door." Her eyes clear a moment later. The gate alarms start blaring.

A cacophony of sounds as the vast majority of the household runs outside. The vampire brothers beating us there. We come up to the gate and a familiar voice grumbles, "And we didn't just go inside because?"

"Because, as has I've said multiple times, our magical signatures are significantly stronger and less identifiable now, not to mention Aggression is a stranger. I don't know about you, but if three unknown beings suddenly popped up on your property, I'd be quite defensive." Samael's voice is flat as usual, but there's a hint of amusement to it.

I push through people and stare at the troupe standing outside the gate. Damien and Phil look like they've been through shit, their clothes torn and bloody. Shadows haunt their eyes and Damien is cradling one arm against his chest.

My attention only remains on them for a moment before my eyes fall on Samael. The lord of the house also looks like shit, bloody, dirty, exhausted. But there's a slight light coming off of him I've never seen before. Though, the most unexpected thing is the cloak of feathers draped across his shoulders. He shifts his weight and the feathers move, revealing that they're wings.

There's a fourth man with them, his eyes as silvery and his hair dark as night. He's observing all of us with an unnerving amount of focus. I do not know who he is, but in his arms, he's holding Lilith. Her head is leaning against his shoulder and her eyes drooping. She looks the worst of all, her skin sallow, her eyes dull, and when she looks over, her eyelids flutter for a moment before closing.

"What in the hells happened to you?" Roland asks, though nobody is moving to open the gates.

Damien growls lowly, "Let us the fuck in so we can all get some gods damned rest and we'll tell you."

I open my mouth to argue but Lilith beats me to it, "Deimos, be nice or no cuddles," She inhales deeply and her eyes snap open, "I smell bacon."

A heartbeat later, Lilith is on this side of the gate; the metal swinging open with a flick of shadows. Though still looking like shit, the young woman prances forward then pauses, the others walk through the gate and she skips back to grab Damien's hand. "Keep up if you want any bacon."

He grumbles about annoying hellions but is smiling as he follows along behind her. Once they disappear inside, I turn to Samael and Philip, "What in the world?"

Samael smiles, "Our souls are healed. This is Errill, a dear friend of Lilith's. I began mending the seal on our way here, though there are more steps to be taken. Let us go inside and we'll sort out the details." He waves at the kitchen door.

Leah Mortimer

Three Years Later

It's amazing how little time it took for the Veil to be mended in the end. Three weeks of recovery, a quick blood rite at the origin, and everything stabilized. Unfortunately, those beings which had made their way across needed to be collected. It turned out to be a far more arduous task than expected. While the Twins gathered those that remained in the city itself, Lilith and Aggression roamed the woods and countryside.

Fate decreed that a few creatures, most animal-like, were to remain behind. Samael took time to teach Aegis agents how to defend against the monsters. In addition to the training, they left a trusted demon to provide assistance in the future.

Samael formally turned over the leadership of Aegis to my family, stating that he cannot remain on this side of the Veil. Their duties lay elsewhere, though they left us with a means of contacting them should we need their help.

Despite the decree to stay in Hell...

The door to the study opens and I look up.

Dancing through the door, Lilith skips to my side and plops into a seat across from me. Her hair lies in a braid over one shoulder, and she's wearing an outfit that I think of as her signature look. A fitted but stretchy top, baggy pants, a long vest, and bare feet, today the cloth is a lilac that makes her emerald eyes pop.

"Leah, darling, how are you today?" the Queen of Hell asks with a cheery smile.

I chuckle and set down my pen, "I'm doing well, I've been working on the records of what happened when you returned. What brings you here?"

"I'm just bringing you a message!" she says happily, "Next month a handful of beings are being granted passage to your realm." She holds up a file, "These are all the things you need to know about them."

I take the packet and flip through it, sure enough, there are details on five different beings, their habits, and weaknesses. I look back up at her, "Usually, a messenger is sent with this sort of thing. What happened to you staying in hell?"

She rolls her eyes and waves a dismissive hand, "I'll stay in Hell when there aren't fun things to do here."

I chuckle at that and close the file, "What trouble are you getting up to this time?"

"None," comes a grumpy voice from the door.

We both look over and Deimos is standing there with his arms crossed, glaring over at Lilith. I smile, "Ah, Deimos, seems you're right on time."

Lilith shoots me a glare, then looks at Deimos and smiles sweetly, "Aww, come on, Dem, I was just going to go to the fair. You know, the one you and Phobos took me to?"

He scowls harder. Her grin widens and then, as always, Deimos relents and sighs, "All right, fine. *We* will go to the fair, and you will not leave my fucking sight. Last time you came up here, you started two brawls and burned down a tavern."

Lilith jumps to her feet, clapping excitedly and prancing to his side, "Yay! I want cotton candy!"

He sighs and puts an arm around her shoulders, "You know you're spoiled, right?"

She leans into his side and giggles, "Of course I know, but you're the one that spoils me so you can't complain."

He chuckles and kisses her head, "Fair enough."

I return to my paper and finish the paragraph.

Despite the decree to stay in Hell, nobody can keep Lilith from doing what she likes. So it's often that we get visits from her, which always leads to mischief. According to Sarah, some things never change; Least of all Eternals."

The End

K.A. Shady grew-up in a very large, blended family. Being the second of 12 kids, most adopted directly from foster care, their life was always very hectic. To occupy their younger siblings and themselves, they would act out elaborate stories revolving around brave heroes exploring fantasy worlds. By the age of 10 they realized they wanted to be a writer, so they started transcribing the adventures they had with their siblings and put together a variety of short stories.

Kyra spent their adolescence in Georgia, but after living there for over two decades they were ready for a change. They moved to Nebraska with their wife in 2019. When they're not writing, they're traveling to new worlds by way of books, battling monsters with their PC, and organizing their next DnD session.